To the
Depths

The horrors will continue in the next installment of the *To the Depths* series:

Coming soon!

To the Depths

Beth Rhydo

First paperback edition: June 2026.
Cover Designs and Character Art by: Macarena Vega — @mav.a1209 on Tiktok.
Developmental Edits by: Tawnysha Greene.
979-8-9956198-0-2 (Paperback)
979-8-9956198-1-9 (EPUB)
979-8-9956198-3-3 (Hardcover)
Manufactured in the United States of America.

READER DISCRETION IS ADVISED

The following material contains graphic and mature content intended for *mature audiences* only.

Content Warnings:

- Death
- Prostitution
- Sexual Assault and Rape
- Torture and Asphyxiation
- Graphic Violence and Bloody Gore
- Bestiality and Animal Attacks (Wolf shifters)
- Forced Pregnancy, Stillbirth, and Sterilization
- Child Abuse
- Dismemberment
- Depression, Grief, Night Terrors, and PTSD
- Cults, Religious Trauma, Living Sacrifices of animals, shifters, and humans alike

This book also contains consensual, explicit sexual scenes between consenting adult characters, as typical in an Open Door Romance.

If these themes are too overwhelming for you as a reader, please proceed with caution, or close this book and protect your peace. Life did not hold anything back, neither did I.

Remember, above all, that your mental health matters.

To the dream-walkers and
those who choose to heal:
May you see the past,
and command the future.

I love you,
to the Depths—

My pretty birds,
my little wolves, and
my cycle-breaking witches.
This one is for you.

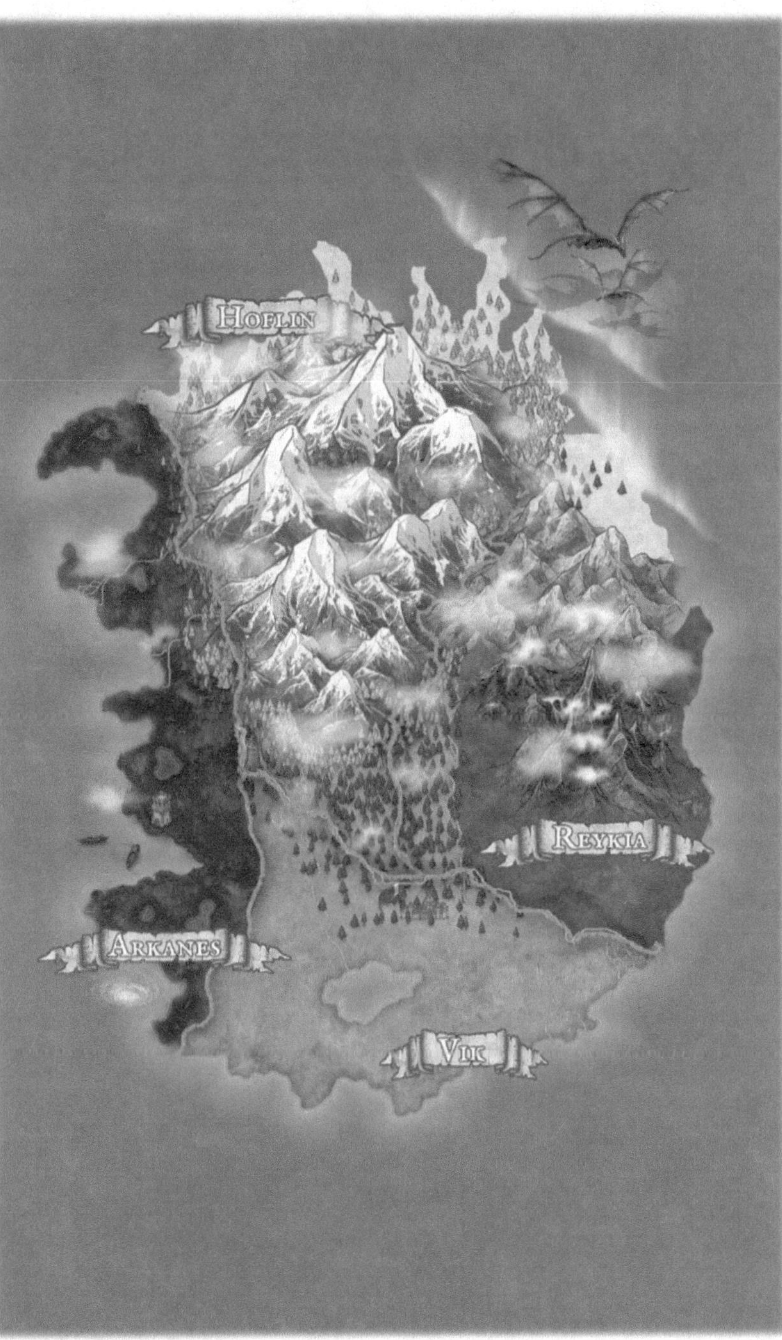

Hoflin
Reykia
Arkanes
Vik

Chapter 1

Brynn

"Brynn, my child! Thank all the gods you are here!" The frazzled woman gasped, out of breath. Her hands were full of bloody towels as she answered the large oak door.

"You should have called for me when it first started, Ms. Thyra." I reprimanded as I edged past her into the dimly lit brothel and let my dusty hood fall to my shoulders. The damp air was saturated with the scent of oils, incense, and active bodies; pungent as always.

"You know very well, Miss, that I have delivered my fair share of babes in the last twenty-six birthing seasons you have been alive without needing a healer like yourself." Thyra huffed as she closed the door.

The oak groaned as it sealed out the noise of the bustling street; merchants' preparations were in full swing as they set up their carts for the day.

Thyra shook her head, worry and despair already transforming her round, ruddy face. "But this one is…"

"Different. I know. I am sure he is just like his father Sondre already." I sneered as I headed up the stairway without further invitation needed.

Of course, that violent bastard would have violent offspring.

"Disgusting man," I murmured.

I knew this brothel, and those that frequented it, better than most. Lately, Sondre, the Commander of the King's Guard, spent his time during his favorite sessions maiming the women to the point of needing a healer afterward, inflicting pain his favorite aphrodisiac. I often arrived to find the women bloodied and broken. My visits were becoming far too frequent to put girls back together in his wake. As wretched as he was, there was little resistance to his tactics anymore.

Only once, I had ever convinced the pleasure house's owner Madame Ahmila to stand up to him. In return, Sondre had barred the entire military from coming to the establishment and threatened any merchant that conducted business with the women. None of the courtesans could earn their wages. The few shopkeepers who tried to keep the ladies fed were brought out to the square to be flogged or publicly executed for going against the Commander's decree.

After a month of Madame Ahmila not relenting to Sondre's tightening grip, women in the town started to go missing. Unable to satiate their hunger at the brothel, the King's Guard sought other ways to find release. Now with no need for restraint, their victims were found down river more frequently. Without a localized place to be found and healed, the women succumbed to their injuries long before they ever made it to the riverbanks. Madame Ahmila's daughter was one of the girls discovered on the shoreline. Stricken with grief, Ahmila yielded to allow the Guard to satiate their darker appetites during their sessions, on the condition I was permitted to heal the women afterward; my visits had become daily ever since.

"Hush, child, his men are here!" Thyra chided.

"They are *always* here." I whispered over my shoulder as Thyra wheezed up the stairs behind me.

My arm brushed one of the velvet curtains in the doorway as I turned back. Ahmila refused to have doors in her brothel and hung curtains in every doorway instead. *No damaging the merchandise without paying the fee, any session can be interrupted as I see fit!* Ahmila would always snap if patrons protested not being able to lock a door when they paid for the time. Even the King dealt with the curtain rule, if he visited. Madame Ahmila, however, did not interrupt nearly as many sessions as she should; we already had lost three girls this week to two of the most ruthless and demented clients.

Sondre and Prince Hurthur were the highest paying customers; they found ways to satisfy their most sinister of urges here, always willing to pay a handsome fee. The three women that had just died were rarely requested, and Madame Ahmila claimed their *sacrifice* would keep the other more profitable women safe and motivated to earn even more, with enthusiasm. I had been forbidden to aid the three girls as Sondre and His Highness had specifically paid for the deaths ahead of time. The three corpses were barely recognizable, defiled in the most horrendous of ways, even after they had succumbed to their injuries.

Sickening.

An officer in the King's Guard stepped out from behind a thick curtain covering the first doorway, at the top of the stairs, and snapped me out of my darkening thoughts.

"Brynn! I did not know you were here, my sweet." The approaching officer beamed, brightening his already flushed complexion.

A genuine smile warmed my face in response.

Officer Magnus was one of the few who always had a kind word; the wolf shifter was a little rough around the edges but intentionally gentle when it counted. He was a rarity in the Guard.

"Baby duty, Sir, my apologies." I started to rush past him, but a glance at the woman behind the curtain gave me pause. I held up a finger for him to wait as I reached into my shoulder bag to pull out a small glass jar of salve.

"Twice a day for the next week." I said slipping the jar into his hand. I glanced at his groin and back up to his eyes with pursed lips. He had an uncomfortable few days ahead of him.

"Damn the Depths, Shay!" He barked, whirling around to shoot a glare back into the room.

The curvy brunette slipped on a sheer robe and tied it with a braided leather belt, unfazed.

"You know I am training the new lads next week;" He bemoaned, "It will be hard enough without my bits chaffing all afternoon in the heat."

"You asked for *the best*, love. If you wanted *clean*, order a young one next time." Shay quipped as she tossed her loose waves back to reveal an unamused expression. With a shrug, she left with her payment.

"I am sure Caraway would be happy to see to your needs next week, once that has cleared up; I know you are a favorite of hers." I patted Magnus on the shoulder and continued up another flight of stairs.

I did not have space in my mind to feel sorry for him today. A healer could drain their reserves dry if every itch or burn was tended to by magic; this birth would demand all I had to offer. Magnus would have to deal with a natural remedy for his folly.

"Did I hear Brynn Ulfhild's voice?" A stout man with even his chest hair starting to grey rounded the corner.

I stifled a groan at the sound of the treasurer's voice. The man believed he was the goddess' gift to women, even the ones he did not have to pay; his slimy persona made my skin crawl, and never in excitement.

"I've got three beauties waiting for me in there, got any of them candies?" He asked, wiggling his bushy eyebrows, a foreign substance was caked in them that I did not dare venture to guess what it was.

The *candies,* however, were one of the main requests from the patrons in this establishment. My blend of herbs and roots, mixed into honey drops, which helped improve specialized blood flow and elongated the men's performance time, were always in high demand whenever I visited.

"Treasurer, a pleasure, *as always*," My smile was all teeth as the corners of my mouth refused to curve. I tried to suppress my gag reflex from the rancid smell coming from the tight braids on his head. I handed him an amber sweet from a pouch at my waist and, unfortunately, grazed his damp palm. "Here, this time, let it dissolve under your tongue for a better effect."

"Can I get two?" He begged while following close behind me. His pants were still half laced, his flaccid penis swaying as we walked up the hall.

I saw the women in his suite first, waiting on the chaise lounge. Caraway was sitting with her head in her hands to massage her temples. Her blonde curls shimmered in the light at the movement. Seated next to Caraway, Liv had rolled her head back to stare at the ceiling and sighed, her knee bouncing impatiently. Then, there was Sif, in all her glory.

While the other two were naked, Sif wore a white chiffon dress cinched at the ribs with a leather bodice. She twirled a crop between her fingers as she stood leaning against the backrest. She brushed her dark brown hair behind her ear and locked eyes with me before tapping the other two on the shoulders with the crop to seem interested. Treasurer Melik was their least favorite client as he never knew what to do with the rising number of women he would order. Sif was one of the more expensive courtesans to purchase time with and was usually out of his price range.

He must be growing bolder with how he swindles money from the crown.

They all straightened as the King's treasurer walked in behind me, still muttering about two sweets, or even a third.

"Melik, good sir," I paused to glance at him without reaching into my bag again. I motioned my chin to his favorite appendage between his legs. "If *it* ruptures with two and you lose that head you are *so fond of*, do not say I did not warn you."

The rotund man shuddered, and the movement made a slight flapping sound.

Caraway turned away to hide her grimace.

Sif snapped her fingers; Caraway and Liv stood and started toward the main bedroom.

"One is fine then, yes, yes. Thank you, Brynn." He blushed as he placed the sweet into his mouth and looked greedily at the women before him.

"May I?" I asked the ladies, already crossing the room, and pointed to the doorway leading to the courtesans' personal bedrooms.

"Of course!" Chimed in Caraway, "She is in my room for delivery."

"I knew that!" Thyra huffed as she finally caught up to us, "This way, Healer. Sif, the side room is free now for you all to proceed."

"I will be back later." I placed a hand on Sif's forearm as she reached for me. She lifted her free hand to my face and kissed me in greeting.

"Before my skin smells like his." She whispered against my lips before kissing me again with a smile.

I gave her hand a squeeze once her grip drifted to my wrist. I leaned closer to let my lips brush against her ear.

"It is only a light dose. He will not last long." I breathed.

I felt her stifle a chuckle against the skin of my neck, then she pulled away with a stern face as if I had just shared something serious.

"We await good news on Asta." She said, her eyes still gleaming with mischief.

With a nod, I followed Thyra into the discrete hallway behind one of the panels in the wall.

"How bad is Asta?" I asked, once we were out of earshot of the treasurer's session.

"Bad. I don't know if you can even save her, Healer. The baby isn't going to make it either, I think. I have delivered many babes before, but this…" The woman searched for the right words, but I knew where her mind had gone; Nothing about this pregnancy had been typical. "This is wrong, it won't live. Shouldn't live, the way it is trying to come into the world. The goddesses will never allow it."

Not a terrible outcome if it did not.

I tried to shake the dark thought out of my mind, but I could not lie about how I felt about this birth. Most women took a contraceptive tonic that I brewed for the establishment regularly, which naturally prevented most pregnancies. A collection of vials for the men to ingest when they arrived were available as well. But Sondre…

Sondre paid to *breed,* unobstructed and unhindered. Sondre wanted this child. I knew it was not the baby's fault its father was a monster, but this world did not need a smaller version of Sondre's darkness within it.

The hallway and surrounding stairways were blanketed in layered rugs and tapestries to dampen the sound between the business side of the establishment and the living quarters. The image of one tapestry caused my chest to tighten as we walked; It depicted the Night Wolves of the neighboring kingdom. A Night Wolf's unintentional first action in life was the death of his mother in childbirth, which earned him a curse from the goddess of Death. Their pitch-black coats blended into the threads of the sky belonging to the darkest night of the solstices. The molten eyes glowed red and orange in the tapestry, full of wrath and murder.

This was the bleak reality of what would happen if I failed; As a healer, it was my duty to bring mother and child safely through the birthing process and prevent such creatures of darkness from being created and roaming the kingdom. The reminder of that became all too real as we climbed the final flight of stairs and were met by muffled screams. I quickened my pace past Thyra, pulling vials out of my bag as I went. As soon as we entered the room, the girl in bed howled for me.

"Get it out of me!" Asta's wide eyes were bloodshot from straining, "Get this damned monster out of me!"

She grasped the blood-soaked sheets until her knuckles whitened. Her amber hair was plastered to her forehead; It was stained with crimson streaks as she clawed frantically at the form coming out of her, then wiped the sweat and hair out of her face.

"It shifted." I said, barely above a whisper.

What the actual fuck.

I whirled around to Thyra in a rage.

"Why *the fuck* did you not tell me it had *shifted*?" I rasped.

Thyra only stood there. All the blood had drained from her face.

"When I left, it had not—It is splitting her open, Healer." She choked as she wobbled at the sight.

Newborn wolf shifter males were nursed a tonic weeks after birth to induce their first shift to prevent any harm to the mother and child during labor. A shifted babe in the womb would mean near certain death for the human mother, and, most likely, the child as well. I had suspected she carried a boy the way it tussled within her over the last months but for the boy to have already shifted…The red eyes of the Night Wolf tapestry seared though my thoughts, challenging me to prevent such a curse from unfolding before me.

No…

"Great Tyr above, help me tend to your child." I pleaded in hopes the Old God would hear me.

I shook off the shock and went into solution mode.

"I am here, Asta, eyes on me." I commanded.

"She is burning, Healer!" One of the maids pleaded, as they all caressed Asta's forehead, arms, and back with cool rags. "We told her to rest, but she keeps trying to get up."

"Move her to the edge of the bed, then everyone out." I ordered as I walked around them to kneel at the bedside.

The maids scooted Asta closer, a leg now on either side of me as I rolled up my sleeves to prepare the area. Blood already caked her thighs.

"Except you, Ms. Thyra. Bring me the water before you go." I insisted.

"You heard the Healer, everyone out, go! Go! Shoo, all of you." Thyra waived her hands at them, suddenly coming back to the moment, even swatting at the maids with a towel to herd them out.

"Cut it out of me." Asta hissed.

Although it was a practice permitted in other kingdoms, here in the South, our goddesses frowned upon such *unnatural* approaches to birth. Regardless of how well a Southern healer would tend to the mother after removing the babe with a blade and healing afterward, both mother and child would mysteriously fall ill, and their lives would be forfeit to Valdis, our Goddess of Death. Neither Dahlia nor Valdis permitted taking complete control over the matters of life or death in such a way.

"I will take my chances with Valdis' sickness later. I know you can do it, cut it out of me!" Asta demanded.

She is not thinking clearly due to the pain. I will not condemn her to such a fate and watch her die, helpless to stay Valdis' hand.

I rubbed a numbing salve I had grown immune to in my hands then down Asta's hips, inner thighs, and around the crowning head of the beast trying to come out of her. Asta released a sigh of immediate relief as her shoulders sagged slightly.

"You've torn badly, Asta." I said quietly, in as soothing of a tone I could muster. I put my fingertips close to the child's skull, but there was no warmth as my magic reached out to sense a heartbeat.

A cold darkness seeped from the babe deep into the bones of my arm; it was not the usually taxing sensation of magic usage.

Something is terribly wrong.

I closed my eyes and pushed my magic further, letting my hand rest on the deformed head as the bone shifted under my touch.

"Asta…" I opened my eyes to search my dear friend's gaze, but found the unfortunate fact we both already knew to be true etched into her features.

The child was dead.

"I won't have to hide it if it is already…truly…*dead*." Asta's voice hitched. "Sondre forced me to drink that damned tonic to make the babe shift early this morning. He was trying to get the little beast to kill me. He said I would be remembered for my *sacrifice*; a price he is willing to pay to usher in his cursed child. He gloated that he wanted his own pack of those horrid Night Wolves as he held my chin and forced the liquid down my throat. But in his haste, he has killed the boy, hasn't he?"

My pursed lips were answer enough for her.

"Then get, this abomination, out." Asta croaked.

"Okay. Breathe for me. Listen to me, no one is killing you today." I said with authority that filled the space, even as my heart stuttered.

Sondre has openly admitted it now; this is what he wants.

There had been rumors that Sondre was attempting something sinister. Roderick, my raven-familiar, had repeated things he would hear whispered around town, and the tone of conversations had been growing darker as of late. Roderick's recent reports rattled in my mind,

The power of a mother's blood.

Cursed children.

The goddess Valdis must not find out.

Kill the mothers.

Kill the mothers.

Kill the mothers.

A gasp broke the repeating sound of his warbled voice in my thoughts. Thyra had paused at the entryway as she returned with a pail of water, petrified by the gory sight before her.

I did not break from Asta's gaze, "Time for you to go, too, Ms. Thyra. Leave the pail and *go*."

Thyra opened her mouth to protest but quickly frowned when a raven, with crimson glinting in his wings, flew in from the open window and landed on the back of the chair closest to me. Tension released from my shoulders as Roderick hopped closer to me and croaked a greeting.

"Cursed beast." Thyra muttered and scurried out of the room, clutching the rowan sprig pinned to her apron. She believed the rowan would keep away the dark spirits attributed to Roderick's kind; little did she know, Roderick enjoyed the tea I would make from the berries, completely undeterred.

I nodded to the raven and wet a towel in my hand to wipe away some of the smeared blood from Asta's entrance to see what I was doing. The bird landed on my shoulder and tucked a loose strand of auburn hair back into my braid.

"Breathe with me, Asta." I coached.

Asta's ragged breath eventually linked with mine as Asta's pain began to ebb into my hand. I hooked the tension in her body with my power and pulled slowly. I squared my shoulders as her anguish filled me before my healing magic soothed it away from us both.

"That's it, let go. Good girl. Look at our pretty bird." I soothed.

As Asta gazed at the raven, her panic eased, and her body relaxed slightly.

When she and I dared to go on picnics together outside the walls of town, Roderick was always with us. Whenever she was afraid of the surrounding forests, I would remind her that our dark guardian was flying overhead, and it would put her mind at ease. I needed that comfort for her now and shrugged the shoulder on which Roderick was perched. He opened his majestic wingspan to get her attention and shifted to cause his red tipped feathers to catch the light.

"Proud bastard, always making things about you." Asta whispered as she let a soft chuckle loose from her chapped lips.

While she was distracted, I moved my hand further away and tendrils of power floated from my fingertips, like a mist catching the sunlight. The golden tendrils covered the baby's head and eased into Asta, numbing all sensation.

All healers were taught how to tap into their personal own supply of magic causing their tendrils of power to glow *gold*, but they were limited by their own physical strength and health. I, however, strayed from the healer's text in dire times, such as these, and channeled that which was forbidden in my kingdom; I reached out to the magic surrounding me. I linked to the black garnet pendant around my neck, a temple blessed talisman hanging from Caraway's small mirror, the mirror itself, the passion and bodily worship in the rooms around us, and the bones of the lost beneath the very foundation of the pleasure house. The strength of life and death coursed through my veins as I channeled it into Asta's womb. The babe's head and shoulders compressed as the light shifted into a crimson glow. I began to remove the fetus from her, my magic crushing the bones of the stillborn creature until it was able to come out easier. Asta let out a relieved moan once the rest followed. Roderick fluttered to the floor and pulled a towel close by to wrap the deformed creature.

"Thank you, my lovely helper," I said quietly as I placed the mangled form into the towel. "A bit more, sweet girl."

Tendrils of deepening ruby power entered Asta again to make quick work of the afterbirth. The door creaked open, and Thyra came back in with more towels. In an instant, my magic defensively shifted back to gold of its own accord as it unlinked from outside power sources, and I felt the tax on my frame increase with a startled gasp.

"I cannot wait outside while another one of my girls dies." Thyra protested, her eyes misty.

"She is not dying today." I professed. The light vanished from my hands as I turned to the emboldened intruder, knowing full well she was not ready for our current reality. "Here then, if you choose to stay, wrap this up for me to take."

I offered the bloody toweled mess to Thyra.

Unquestioningly, Thyra reached for it but gasped, stumbling back once she caught sight of the mutilated child.

My expression hardened as I set it down on the floor next to me and refocused on my work. Asta continued to bleed, and I reached into my bag for a dark amber vial embossed with the sigil of the Night Wolves on the side.

Thyra murmured a prayer as she perceived its origin as a thick cloudy liquid spilled out into my fingers.

"Valdis and Dahlia spare us." Thyra touched her forehead then navel with shaky fingers.

"You can leave them out of this. Don't be superstitious, Ms. Thyra. She will bleed out if I do not have a little help. If the Night Wolves can help, then so can you. Take the babe and get out." I ground out, the exasperation deepening my voice.

As a healer, I was forced to learn the healing properties of *anything* that could be of use; ironically, the harbingers of death to the East, who I tried so desperately to prevent the furthering of their curse, could provide assistance with the most drastic of healings. I had traded much for this vial, and it had saved many lives already. I did not have the luxury of such moral dilemmas when finding ingredients to help my patients.

With shuddering breaths, Thyra gathered the soiled towels and the cursed bundle to rush back out of the room, mumbling more prayers to her goddesses.

I rolled my eyes at the woman as I slipped my fingers into Asta and coated her inner walls with the liquid. Asta's body shook violently at the foreign presence, but I assured her that we were almost finished. The healing was instant as the solution soaked into her tissues and stopped the bleeding. There was no need for stitching or cauterizing with this vial.

"Healer's help or not, no working for a few weeks, okay?" I warned as I withdrew my fingers and ran my hands up Asta's thighs, mending any cuts and scrapes with other salves as I went.

Asta slumped from exhaustion as the last of the mending was complete. I pulled down her night shift to offer her a little privacy now that the ordeal was nearing its end.

"Come, up we go, Asta. We need to move you to your room before Caraway gets back. The Treasurer never lasts long; the maids can freshen up her sheets once we leave." I said as I gently slid an arm under Asta's legs and around her back to lift her frail frame up with ease.

Asta put her arms around my neck but that was all her energy allowed her to do. Asta was one of the smaller women in the brothel, subject to more than one man's need for dominance. Not only was she a friend of mine, but a frequent patient. I carried Asta to her room, weaving tissue and lessening inflammation with subtle golden tendrils of magic as I walked. Asta rolled her head to rest on my shoulder.

"Will you burn it?" Asta asked quietly, her breath tickling my collarbone.

"Yes, sweet child." I replied kissing her forehead; the sweat and blood left a tang on my lips, but I did not pull away. "It was deformed so we cannot offer it in the local temple with the Solstice approaching. But I will burn it, don't you worry."

"Not to his gods. Do not take my boy to Sondre or his hateful gods." Asta pleaded as tears filled her eyes.

"I would never." I promised.

The bastard will never see what his twisted greed had created.

"Valdis and Dahlia don't deserve my baby boy, either. They did not intervene; they did not stop Sondre. I called to them when he forced me to drink that tonic. But they did nothing," She alleged, sorrow weakening her hatred.

I felt dampness on my chest as her tears fell.

We passed the Night Wolf tapestry and Asta took a shaky breath, "Will you bring him to your deity in the forest?"

"Bless the Depths!" I coughed on the laugh that caught in my throat. "Aksel will be amused that you think him *a god*. But, yes, I will bring your boy with me to the forest this afternoon to be offered up; his soul will join your ancestors in the Depths and wait for you. I will not need a temple's blessing in the East. Our pretty bird will join me and watch over your son and me. The words will be spoken, my dear, and he will be at rest."

I consoled her as the raven flew ahead of us into the room with an answering croak.

Her room was cramped like the others. A little bed touched the three walls in the back, and I had to turn sideways to slip past the small dresser. It was covered with small trinkets from her past favorite patrons and a couple from our closest friends. A carved wooden dragon was in the center of her collection. Rune had taken the role of Asta's protective older brother and had whittled it for her during a picnic the three of us had last year; he had spent weeks trying to find the right mossy dye from passing merchants to stain it the color of Tyr's green scales. As a member of the Guard, he spent many nights here and the nearby tavern to break up fights and protect these women. He only frequented Sif's chambers now but looked after each of the girls all the same.

"Now, rest." I said, setting Asta down on the lumpy, straw mattress. "I will speak with Madame Ahmila about some time off, starting you back in the kitchens first would be best.

The tearing has healed, but it will still take time for your body to adjust; there are limits to what I can do. Nature must take its course as with the aftermath of any pregnancy."

"Thank you, Bry." Asta whispered as exhaustion took her deeper into a dream state.

I pulled a blanket over the young woman's petite shoulders.

"Burn him..." She mumbled half awake.

"I promise, he will be burned." I swore as I brushed the curly amber hair from Asta's pale forehead to press my lips against it for one final kiss. "Sleep. May Tyr, Your Protector, watch over you. May his wings shield you, and may the light of his fires burn away your fears, my sweet sister. Ms. Thyra will be up to help bathe you later and wash away the pain of today."

We may not have the same parents, but, in the brothel, I had raised Asta like a little sister since the day Asta was dropped off at this doorstep. Her mangled flesh was just as tattered as her clothes, once the Guard had used her up and left her here. Half of her bones were broken when her family had missed protection payments to the King's Guard. Asta was given to Madame Ahmila to pay off the family's debts once she had her first bleed and could be worked and bred at the brothel. My blood boiled every time I remembered the worthless people who had sired her; whenever I passed their lonely, unmarked graves in the cemetery, I spat on the cursed ground where even grass refused to grow.

Fuck them, for all eternity.

I motioned to my winged companion as I walked out quietly. Roderick flew to my shoulder and nuzzled the side of my cheek with his beak. He warbled in hushed gravely tones and nipped at the loose auburn strands at the nape of my neck as I worked my way to the exit of the brothel. Thyra waited impatiently near the large oak door leading to the street, struggling to maintain composure as she fiddled with the wrappings around the swaddled child. She carefully handed the bundle back to me, and I gently put it in an extra bag slung across my chest. Death was an unavoidable part of the job, regardless how good I got at the craft, but this next part never got easier.

"She is sleeping for now. I will be back for my usual check-ins to speak with Madame Ahmila tomorrow. I need to see Sif later; plus, there is that business about the pup in the hallway." I said nodding to the floor above us, where a soft growl sounded in response.

"Don't rush back." Thyra motioned to the lump in my bag, the muscles in her throat constricting. "Handle that, Healer, before the Commander comes looking for the child. He will want to know what went wrong to be more successful with his next pup. It will take days for you to get far enough from the Commander, if you go on foot..."

"Commander Sondre, with all his breeding plans, can go fuck himself. The day we all stop cowering to that evil man is the day we stop risking our girls and burying their children." I replied as I gritted my teeth and I took the rag Thyra offered for my bloodstained hands.

Even she suspected his intentions for this child and future pups, yet she stayed silent...

Fantastic.

I wanted to scream in frustration at the whole situation but taking it out on Thyra would not help anyone. We needed to not allow Sondre to pit us against each other when there were so few allies to be had. I let a sigh release my unspoken condemnations.

"I will travel with Rune," I shook my head at her attempted protest, "Which *will drastically* shorten how long the trip will take. We should be back before most of the girls' shifts start tomorrow night."

Thyra simply nodded, worry deepening the wrinkles around her eyes.

I paused and forced myself to see the woman behind the flustered façade. The way her brows knit together betrayed her; she was scared, just like the rest of us. Her slightly swollen ruddy hands, from always cleaning with too hot of water, were trembling. There were more white strands mixed in with the ginger hair around her temple and knots at the nape of her neck from not taking time to tend to herself instead of the women within this building.

I tilted my chin to the small worn twigs peeking out of the front pocket of Thyra's apron, resituated after her recent prayers.

"While I am out that way, I will try to find more rowan berries for teas. Maybe even bring back a fresh sprig for you, if you'd like." I offered. There was not much I could do for her, but this small gesture lit up her face.

"Dahlia bless you! I'll need as much rowan as you can spare me to rid the place of the spirits that little one has brought with it. Those woods you go into, though, for burning…" Thyra said with a wary eye at the raven nipping at my hair. "They be unnatural, Healer, unnatural."

"Unnatural." Roderick croaked in a tone mimicking Thyra.

The sun caught the subtle reddish hues of his dark wings as Thyra opened the main door to the street. He nudged my jaw with his beak once more before taking flight as he warbled; the sound was far too akin to him muttering under his breath at Thyra as he flew off.

"Then it will be the perfect place to burn this *unnatural* thing, will it not?" I replied as I gently tapped a hand on the bag and walked out.

Chapter 2

Roderick

Brynn paused on the steps to watch me fly above her, before turning to Thyra to say final goodbyes. Sif peered over Thyra's shoulder and called for Brynn; the sheer chiffon clung to her skin, damp with sweat. Her hair was disheveled, but it could not conceal the concern in her furrowed brows, even as she tapped Thyra with the crop to get closer to Brynn. Worry filled Sif's gaze as her eyes traveled from the bundle in Brynn's satchel to the strain in Brynn's expression, but she kept all that at bay as she teased Thyra until the flustered woman left the two best friends to whisper amongst themselves. They started to argue about the safety of Brynn's plans. Knowing Sif's protective nature was only second to Rune's and my own, I stopped my circling to give the women privacy and glided over the town.

Preparation for the autumn solstice and the yearly arrival of each kingdom's deities in the South had taken over the surrounding buildings, shrouding them in gloom and anticipation. The usual bustling sounds from earlier this morning were now muffled by the black banners over every window and door. Young boys in rags argued who would be Skai or Sverre, the North and West's deities of Death, and who of their friends would be sacrificed to them. Little girls wove dried flowers and sticks in their hair to resemble the horns of Dahlia, the South's Goddess of Life. A child draped a funeral cloth over her shoulders and smudged ash over her eyes to depict Valdis, the Goddess of Death, as she raised her dirty hands to cast a plague upon the fountain in the square. Screams filled the air as the children sipped the water and fell over in dramatic death scenes. I had seen Valdis' last curse upon the kingdom after the birth of a Night Wolf and did not remember the giggling that accompanied this reenactment.

Black flags hung between the buildings across the square and snapped in the breeze as townsfolk readied their meager offerings in hopes to appease the arriving deities. Smoke rose from the temples as the fires for sacrifices were prepared and the spaces were purified.

I only had a few days until I would be needed at the main temple of Vik for the Council of Deities, but I forced myself not to be in a rush. I flew down to perch on the baker Ivan's cart. He squinted his yellow reptilian eyes at me and a curse rolled off his forked tongue as he refreshed his stock. I puffed out my chest and readjusted where my wings rested against my back. I leaned down and snapped my beak shut near his eye, too close for comfort as he grunted and retreated back inside.

Another healer briskly walked by her ivory apron notified others of her trade. The hem was stained a dingy brown from years of mud and blood, adamant on leaving their mark on her life. She paused at the stall, her breath shaky as her hands trembled. The muted sun peeked out from the clouds and reflected on the bruise under her left eye. I hopped closer as a voice rang out across the street.

"Healer!" The voice boomed causing the healer to jump and spin around. It belonged to Alaris, one of Sondre's vermin. The wolf shifter crossed to the cart and towered over the petite woman. "Well?"

In his shadow, the woman's eyes filled with tears.

"No," The healer whispered. "No, sir. I could not save her. The bleeding was too great."

"And the baby?" Alaris seethed.

She only shook her head as a shiver racked over her frame. The magic she must have expended in attempts to save another mother and child now demanded payment from her small build.

"Swear to Valdis you did not execute the child after it killed its mother." Alaris demanded as he grabbed her arm and yanked her frail form against himself.

Blood slowly drained from her face.

"I swear it, may my goddess see the truth in my words or strip me of the power to heal." She breathed, as her gaze lost its focus and her knees buckled slightly.

Alaris seemed to grow aroused by her increasing weakness as his hand traveled from her arms to her waist and pressed against her.

"Swear to me, your life, not your power, depends on it." Alaris ground himself into her hips, earning a frightened whimper from her.

I had seen enough.

I spread my wings and reached for his face with my talons. He released the girl to bat me away but not before I shredded his cheek to ribbons. I croaked and beat my wings to hover in front of his face. The satisfying squish of his eye popping under my grasp was almost too tantalizing to ignore. The same realization was enough for him to turn and leave, mumbling his plans for the healer later.

I landed on her shoulder as she watched Alaris' back. His blood soaked from my talons into her sleeve, but she did not seem to mind as she leaned her head against my wing.

"Thank Valdis for you," She breathed. "The goddess' wraiths will be busy if that man gets his way. I can only prevent so much."

She remained for a beat, relishing the moment of protection while she regained her bearings. Heaving a sigh, she peered up at me.

"We must both get back to our duties, lest Death catches up to us." She claimed, as she offered a blueberry from her apron.

I accepted her offering with warbled thanks and took to the skies again to return to Reykia.

The forest on the edge of town was where the energy over the gods' arrival abruptly halted. The woods were eerily quiet as I flew above them. Shadowed figures roamed below the canopy of trees; a creature shrieked and its leathery wings caught the cool sunlight that rested below the nearby mountain ridge. The sun would not set for another few hours, but it did not keep the darkest of beings at bay. The woods groaned under the weight of the predators stalking through their canopies.

I passed a meadow of purple lupine flowers and hatred filled my core. At the border of our two kingdoms, Brynn had once routinely practiced her magic, healing the fauna and small helpless creatures within the meadow, away from the suspicious eyes within town. It was here that I had revealed my true form to her for the first time when Sondre had followed her to the border. My flight ahead was long and I allowed my mind to wander through the memory of that fateful day, years ago.

Sondre and his men had whispered their assumptions for weeks that she had been a witch. I had tried to warn her, but, while confined to this bird form, I could only croak out small sentences. Back then, Brynn had begun testing her limits healing patients at the edge of a battlefield, once she had convinced Rune to allow her to accompany him and help the cause against the Northern Kingdom of Hoflin. Many of the enemy prisoners, in the tent where she was stationed, had wounds that would have been beyond the power of a typical healer of her training. Even for her mother Bodhil, the head healer of the Royals, it would have drained her reserves. Brynn, however, patched up each of the winged soldiers of the North without a single fatality in her tent. This fueled Sondre's suspicions that she drew magic from sources outside of herself. Once they all returned home, he began tailing her for evidence against her; when he could not find any, he resorted to violence.

It was Aksel, Alpha of Night Wolves, who was the first to hear Brynn's screams. As I coasted on a cold breeze, the shadow beneath me had raised his colossal head and turned his attention toward the meadow, his ears erect as he listened. A growl reverberated through the trees as another shadow appeared at his side; Gunnar, Aksel's second in command, was just as formidable in size and unbridled by the politics of being alpha.

"One of your humans calls for aid." Aksel lifted his gaze to me. "Gunnar, go with Roderick to ensure no crime befalls her on our land. The goddess Terōta grants you clemency, handle it discretely, but quickly."

Gunnar needed no other encouragement to enact justice and took off before me; his onyx coat blended with the underbrush. Luckily, I had already been on my way to meet Brynn from my time in the East when I reached the meadow and heard her screams, myself. Sondre was in wolf form on top of Brynn; she held her forearms crossed above her head to protect her neck as Sondre's fangs tore through her skin. Blood covered her face and matted her auburn hair. For the first time since I had discovered her, there was terror in her emerald eyes. Their fight had rolled over the invisible line between our kingdoms and Sondre was now in *my domain*. I did not think, I simply shifted.

I felt my wings magnify as they elongated from my bare back. I barreled into his large form from above, knocking him into the grass. I planted my boots into the ground in front of Brynn and unsheathed the long black sword that materialized between my shoulder blades. Disorientated, Sondre rose to his feet and stumbled back in shock.

"A Blood Raven." The grey wolf spat as if it was a curse. "You will regret this, *witch*. It is my right to breed you; I will put a pup in you yet."

I loosed a dagger from my hip, and it found purchase in his shoulder.

The wolf howled in pain and ripped it from his flesh with his maw.

"You're on Reykian lands now, dog." I seethed as I pointed my sword at his face that dripped with blood, *her blood.* "No title will save you here."

It may have been a bluff; killing a fellow commander of a neighboring kingdom would have had severe consequences for me with my own leadership, but he did not need to know that. He recovered and lunged for me. I caught his maw with the edge of my sword and sliced through his cheek as I stepped out of his trajectory. His blood mingled with Brynn's on his teeth.

I wanted him to choke on it.

He launched himself at me and I beat my wings to meet him in the air. We collided and my sword pierced his thigh, but he snapped his teeth close to my face, clawing at my arms. I banked, causing him to fall away from Brynn. The ground trembled at his impact, and the satisfying crunch of his bones breaking under his weight filled the space. He yelped and staggered back, favoring his hind leg.

I landed in front of Brynn, again, and spun my sword, droplets of his blood flicking off.

He glared at her again, as if he blamed his new pains on her alone.

A branch snapped on the edge of the clearing, and I realized the rest of nature had gone silent. Sondre's eyes widened as he realized it too. The birds had stopped their chirping in the meadow, the breeze had stilled, even the hum of the bees pollinating the flowers had ceased. We both turned to the sound of wood snapping to find death incarnate snarling with his teeth bared.

Gunnar, took you long enough.

The Night Wolf's massive incisors of black garnet were in stark contrast against his frothing white teeth that gleamed in the setting sun. Saliva foamed at his mouth as he snapped his maw and lowered his shoulders. The muscles tensed under his midnight fur as the power behind his attack built.

To his credit, Sondre turned toward the beast and snarled in return.

"One day, your guardians will not be there to save you from me." Sondre fumed without turning his head from the larger threat.

"Luckily, for her, today is not that day." I retorted and took a step toward him. The heat of the kingdom's barrier singed my skin as I closed the distance between us.

Gunnar bolted across the clearing and barreled into Sondre. The grey wolf stood no chance as he was half the size of Gunnar. They rolled in the grass, a blur of teeth and fur. Gunnar's jaw clamped down on Sondre's shoulder and shut like a vice. The Night Wolf shook his head violently, ripping flesh from bone, as howls of pain filled the air. Gunnar flung Sondre to the side as the grey wolf landed on his injured leg. Scrambling back up, Sondre fled with a huff, leaving us in a moment of silence as I dared not turn my back on them yet. Gunnar glanced over at us, blood pouring from his mouth as he rolled a chunk of Sondre's shoulder off his tongue. The Night Wolf's eyes shifted to Brynn's form behind me before he turned to follow Sondre deeper into the forest.

Brynn's cough, as she tried to rise, made me spin and sheath my sword.

"Depths." I knelt by her side and helped her sit up. "Brynn, are you alright?"

She peered up at me with those blood-streaked emerald eyes and tried to scoot away in trepidation. Over the years of watching over her, I had always wondered how this first time meeting her in my true form would play out; this was not what I had in mind.

The shivers of shock brutally shook her frame.

"Who…Who are you?" Brynn stuttered as she cradled her arms against her torso.

I bowed my head to her.

"Apologies. Roderick, at your service." I said as softly as I could, attempting not to startle her further. "But you can still call me your Pretty Bird still, if you like."

Brynn gasped in alarm and tried to distance herself, her feet slipping in the pool of blood.

"I do not know what you are talking about, Sir." She whispered, breathlessly, as her gaze landed on my wings, then back to my face in bewilderment. "This cannot be real."

"I know, it is a lot to absorb; I had hoped to tell you under different circumstances…" The words spilled out faster than I intended. Trying to defuse the tension, I stood to give her space. "Try to contain your amazement, Brynn. It is I, as I live and breathe, your ever present, delightfully pretty, guardian."

She did not take the bait and standing made her seem even smaller beneath me. My expression gentled as I extended my hand to allow the first move to be her choice.

Timidly, she slid her wet fingers against my palm, and I helped her to her feet.

"Here, my darling," I said quietly, as I turned my back to her and spread my wings.

She studied my feathers, where each red tip was, how they moved, identical to the bird that whispered warnings to her and brought her herbs on her morning walks. She hesitated then reached out and touched my wing. How many times had she pet these feathers over the years as I comforted her, brushed her knuckles against my chest as I nestled into the crook of her neck. A slight shiver fluttered down my wing to my shoulders at her caress. I turned slowly and read the recognition flooding her face. I placed a hand against her cheek, and this time she did not flinch.

Tears of relief brimmed her eyes, mixing with the kohl and blood.

"Brynn, you're safe. Mm?" I hummed.

She let loose a sob and buried her head against my chest.

I wrapped my arms around her, and she crumbled in my embrace.

"You saved me." She choked out between shaky breaths.

"And I always will." I murmured into her hair. I let her take a moment to steady herself before leaning back. "Let me stop the bleeding though, dear one."

I knelt to the hem of her skirt, and she steadied herself with a hand on the collar of my leather vest. I tore away several strips to bandage her arms but felt her fingertips trace the curve of muscle on my exposed shoulder.

"So, you're a Raven-shifter?" She sniffled as she tried to collect herself.

I nodded as I tossed the dirtied hem to the side to tear fabric strips clean enough to bind her arms.

More recognition settled in her face, "Wait, this *whole* time?"

I looked up to see her expression contorted as an onslaught of emotions plowed into her, surprise, embarrassment, disbelief, aggravation, amusement, and—

Wait a second, is that…

Arousal.

A blush flared in her cheeks as I watched realization settle into her features and I knew she must have been recalling the times she called me in from the window to perch on the edge of her bath to talk to me while she lathered herself, or the times I had flown over when she was swimming in the river during the summer after a long hike, or during the nights she pleased herself testing Sif's latest instructions and made the sweetest of noises in the dark as I nested in the tree outside her room.

"The whole time." My gaze heated at the deepening crimson on her cheeks blending in with the blood.

"I should have known." She let out a nervous chuckle and winced at the pain in her ribs, bringing us back to the current predicament. "Now add that Sondre wants to kill me for making flowers grow, this day just keeps getting better."

"You're in shock." I claimed as I tore off another strip of cloth. Her chemise underneath clung to her legs, soaking in the blood from the fresh scrapes. These would not scar like her arms, but I could see where Sondre's claws had met skin as she scrambled backwards on the grass.

"And you're a *man*." She shook her head as I stood to bind the lacerated flesh of her arms. A soft whimper escaped her lips, but she obediently remained still.

"Observant." I answered, unable to hide the slight smirk that tugged on the corner of my lips.

From the last week on the battlefields and testing her abilities in the meadow, I knew she would be too depleted to fully heal herself on her own for some time; I needed to get her to another healer.

I took off my leather bracers and slid them onto her forearms. They were much too big for her, strong as she was, but they would keep everything tightly bound and limit questions when she arrived back in town.

"If I speak out against him for this…I will have to explain *why* he attacked me…" She whispered as she stared absentminded at my hands tightening the leather laces.

"Your kingdom is not kind to witches." I replied gently. "You...would be welcome in my kingdom. We do not have many witches, but you would not be hunted the way you are in your city. Several have sought refuge over the mountain pass on the outskirts of the lava fields in Reykia. They can practice freely…"

"No." Brynn cut me off and raised her head. Determination hardened her features under the drying crimson, making her a fearsome creature to behold. "I cannot leave the women in my city to Sondre's mercy. If I was not there to heal in the lower levels, most of the residents would be dead by now. I cannot do that. I will not, Roderick."

Hearing my name on her lips set my blood ablaze. I knew, in that moment, I would do anything to hear her repeat it. I took her chin in my grip.

"You cannot heal anyone if he kills you." I warned.

"Good thing I will have an ever-present guardian then, huh?" She said pushing against my grasp in challenge.

There she is, my brave woman.

"I won't be able to leave you alone now, you realize that?" I raised an eyebrow as I let my hand come to rest on the bracers again.

Her gaze drifted down my jaw and neck before lingering on my collar and the tattoos that decorated my skin. She followed the inked designs down my arms. I tried not to flex under her gaze; the ridiculous bird instinct in me wanted to puff out my chest and claim all her attention, to distract her from all her recent horrors.

"That does not sound like a *terrible* fate." She mused as she stumbled slightly. She cleared her throat and blinked multiple times.

Blood loss, Roderick. Right, focus.

"We…" Her eyes rolled back slightly before refocusing on my face. "We should go to the river. There will be too many questions if I show up in town looking like this."

"The East bank. Reykian soil." I interjected. "I cannot remain in this form once I enter your kingdom unless directly

41

permitted on a mission. I can carry you, if we stay on this side of the border."

"A curse?" She asked as she took my arm for balance. Her fingers were cold against my bare skin.

"A leash." I answered firmly. I glanced down at her uneasy pace and wrapped an arm under her hips. In a fluid movement, I lifted her up.

She steadied herself, her arms around my neck, and squeaked in surprise.

"It will take hours to reach the river at your pace, you'll bleed out; we will fly." I tried not to laugh at the sound that just came out of her. "Do you think Rune is near enough to meet us at the river so he can escort you home?"

"He is going to be pissed." She muttered as she nodded. She rested her head against my chest as we took flight. Her warm breath caressed my skin as she relaxed into my embrace.

"Good." I answered.

We were going to need his rage to keep her safe. Her rapid breathing slowed as we flew, and she slowly closed her eyes. Having a moment to think, I quickly realized another healer would start asking questions, questions Brynn could not give answers to without endangering herself. I reached down my own bond to the swirling darkness within me.

Lerevna.

"This better be important." A strong female voice answered in my mind.

"Brynn is injured. Send a wolf with a vial to the river. He will be able to scent where we are easily enough from her blood." I ordered. *"Oh, and a dress, we will need to burn this one."*

There was a frustrated sigh then silence on the other end. Howls in the distance filled the air as the Night Wolf pack communicated.

"Daegon is...busy with me. Gunnar is on his way back to you now; he will have company. He claimed he is finished with...the 'problem'? The Commander?! I swear to Randgrid if you two killed off another kingdom's official, again, without directed orders, I will flog you both. I expect a full report on this once you return." She answered.

I felt the bond grow cold as she blocked me back out. Brynn would be able to apply the healing potion to avoid any undue attention back in town.

This could work.

Gunnar indeed met us there and was accompanied with his packmate Brede and the pack's witch to help heal Brynn. The Witch even had brought a thin black dress for Brynn to wear; thankfully, they were of similar builds.

Rune was furious when he arrived, snarling at the Night Wolves and myself until Brynn calmed him down enough to stop him from trying to kill us.

Not that it would have been a successful attempt...

Rune wasted no time lifting Brynn onto his back before taking off toward Vik in a sprint. The look in Brynn's eyes as she glanced over her shoulder at us on the bank still haunted me to this day. Her gaze held so many questions that I was still trying to answer all these years later.

A growl below broke through the fog in my mind as I relished the memory of her closeness and the sound forced me back into the present moment. I had been flying for hours since leaving Brynn at the brothel and had let the daydream overtake my thoughts to pass the time.

Beneath me, circled a pair of Night Wolves with their great heads pointed at me as they snapped their maws skyward. I tilted into a dive toward them and shifted at the last moment to land between them. The corner of my wing caught the larger of the two in the mouth as my wingspan extended to its full length.

Remaining in bird form always felt cramped, like wearing a glove that was too small.

"Gunnar. Delightful for you to wait for me." I crooned at the massive beast as I dusted off my black trousers post shift.

"Shut it, bird boy." Gunnar snapped. "The Alpha has been looking for you. He wants a report before the deities are set to cross the Southern territory."

"Well, good. There is something he needs to hear, beforehand." I strode past them and adjusted the sword on my back.

"Spit it out, Roderick." Daegon, the leaner of the two wolves, snarled.

"Brynn will explain what he needs to hear, when she arrives. She is on her way." I looked over my shoulder at the beasts of death. "Try not to eat the messenger, yes? It would be a shame to spill blood this close to the solstice. We would not want to anger *High Lady Braxcia*."

With a synchronous huff at the mention of our Goddess of Death, they followed me into the darkened clearing.

"Is Brynn's *mate* with her?" Gunnar asked.

My skin bristled at the term.

"We do not know for certain that copper wolf Rune is her mate." Daegon corrected.

"She will be with *him*, yes." I answered as I rounded a downed stone pillar to enter the abandoned temple in the middle of the forest. The scent of burning herbs filled the air as a witch's chant whispered through the leaves.

"The Witch is here?" I asked as I walked.

"She insisted. Brede agreed." Gunnar retorted with a grunt.

Brede, a fellow Night Wolf, had claimed the Witch when she arrived at the Reykian court from the southern pits. The mighty beast of death was an obnoxiously smitten pup around her and often agreed to her requests.

"Of course he did. Well, good. It is about time these two women meet again." I mused as the incantation grew louder around us.

Chapter 3

Brynn

The cool breeze nipped at my bare shoulders as I tugged the cloak closer around my neck. I fidgeted with Roderick's leather bracers that I had cut down to fit me. They hid the scars from that attack years ago; yet, my forearms always ached as we approached this part of the kingdom. Usually, the movement of the massive wolf beneath me would have lulled me close to sleep by now, but, today, my heart was tight in my chest as we travelled through the brush. I leaned forward against Rune's back to gain some of his warmth and become less of a target in the woods.

"You know, I can walk." I mumbled half-heatedly in the fur of the rolling shoulders near my head. I did not want to, and it would slow us down considerably, but I knew his morning had been just as long as my own.

"You could be quiet and rest too." Rune rumbled from between my legs; his deep growl reverberated through my body.

The sensation vibrated down to my bones causing me to grunt and sit up slightly.

We had been walking for hours outside of the city. The icy blue river that separated the two kingdoms churned next to us, edged by tea-leaved willows and downy birch. The Southern Kingdom of Vik was under our feet with the Eastern Kingdom of Reykia just across the water, providing its own gloom in the trees as the shadows shifted and the woods creaked. Crossing the glacier runoff was forbidden but scouts rarely dared to venture out this far to enforce such rules. The stories of the woods kept this place uninhabited except for the creatures that lurked in the dark.

The cold river was shallow ahead of us, before dropping into a series of waterfalls. This was our usual place to enter the neighboring forest of Reykia. From here, I could see the snowcapped mountains of the Northern Kingdom of Hoflin cutting into the overcast sky. Hidden from sight was the Western Kingdom of Arkanes with its black beaches and trade ports.

"We will have to make it back tomorrow before the rains cause the river to swell," I said, half to myself, as I looked at the darkening sky on the horizon.

My grip tightened in Rune's honey colored fur as he leapt from rock to rock across the river; a single slip would send us into the freezing water. The spray of rapids below bit my cheeks, causing them to burn and redden from the chill. Visually, there was little difference between the two sides of the river; yet, as the view of Vik was lost as we went deeper into the wood, the dread in my body eased.

Over the next several leagues, we would weave in and out of the winding kingdom barriers but there would not be a single person to cross our path. Here, I would not be hunted for *what I was*, simply hunted. It brought an odd comfort with the growing anticipation of becoming a different kind of prey. A dark smirk pulled at the corner of my lips at the irony of being safer surrounded by the creatures of nightmares than to near those in my own city.

My hands glowed a blueish green as I pulled from the power in nature surrounding us and ran them through the streaks of white highlights in the fur along Rune's back. A relieved growl rumbled beneath me as tendrils of healing magic penetrated his hide.

"You have more injuries than last week." I stated, partially in reprimand, as well as out of curiosity.

"*There is unrest within the ranks. Your father sent Halsten and I to handle it.*" Rune's voice sounded in my mind. There was an edge to his tone and bitterness dripped from the bond at the mention of my father.

I sighed and continued healing him. He rarely spoke aloud once we were on Reykian soil. He did not share my enthusiasm for walking through *enemy territory.* When he had found out this was my ritual, he made me swear never to go without him, again.

In the last seventeen years since we officially met as nine-year-olds, we rarely spent more than a few days apart, especially after Sondre's attack. Once I was allowed to start practicing my healing in the pits, we had an immediate connection; he had become my protector and I, his healer. I had grown up as Commander Ulfhild of the King's Guard's only daughter and was raised under his wife, the Head Healer. Rune's childhood was that of the pits, before they were shut down, dungeons created to weed out any weakness in the pack. Never claimed by a wolf in the higher ranks as a son, Rune was raised by the healers and soldiers from the years ahead of him, just like many of the abandoned pups of the pit litters every birthing season. In the years since, no one had acknowledged Rune's pedigree, even though there were undeniably striking similarities in some of the Guard's wolf forms. The brotherhood within the younger ranks of the Guard was strong, many shared a father without even knowing it. According to Rune, he had grown up as an orphan, without a family, until I came along and we made our own pack.

"Has Sondre approached you about Asta yet?" I asked as I focused on knitting a torn muscle back together.

"*More so inquired about the pup, but, yes, he has. I said you mentioned she had a couple more weeks before giving birth.*" His voice echoed in my thoughts as I pictured the sinews in need of mending in his hind leg. "*He is invested in that child you carry with you. Did he really force it to shift prematurely?*"

I allowed the image of the thing I had removed from Asta to fill my mind for him to see. His breath caught at the sight of it. The baby's skull was half exposed through the taunt skin barely containing it. A row of canine teeth pierced through one side of the semi-human face. The creature's skin was a blue tint under the blood, with the umbilical cord wrapped tight around its throat. It became more grotesque the further down I showed him. The spine had ruptured from the back, broken in several places. Patches of fur marred the baby's soft skin. Its hands were half fingers, half claws, which had scraped gashes all along the torso. In its frenzy of shifting, it had clawed through Asta's womb as well. The lower half had never developed skin as bare muscle and bone protruded out of the small frame. The toes, feet, and would have been tail, were a lifeless black that streaked up its contorted form.

Rune shivered under me.

"*Depth, Regh. How did it become so twisted? I have never seen any pup do that.*" He asked internally, trying to push the image from our mind with the overpowering scent of the meadow ahead.

Our year's littermates' nickname for me growing up stuck, regardless how much time had passed. I had been known as the Runt Guardian, as I focused on the smallest and weakest when I came to heal in the pits. The tonic to cause a newborn to shift, which Sondre now abused, was not made available to the pit's litters; triggering the first shift at a young age made it easier for a wolf shifter to learn how to change between forms early on. Many young pups had difficulty shifting and were put in the ring with their older pack mates to adapt or be killed. I spent many nights patching up the young wolves that had barely made it out of the training grounds, not all were so lucky. *Runt Guardian* slowly evolved to *RG* and then *Regh*. A plague sent by Valdis had wiped out many of the young pups from our birthing season, all too frail to fight the sickness. Rune and I had been helpless to save them all that time. The nickname still brought a warmth to my chest, even though so few were left to say it.

"The tonic to make a pup shift has always been meant for *after* they are born." I answered out loud, refusing to be silent about the Commander's atrocities, even in Rune's company. "Sondre had hoped the babe would shift *in labor* and kill Asta by forcing her to drink it early."

"Kill her?!" He bellowed, forgetting his goal of stealth entirely.

"Yes, to create his own Night Wolves through the forbidden blood rite of prenatal matricide. The bastard even bragged about it to her—" I said, shaking my head and leaning back to look up at the sky. The words caught in my throat as there was no sky to be seen; darkness spread out above us.

Sensing it too, Rune tensed beneath me and stilled.

During our distracting conversation, something had crept into the treetops above us. My heart pounded as I searched the canopy for any sign of what may have approached. Three pairs of amber eyes blinked above me, and I froze.

Don't move.

The serpentine beast was coiled in the canopy above us, clutching a thick tree with its only two visible legs. It was three times the size of Rune, covered in scales with an array of horns down its back. The long talons pierced through the wood with ease, and I knew it could puncture us both without much effort. The clicking sound coming from its mouth full of fangs caused my ears to ache as it echoed through the woods. I felt Rune's muscles bunch between my thighs as he readied to attack.

"Don't you dare move." I insisted, as I ever so slowly lifted my leg over his head to slide off his back, keeping my face directed at the nightmare above me.

"Get your ass back up there!" Rune screamed at me.

As soon as my feet touched the ground, the beast released something from its maw. It thudded on the ground next to me with a squelch. Fingers trembling, I crouched down without turning my head from the creature. I patted the grass until my palm landed on something cold and wet. I raised it between us and let my eyes flicker to it long enough to register what was in my grip. It was a severed human hand covered in saliva. A bent oath ring of braided silver was clamped into the flesh. A shiver racked my spine as I looked back at the beast.

"Where is it hurt?" I asked Rune, his senses far more attuned than mine in his wolf form.

"You've got to be fucking kidding me!" Rune snapped as a low growl came from his frame.

"Answer me, you stubborn fool! Before it tries to eat us!" I screeched back at him as his ears went flat.

"I can smell old blood in the trees to your left. Human blood. Wait, its right shoulder smells infected. Above you, to the far right." Rune relented.

With a sigh of slight relief, I let my magic course through me; I pulled from the waning light of the nearing solstice's sun and the tendrils of power coursing from my frame shifted to a pale blue. The creature did not take its eyes from my face as my magic reflected in its gaze and penetrated its wounded shoulder. The rotting flesh made me want to gag but I gritted my teeth and pushed deeper. My magic at last found an arrow tip of iron rusting in the puss filled gash. As I pulled it out, the beast clicked in approval and its forked tongue flicked in and out of its mouth. I mended the glimmering dark scales until the beast snorted.

I jumped at the sudden noise and cowered into Rune reflexively.

The lindworm, however, turned its head from me and reached for a nearby tree to slither away through the canopy, miraculously without a sound other than the whispering of leaves.

I melted into Rune's fur.

His fury radiated through him until I lifted the severed hand to his eyes and pointed to the braided oath ring around the wrist.

"*Silver.*" I was too breathless to speak aloud. "*The few times I have seen that creature, the visits have always been transactional. Silver means it is hurt; it was asking for help, for healing.*"

"*And if it was a gold necklace around a detached head? What, it would have eaten us?!*" Rune asked incredulously.

"*It has never brought gold before. Bronze is a warning. It only brought bronze once...*" My thoughts trailed off as I saw the meadow from between the trees. "*It knew Sondre was hunting me that day. I did not understand at the time...*"

"*Depths, Regh...*" There was an ache in his voice as he nuzzled me and helped me onto his back.

"No offering means it is a different lindworm and most likely it will try to eat us." I tried to lighten the mood. I slid the oath ring off and tossed the severed hand into the brush; bent or not, one of the traveling merchants would trade for the silver. *"So half-eaten bits are a good thing."*

He just shook his head, and we crossed the valley in silence. Once we exited the tree coverage, my shoulders started to relax. It was less likely now for something to drop down on us.

"Kill the mothers!" A voice croaked above us, sending Rune in a whirl to snap at the direction of the voice.

"Don't eat Roderick!" I exclaimed, pushing Rune's snout down as his teeth barely grazed the approaching raven's wing. "This trip has been tense enough, you are undoing all my work."

I swatted the top of Rune's large head, and the teal tendrils intensified into his skin. My anxiety lessened as I noticed no feathers were sticking out of his maw and released myself into healing his frame.

"Plus, Roderick was there this morning, and he was helpful." I added in defense as I lifted my arm for the raven to come in for a landing.

Roderick instead glided ahead of us toward the kingdom's barrier.

"It does not give him the right to sneak up on us right before we go into that wretched clearing, after almost getting eaten, for Depth's sake." Rune grumbled in my mind.

"Since he did not try to pluck out the lindworm's eyes, he probably did not realize what just transpired." I defended internally with a smirk.

Roderick tightly tucked his wings in for a spin and shifted in a plume of black feathers. His boots landed gingerly in the grass, and he turned to face us.

My breath caught as I saw his dark wings stretched out, no longer confined to his hexed bird form. There stood one of the most handsome men I had ever seen. His collar length, wavy, black hair was cut short on the sides of his chiseled face. His predominate brow cast a shadow over his chocolate brown eyes wreathed in black that scanned the clearing intently. Reddish hues warmed the dark stubble on his jaw that hid some of the scars decorating his rugged face. From his broad shoulders sprung his glorious wingspan, nearly twice the length of any of the shifters' I had healed in the medical tents for Northern war prisoners. His red tipped black feathers caught the fading light. His leather armor revealed his bare arms covered in inked binding runes and staves, his light scars from his bout with Sondre blended in with the plethora of old wounds peppered all over his body. A long black sword was sheathed between his shoulders. Near his scarred hands, calloused from the sword's use, were daggers strapped across his belt and down his thick thighs into his leather boots. A grin broke his solemn expression once our eyes met.

"I will get down here." I hurriedly swung a leg over Rune's shoulder to hop down; the soft ground cushioned my drop from his lofty back.

Roderick opened his arms, and I hurled myself into his embrace. He lifted me up off the ground and he held me tightly. It had been weeks since Rune and I were able to come out here and seeing Roderick in his raven form was just not the same. I hated the unnamed warlock who had bespelled Roderick to be confined in bird form when bidden by his leadership. I wanted him out and free like this every chance I could get. I threaded my fingers through his hair and let out some of the tightness in my chest in a contented hum. The smell of crisp snowy mountain air, fresh sage, and warm amber washed over me.

"I was hoping you would be here." I murmured into the crook of his neck.

"Cannot let angsty alpha Aksel get all your attention." I felt him breathe deeply as if to absorb all of my scent as well and make up for the time apart. A soft groan escaped as he squeezed me tighter. He pulled away enough to kiss my cheek. "He is not far behind me and will meet us by the old temple."

I kissed his jaw in return, his scruff tickling my lips.

"Thank you." I leaned back enough to look at him, my arms still resting around his neck.

The warmth of his eyes helped ebb the unease that had been building within me the entire trip. He kissed my brow and reluctantly set me back down on the grass. I turned enough to look at Rune, his disapproving glare still obvious in his wolf form. Finding me bloody in Roderick's care all those years ago had kept Rune from ever fully warming up to Roderick.

"Are you going to shift to talk to them?" I offered.

"*Absolutely not.*" Rune growled mentally. "*You and I have both seen the darkest of beings on this side of the river. I will not get caught unaware.*"

"Right, not like how Roderick just caught you unaware." I teased as I patted Roderick's firm chest. It was always startling how different it felt compared to stroking his feathers in bird form. It brought a blush to my cheeks, and I lowered my hand.

The red tips of his feathers were magnified by the sun in this forest; here it was obvious he was no ordinary raven shifter. He sensed my gaze and stretched out his wings in all his Blood Raven glory with a smug smirk. He tucked them back and slung an arm around my shoulders.

"Come, there are many things to discuss." Roderick whispered close to my ear.

I felt pure hatred and instinctual dread pour through the bond.

"*Fuck, overreact much?*" I shot at Rune in surprise, but he was not looking at either of us.

I felt Roderick's muscles tense as well, and I followed both of their gazes. The reason for the shift in their moods slinked into the clearing.

A black fog poured out from the woods and seeped through the grass ahead of us. I felt a golden heat rising from Rune through our bond, but I pushed back against it as he positioned himself in front of us.

"No." I said firmly. "Wait until we are back in the woods, save your strength."

Roderick's arm fell as I rolled my shoulders; I strode over to pat Rune's side and walked ahead of them toward the fog. Rune's snarl grew louder with every step. The fog sped up to meet me, and, for a moment, it enveloped my body whole. Rune exploded, snapping at the air around me until it dissipated enough for him to be able to see me again.

"Rune," I chided, "I'm *fine*."

The fog carried the scent of leather, tonka bean, and a hint of cedar embers that I breathed in deeply as if I was curled up next to a fireplace in a cabin deep in the woods beyond. I ran my hands through the fog as it caressed down my skin and eventually returned to the ground. It covered my boots as I continued to walk; Roderick fell in step next to me. His wings ruffled against his body and scattered the black fog around us.

Occasionally, the shadows reached back up to my fingertips, and Rune snapped at the darkness sporadically.

"Seriously, stop trying to eat my escorts." I scolded Rune.

"*I hate this thing.*" Rune's disgust echoed internally, as he eyed the dark tendrils which whispered up to my shoulders and through my hair in a momentary breeze.

Roderick swatted it away when it neared his wings.

"Ah, but do you hate it more than Aksel?" I asked over my shoulder as I crossed the tree line.

"*There is very little that I hate more than Aksel.*" The hair on his neck stood up, adding a cubit to his massive frame as the depths of his loathing reverberated in my mind.

I stroked his side once more as he came up next to me. I tried to send peaceful sensations down our bond as we walked together up the familiar dark path, but they hit a wall around his wolf mind. He sensed a threat and the animal within him was in control.

"You and me both," Roderick agreed, already knowing Rune's answer without him voicing it aloud.

"Aksel has helped me save more lives than either of you two *combined*." I defended.

Rune and Roderick both raised a lip in a sneer at the same time.

"He's still a dick." Roderick quipped as he ducked his head to pass under a branch.

Rune rumbled his agreement.

"You two are hopeless." I grumbled down the bond.

I could not hate Aksel simply based on what he had been created to be. The potions he provided had meant the difference between life and death for many of my worst patients, Rune, Roderick, *and myself* included. I did not let his condition undermine that fact. Night Wolves could be sired by any wolf shifter.

Depths, even Rune could sire one.

The pups' first act in life was the death of their mothers in labor, the unholy and unintentional blood rite. The gods and goddesses of Life and Death did not take kindly to such a heinous act upon entering the world and cursed them to be the harbingers of death, their fur as pitch black as the Depths from whence they came. As a healer, I would not wish that fate on any wolf pup, nor did I vilify them for the life that was thrust upon them.

Often times, after a Night Wolf was born, the kingdom would be struck down with a plague as the gods and goddesses took out their wrath on the disruption of nature. Rune still blamed Aksel and his kind for the loss of our year's littermates in the pack when the sickness took hold in our childhood. The young Night Wolf responsible was found and offered to Valdis to appease her fury. The child, born with the burden of killing his mother by no intentional fault of his own, was slain on the temple altar, ending the blight and my respect for the deity. The sacrifice had changed our lives in a way none of us could have foreseen.

Roderick's hand grazed the back of my neck tenderly as my shoulders tightened at the memory of the little boy's black fur matted with blood that flowed down the stone altar. My father had made me watch to understand my duties as a healer to protect the pack by slaying any threat to it, regardless of age. Bodhil had protested his methods, claiming it went against what she taught me as a healer. He had not listened, insisting he knew what was best for *his* daughter. That day, he stood behind me and held my chin to watch the priest slay the young Night Wolf. I had glanced to where the plagued litter was piled near the flames to be offered to the gods and cleansed. Rune's young face had been tear-stained as he was forced to place his brothers on the pyre for Valdis. His fierce emerald eyes had found mine.

"Never again," He had sworn down our newly established bond.

My gaze shifted to the deformed sack now bound to Rune's muscular adult shoulders.

Had it been Sondre's doing last time too?

I only had delivered one Night Wolf in my years as healer since then when I was eighteen. My instructing healer cut the babe's throat before it was fully out of the birthing canal as soon as she knew the mother had died. Frantically, I tried to heal it, tried to restart the mother's heart, but I lost them both when the other healer intervened. In a stoic tone, my instructor told me that Valdis had willed for the mother to die and Dahlia would not condone a Night Wolf living in her lands; it was part of the pain and wonder of birthing wolves, an honor only allowed to select healers steel enough to do what was necessary for the sake of the kingdom. The wolves were our strongest assets of defense, comprising much of the kingdom's army and the entirety of the elite King's Guard; they were also our greatest liability to anger the gods if they upset the balance of nature. I had sprinted into the woods with the slain babe cradled in my arms, knowing no one would dare follow me though the dark trees. I fell to my knees in the abandoned temple and pleaded for the Old God Tyr to stop this needless massacre of wolf pups in the name of *religion and fear.* Tyr did not answer himself, but he had sent Aksel to hear my pleas. Ever since, I promised to bring him the innocent killers whenever I came across them.

Chapter 4

Brynn

The black fog was a stark contrast against the white bark of the trees surrounding us. To the locals, the white trees were a sign of a hex upon the woods. It was said that the wind of Reykia gave a voice to the dead. Through my nature studies to be a healer, I knew the leaves of the aspen and poplar trees were what whispered in the wind, but it did nothing to still my rapid beating heart. I reached deep within myself to lend some peace to Rune as we continued and got a huff in response; he did not like it here as much as I did. A small stream babbled in the distance, on its way to the river, adding to the eerie melody of the forest. Every time we traveled this way, we would stop at the stream. The tradition may have seemed reckless to some, especially with how forbidden the forest was, but it was our custom all the same.

The stream parted against a large black stone covered in ornate carvings. The ones at the bottom had been smoothed down by the river and were barely visible. Rune and I knew the prayer etched there by heart already and whispered it down the bond in synchronicity.

I glanced up at the wolf next to me. The once young pup had grown to be one of the King's elite hunters. A streak of white fur went across his left eye, down his shoulders, and to his tail; the rest of him was various shades of honey and copper. The thick fur hid the numerous scars that decorated his muscular frame, a scroll depicting the brutality of the castle's customs. He lowered his head and nuzzled the grave marker. The woman we loved dearly had died in this spot, tracked down by a previous generation of hunters. The irony was never lost on us.

Rune had given the carvings on the stone as a birthday gift years ago. Tyr's scaled form coiled around the stone as a permanent guardian and silent promise for justice. It had taken Rune weeks of hushed excursions into the forest he hated so much to etch in the staves and lettering. It helped soothe some of the pain of her passing. I waded into the water to kiss the *Yrsa* carved into the stone as Roderick waited on the bank.

This was the first place I had met the beautiful bird when my mother Bodhil had brought me here to pay my respects on an anniversary of Yrsa's death. He had been flying overhead and came to roost above us as Bodhil sang a prayer to the Old Gods.

In the years since, the Blood Raven has watched over me, my protective shadow, repeating warnings he heard around the town.

Our trio continued deeper into the forest until we came upon a line of stone pillars reaching toward the sky. A barely perceivable golden hue covered me again as Rune threw a protective shield over me. This time, I submitted to the covering as it soaked into my skin. Tyr's abandoned temple was near the hunting grounds of multiple species far worse than the lindworm we crossed paths with that would favor the taste of human flesh. The dark fog pooled at the edge of the stones and beyond, creating a blackened path ahead. Rune stepped closer to me as we walked past the threshold of stones and crossed through a barrier of magic. It crackled over my skin but did not sting, thanks to Rune's protection. Roderick walked behind us, alert and suspicious as always. Inside the circle of pillars, overgrown with moss and ivy, the sun was muted as the light took a cooler tone. Shadows shifted at the corners of our vision, but nothing could take my eyes away from the massive beast before us.

Resting on one of the downed pillars was a black wolf bigger than any in Vik's court. He raised his large head in greeting and watched us approach with his keen eyes. The colors in them shifted between different yellows, oranges, and reds, like the molten lava fields further out in Reykia. The tapestry in the brothel did not do his kind justice. His fur absorbed all light, as if he were a living shadow, with claws of garnet equipping each paw larger than the size of my head.

Below him, leaning against the column, was a woman. The black tattoos of swirls, runes, and staves were in stark contrast to her bright ivory skin. Her chest was bound by strips of fabric matching the wolf's eyes and the hem of her long black skirt looked like it had been dipped in blood. She brushed her ashen blonde dreads off her shoulder as she pushed herself off the pillar and walked toward a stone basin. Carvings that matched the same designs etched into her skin covered the basin.

Rune stopped a few strides away and I continued forward, knelt, and bowed my head. The black fog had dissipated, but a small presence remained pooled where I knelt, not leaving my side.

"Sire." I said quietly, knowing Aksel's hearing could pick up my voice long before we had arrived. The Alpha of the Night Wolves deserved no less respect. "Thank you for agreeing to meet with me."

"Roderick made it sound urgent, but that loud bird does have a habit of exaggerating. Rise, Brynn, bring forth your offering and news." His deep voice rumbled like thunder from a cloud, dripping with authority.

Roderick scoffed in defense and retrieved the pack strapped to Rune's shoulders. Rune glared at Roderick's closeness, but he made no motion to stop him. Untying the satchel carefully, Roderick brought it to me as I started to stand. I kept my head bowed as I took the wrapped deformity out of the satchel and approached the basin. Roderick turned and leaned against a pillar, crossing his arms to watch what was to unfold.

"Hello, Witch." I said as I tenderly set the child into the basin for inspection.

The Witch's bracelets of bone and metal clinked as she reached for my hands as I attempted to step back.

"Tell me, child." The Witch said as her pointed onyx nails gently grazed down my forearm. "Was it dead when you brought it into the world?"

She inspected my face first before hovering a hand over my chest, core, then back to my arm, reading the traces of the magic I recently used lingering in my skin. I did not resist, nor did I pull my arm out of her grasp. Instead, I looked at the colossal wolf above us.

"The babe shifted while still in his mother. It is our custom to wait to issue the tonic until a fortnight has passed to ensure neither the boy nor the mother is harmed in the transition. In Vik, it is meant to be nursed to the child; all of our healers abide by this rule. Commander Sondre forced the tonic upon the mother *before the birth*. The child transitioned in the womb, Aksel; during the struggle, it looked like the cord strangled the boy before I arrived, and he had torn himself open in his panic."

I explained. I knew there would be doubt as Vik's healers were meant to kill any offspring at risk of the Night Wolf Curse.

I looked to the Witch, now hovering a breath away from my face. As much as she tried to get under my skin, I owed this strange woman my life. After chasing away Sondre when he attacked me, the Night Wolves Gunnar and Brede had brought her to the river to help heal me and she inked runes and staves similar to her own along my waist. A protection stave to mask my scent as anything more than a healer decorated my right hip. I had allowed her to needle in a stave of her own making, protection many witches wore once they escaped the breeding pits in the South. An upside-down fertility rune imbued with my own sterilizing magic kept me from ever being able to conceive a wolf. Sondre's threats to breed me had become slightly hollower after she offered me the inked protection hidden under my clothes.

"It was dead when I first inspected the mother." I repeated to her, not backing down.

Aksel was well aware that I refused to practice the disposal of Night Wolf pups; as much as I hated the idea of future warriors being the seed of Sondre, the intentional death of such offspring would have been an offense to Aksel's kind and my own personal morals.

"And you ensured it stayed dead by crushing the skull and shoulders." The Witch whispered, her breath hot on my lips.

Her yellow eyes searched my face. "The magic you used was such a pretty red, an odd color choice for a *healer*, and to kill a child, no less."

Rune growled a warning.

My lip instinctively tugged into a sneer as his disdain coursed through me at the implication.

"As a *healer*, I ensured the mother lived," I insisted. "I did what was necessary to keep her alive. I cannot kill what is already dead."

"Ah, but in Vik, your healers have *gold* magic." The Witch mused and grazed a nail across my forehead to tuck a stray strand of hair behind my ear. "Yet, a pretty ruby red flowed out of you."

"The child was dead; no life came from it when I read it." I tore my gaze from her accusatory eyes as this was not the discussion I wanted to have here; I peered up at the massive wolf above us, holding his molten gaze. I had come here to focus on Sondre's affront to nature, not my controversial use of magic. "It was gone. It was dead, that I will swear to you, Aksel."

"Why would your Commander risk killing an heir, Wolf?" Aksel asked Rune without shifting his focus from me.

Rune rolled his shoulders uncomfortably and strode closer.

"We believe it is to create his own Night Wolves." He admitted cautiously.

Aksel's attention snapped to the copper wolf as he rose in rage, snarling at the thought of such blasphemy.

"To *kill the mothers*." Roderick sounded in agreement from across the temple. He often repeated the phrase in his bird form from hearing it around town in secret meetings down dark alleyways. "It is calculated and intentional, Aksel. I have no doubt after witnessing this pup's mother try to give birth. Sondre means to do the unthinkable. The Guard has murmured about such plans around town for months, but this was the first time I have seen the Commander make a real attempt at this. This is bigger than just little Asta's boy here."

"It makes sense." Rune continued. "There has been dissention in the ranks due to Sondre's recent methods to increase the pack, as many of the mothers have not consented to carry a wolf shifter's baby with the uptick in deaths. He has petitioned the King to bring back the breeding pits to avoid the issue of consent; it has caused a decrease in future Guard members. Less willing mothers means less pups, less soldiers. The King will sign just about anything to keep his military well populated with the growing threat in the North."

The Witch's hiss made Rune pause. She had been one of the last women to find her freedom once the pits had been shut down.

"In the meantime," Rune proceeded cautiously, "More of the pleasure halls have had women who are carrying wolf bastards go missing. All the ones my pack have found have died so far in childbirth."

It was I who now turned to him in surprise.

"I did not want to tell you before I knew more," Rune confessed, "We've only recently discovered the patten. Asta was not due for weeks so I thought we would have more time to figure out the connection. You confirmed my suspicion on the way over here: Sondre and his men wish for the mothers' deaths to trigger the blood rite and create a new Night Wolf pack though the matricide curse."

"Night Wolves were never made by choice. Your impetuous Commander should know that." Aksel growled.

I could only look back to the deformed baby in the basin.

How many of my pregnant patients had been with one of the Commander's wolves? Or worse, the Commander himself? He went to a different hall every night. Are only the ones near full term at risk? How had I missed this?

The Witch watched intently as the thoughts flooded my mind.

"You know what this will mean for you if they bring back the pits, don't you, pretty girl?" She asked as she crooked a finger under my chin to lift my gaze to her.

Roderick tsked in disapproval at the Witch's insinuation.

"I am a healer in the city, Witch. I will be in the pits, healing." I answered dryly.

"Healing the mothers or the pups?" The Witch knew the difference in hierarchy, having lived it herself.

The pups were tended with intention to make strong warriors for the King. The mothers were only put back together enough to be assaulted again to bear more wolves.

She leaned close, her blood red lips brushing the edge of my ear. "They force witches to breed in the pits, how long until they try to rape you, too, *oh, holy healer*?"

Rune lunged at the Witch with a snarl, but he was not fast enough to reach her.

Aksel had leapt from the column at Rune's first sign of movement and landed between them. The forest floor trembled under his weight, and the surrounding birds took flight. Aksel's teeth were around Rune's neck before the Witch could respond. A protective covering surged from me to Rune's throat on instinct, but Aksel did not attempt to pierce the skin. He gripped firmly enough to toss Rune to the side, injuring only his pride. My knees buckled at the effort, the magic demanding payment within me. I felt the Witch's knowing hand on my elbow, steadying me as I regained my footing.

Roderick had pushed off from the pillar, but paused to watch Aksel's next move, hand on his black garnet dagger. There was a fight brewing in his eyes.

"You forget yourself, *boy*." Aksel growled at Rune.

Rune was one of the strongest wolves in the King's Guard, but he looked like a domesticated pup in comparison as Aksel stood at his full height. Power radiated from the alpha and even the shadows appeared to quake at the sound of his reprimand. He bit at the air and foam dripped from his muzzle. Rune's ears went flat, and his tail instinctively curled closer to his body. I had never seen Rune submit to anyone as an adult, but the very trees seemed to yield to Aksel, their branches heavy and dipped low.

"Witch, take the babe and leave us. Do your readings and fire sacrifice, then return to me, immediately." Aksel did not turn from Rune, but the Witch obeyed.

"They will come for you, and not just Sondre and his mutts." The Witch cautioned quietly to me as she rested a hand on the bundle and looked off into the distance toward Reykia. "That will cause *him* to come for you. You are valuable for more than your womb to those outside this kingdom. I fear you do not have much time."

The shadows at my feet stirred in response to her words.

We both peered down at the darkness coating my boots; she squinted at it wearily. An orange tendril of magic wisped from her hand, seeped through my skirt, and caressed the tattoos on my hips. I could sense the genuine worry in her magic. It vanished as soon as it appeared as she scooped up the deformed creature, and with one last lingering look, she departed.

"Who will come for you? Who is she talking about?" Rune groaned as he got back up to his feet and shook off the damp leaves sticking to his fur.

"She is toying with you." Aksel interrupted as I took a breath to answer. "Your goddess of death, Valdis, will never allow this kind of insurrection under her rule. A manufactured pack like that would be an abomination to her, to each of our deities of death. She cannot allow your Commander to succeed. She has killed for less."

Roderick scoffed from across the clearing.

"So, to prevent it, she will cause both the mothers and children to die, every time?" I asked quietly, unable to look up from the empty basin as the future ramifications crashed against my spirit in waves.

How will I save them?

How much time do I truly have?

Aksel came up from behind me, his large chest brushed against my head and shoulder. His heat cascaded through my frame, combatting the anxiety that sent ice though my veins. I felt so small in his presence, smaller still when faced with such insurmountable odds.

"She may. None of my pack's sires tried killing their mates to create a more powerful pack and each of us were still cursed by Death before our first breaths." Aksel's tone softened even as his words remained solemn. "Your Valdis may respond even more harshly to the Commander's attempts to defy her in such an intentional way."

"Why has she not already?" Rune asked as he took a step toward us; his apprehension at Askel's closeness was palpable.

"The solstice has consumed her focus, as it will with all the gods, in the coming days." Aksel resounded behind me.

"What of the other arriving deities? Could my women pray to them to intervene? If they are in Vik for the solstice, they can act. I must be able to give some hope to the mothers back home." The words spilled out of me as I peered up at him, attempting to switch to solution mode instead of panicking. I turned and placed a palm on his chest, his fur enveloping my hand in inky darkness. "Surely, *your* goddesses may step in, as the only Night Wolf pack resides in their court."

Aksel shook his head and looked down at me, his essence enveloping me.

"Braxcia would let the deaths be gentle, young one, but she would spare neither mother nor child to prevent another pack from forming. Sverre, Death of the West, in Arkanes, will not interfere either. He has only one Night Wolf currently in his kingdom from my pack and has no reason to meddle in Vik's affairs. Hoflin's deities will never help; Skai is more likely to kill your whole town if you pray to him for assistance." His sigh warmed my skin as his words made my blood go cold. "The only hope you can offer the mothers is to pray to your own Dahlia of

Life; although, I fear your Commander may have damned them all to death already.”

He gave my chin a nudge of condolence with his snout.

I brushed my hand up the bridge of his muzzle and stroked between his fiery eyes.

“The mother this morning, Asta, thought you a deity…Can you intervene?” I knew his answer, but I was growing desperate. I clung to the fur between my fingers, searching for some strength to hold onto in this.

“My pack cannot undermine the authority of Valdis in your lands. Along the border, treaties are blurred but to go into your city, and enact justice, would set things in motion that cannot be undone.” Aksel cautioned as he leaned into my touch.

“The death of the mothers and children of my city cannot be undone.” The words felt flat as they left my lips. The finality of our situation settled into my bones. I rested my forehead against his fur.

This cannot be the future for my girls.

“We do nothing?” Rune asked behind us, his tension radiated into my mind.

“I refuse to do nothing.” I interjected as I leaned back. I looked into the alpha’s molten gaze and searched for my courage. The deep reds, oranges, and yellows staring back at me stoked a fire within me. “If the gods refuse to do anything, I will heal whoever I can.”

"You cannot heal all of them, Brynn. Not without tapping into outside power that could get you killed. Either by burning out, or worse, by being *found out*." Rune argued. "You were already flirting with that line today and that was only one mother, not the whole town's worth. The townsfolk will only go so long without asking questions about why you are different from the other healers. That Witch will not be the only one wondering why your tendrils can shift away from gold; people will start to notice. Outperforming the head healer and dipping into your witch roots will get you bound and bred for what you could produce for the pack. They are *desperate* for the powerful wolf twins that only witch mothers can carry; if they could make a *pair* of Night Wolf twins from breeding and killing *you*, they will! The Guard will find a dungeon to stick you into, pits or not."

His words echoed many arguments we frequently had on the subject. I did not need Aksel and Roderick joining in on this discussion too.

"We do not have time to get into this again, Rune." I chided internally.

"Because you know I am right." Rune bit back.

"Then I will need help to keep that from happening." I walked to Rune, shaking his reprimand out of my mind.

Human mothers without mystical abilities often only had one child, and it was not always guaranteed to carry the father's shifter gene. Witches were known for their shifter offspring and strong likelihood for twins, both imbued with magical powers. If both pups survived, they were an elite force to be reckoned with, historically changing the tide of many battles against the North.

I will not be turned into a brood mare to be inseminated by any wolf seeking power.

I took a handful of Rune's fur; anger warmed my core and melted away the impending doom.

Roderick was behind me in an instant, with his hands on my shin, boosting me onto Rune's back.

"I used the last of my vials on the babe's mother this morning. May I have another before this nightmare begins?" I hated asking for such an intrusive remedy, but I was out of options. "Please, Aksel..."

"The Witch thought as much. She made several for you to use in your salves." Aksel motioned for Roderick to fly atop the downed column next to us. "The whole pack contributed; this should last you through the rest of the birthing season. If you run out, things are more dire than we realize."

Roderick returned with a satchel of glass vials clinking together; a slight look of disgust marred his handsome face as he handed the precious cargo to me.

"She has been collecting for days," A rare, amused twinkle lit the alpha's eyes. "Most likely in hopes for a favor from you."

"Then I owe you *both* a favor." I claimed as Rune nuzzled my leg to hold on tight. "Thank you, Sire, truly."

Rune did not wait for a reply and took off in a sprint back toward Vik and the mothers we needed to save once we arrived in the morning.

Chapter 5

Brynn

Screams pierced through the darkness. I tried to open my eyes; everything stung as if hot sand lined my eyelids. The smell of the burning pine, singed fur, and charred flesh hit me as I attempted to gain my bearings. An uninvited thought that the raiders had reached us in the night echoed in my mind. I threw off my thin blanket and pushed myself off the forest floor. Rubbing the sleep and smoke out of my eyes, I called for my mother instinctively; my voice sounded strange and foreign.

Only the crackle of trees burning around me answered.

My mind felt foggy as I wondered why I had just called for her; Bodhil would not be nearby, she was across the border. I reached out to wake Rune, but neither he nor Roderick were with me.

We had just settled down for the night in a cave before...

My head throbbed and I pushed back my hair only to gasp at the deep red strands. I regarded the tattoos weaving down my arms and recognition settled into my bones.

Dread coursed through me as I realized this must be a dream.

My gaze scanned the runes twisting around my forearms into my hands, and I knew I was staring at Yrsa's skin. My dreams were wandering through her memories again, as they had so many times since childhood.

"No, no, no! Wake up!" I thought frantically.

I was trapped in her horrors until I could wake, forced to see things as she did. I –she–scrambled to our feet and found that we were already dressed. As I considered reaching out to Rune through the bond to wake me, a voice resounded in our mind in place of his.

"Yrsa, run!" A hoarse voice yelled internally.

"Admund? Where are you?" We cried out in fear. Yrsa's young voice was raspy in our ears as we spoke the words. I could feel her fear coursing through the body we now shared.

"RUN!" Admund bellowed down her bond.

Yrsa's memory took us sprinting through the makeshift camp on the outskirts of town, jumping over burnt bodies on the path. I dared to glance behind us to try to catch a glimpse of this Admund she spoke of, but through the smoke, I saw the silhouette of a woman with wings dark as night, watching us intensely. The *light of the fires made the red tips of her wings glow like dying embers hidden within her black feathers. Runes of kohl adorned her strikingly beautiful face and the flames reflected in her steely gaze. She did not belong in the memory, she felt superimposed within it like I did, eerily out of place.*

Distracted, we collided with something solid in front of us. A surprised yelp escaped our lips as we were lifted into the air by a set of strong hands. We went to claw blindly at the face of the one holding us, but our arms were pinned as we were pulled close into an embrace.

"Yrsa, you're alive! Oh, my sweet girl." The older man breathed as he kissed our cheek in relief.

I then noticed the healer's mark on his neck and tattered robes.

"Father? Oh, father!" Yrsa's voice spoke the unfamiliar words without my consent, but we held on tighter instinctively. Yrsa's recognition of her father washed over me. "Where is Mother? And Bodhil? Admund told me to run, but I cannot find him."

"Your sister Bodhil is with the town healers. She and Mother were badly burned and are among those evacuated. Come, I know a safe way out." He rushed as he set us back down and took our hand to guide us.

As we hurried away, I looked back to the winged woman, but she was gone. In her absence, there was a void; its darkness crept into my core, filling me with dread.

"Admund was out getting herbs when the Southern scouts arrived." Yrsa's father rasped as we navigated through the chaos. "Some wolf in the village tipped them off that there are witches in our camp. The bastard wanted the reward, but this is what he got. The scouts have burned the woods to force us toward their ranks posted in the town, killing any male they have come across without the magical gift and enslaving the women for their pits."

He yanked our hand down as we hid behind a fallen tree. Several soldiers jogged past yelling directions to spread out the search.

"He is leading you in the wrong direction. Head back to the forest." Admund whispered in our mind.

"We should not be going closer to town." We glanced back at the way we came, an ache to follow Admund's guidance penetrated to our very core.

"I can get you to the other healers, they will take you in and away from here. Once they train you with your older sister at the citadel, the South won't come looking for you anymore. You can blend in with the other healers." Yrsa's father said firmly, his usually warm tone was cold with determination.

"But Bodhil's late mother was a healer," Reality sunk in as Yrsa pulled our hand away, "That's why she trains with them. The healers know Mother is a witch, they will not take me."

It was a truth Yrsa's father never seemed to accept. We were outcasts in his healer community after he had wed Yrsa's mother and bore Admund and Yrsa.

"You're running out of time." Admund urged in our thoughts.

Yrsa shook our head and turned to run but our feet were affixed to the ground. Regardless of how hard we tried, we could not lift our shoe. The grip on our hand tightened until it hurt. We looked up at her father in confusion but saw his wide eyes looking past us. Tears of blood streamed down his cheeks as he gurgled. Darkness like a spiderweb crept from the collar of his tunic up his neck. We tried to scream but it caught in our throat. We thrashed against the invisible bond holding us in place as her father fell to his knees before us. Blood now leaked from his ears and mouth.

For a moment, we were transfixed; our thundering heartbeat was so loud it muted the approaching footsteps.

"I can feel your power, girl." A slick voice sounded from behind us. A cold gaunt hand caressed the back of our neck before wrapping around our throat.

We tried to look up but our entire body was still locked in place.

"Wolf!" The voice snapped and a sleek grey wolf trotted out of the smoke. "Take this one for breeding. Her witch blood will give you twice as many pups."

The lust in the wolf's eyes gleamed as it stalked forward.

"I will bring the boy with me to the front to be syphoned until he can be conditioned and trained." The man above us explained. The hand slid down our collar and rested upon our heaving chest as he tsked. "Pity to waste such a good pair on the dogs. Put her with the others you've found."

The wolf growled his reply.

The oily presence enveloped us as he leaned down. His damp skin brushed against the side of our face as his fingers trailed up the nape of our neck. His breath against our ear sent chills down our spine.

"Give my regards to the Keeper of the Pit, child." He whispered before licking the side of our throat.

I woke up with a start, swatting around my face and kicking against the form pressed against my frame.

"Get off me!" I shrieked.

"Regh, stop! Regh—ow! Regh—Regh, it's me!" Rune was shaking my shoulders in his human form as he pinned my legs to the ground to keep me from striking him.

The fight in me settled as I took in my surroundings. The cave was dim, sheltering us from the wind that howled outside in the darkness. There was a small fire with the remnants of our freshly caught dinner from earlier next to it, but no flames devoured the space around us. I was not under a spell; I was under Rune. The twisted being no longer caressed my throat; it has Rune's hands tentatively lingering on my skin.

Rune rolled off, out of breath.

"Fuck, Regh. You tried to take my eye out this time when I went to wake you." He rubbed a light red scratch across his cheek. He sat up and rested his forearms against his knees.

I could feel his exhaustion through the bond as I must have syphoned his strength while fighting in the dream.

Rune tilted his head slightly to acknowledge my assessment.

"*Shit...Sorry...*" I thought in his direction.

He opened his thighs up to me and motioned for me to come closer.

Shivering from the shock of the dream, I gladly accepted his warmth as I curled up between his legs, my back to him, and rested my head against his arm.

He rubbed his other hand against my spine until the trembling started to subside.

"Ah, our night terror has awoken." Roderick's voice echoed off the stones. His dark hair was tussled as if he had not slept much either. His bare torso glistened in the firelight as he ducked into the cave.

I bashfully sat up a little straighter, realizing how loud I must have been if he had gone outside to ensure none of the forest's creatures came looking for what caused the commotion.

Roderick crouched in front of us and offered me a leather wine skin of water. "Here, fresh from the stream, drink. Your voice must be hoarse from all the screaming."

I leaned into Rune's warmth and drank the icy glacier runoff. The frigid liquid cooled my panic, and I steadied my breathing to the rise and fall of Rune's chest.

Roderick grazed his knuckles against my arm before sitting across from us. He rested against the cave wall, his wings stretching out against the damp stone.

"Yrsa's memories again?" Rune asked pensively into my hair.

"The forest raid." I answered.

Ever since I could remember, I was plagued by glimpses of her life, unable to affect the outcome, forced to relive her terrors.

"Anything new this time?" Roderick raised an eyebrow.

"There has been a woman showing up in my dreams as of late. She was there this time." I turned slightly to peer over at Roderick from the crook of Rune's arm. I watched as firelight shone on his massive wingspan, highlighting the various shades of black and red in his feathers. "She had…wings…blood-tipped like yours."

Roderick sighed and lulled his head back against the stone wall. His expression grew grim.

"Lerevna." He breathed. His brown irises glowed in the flickering light like a rich honey on a summer's day as he searched for the right words. "She is a…dream walker. She must be looking for something in your, well Yrsa's, memories."

"So, you know who is tormenting Brynn? Why am I not surprised…" Rune sighed, accusation dripping from his tone. His arms instinctively flexed around me protectively.

"I will look into it." Roderick's tone was dismissive to Rune, but he softened and raised his chin toward me. "Try to rest, Brynn; she will not visit you again tonight."

"How can you be so sure?" Rune interjected.

Roderick tapped his temple.

"You two are not the only ones who can communicate across distances." Roderick crossed his arms and let his head lull against the stone once more.

"*I don't like this.*" Rune's voice quietly sounded in my mind.

"*A bit hypocritical if we judge him over something like this.*" I offered in return. I handed the water to Rune in hopes it would sooth the boiling suspicion within him.

Even though Roderick had been in my life for so long, we knew very little about each other still. Moments like this, being able to simply talk, were rare. I did not want to make it awkward, but the chill I felt in my bones upon seeing the winged woman weighed on my soul.

"Who was she?" I whispered, apprehension constricting around my throat.

The woman I had seen was formidable, and she wanted to know something desperately enough to enter my dreams, unannounced and uninvited. Every muscle in my back began to tense as my thoughts spiraled through worst case scenarios.

Rune grazed his knuckles along my spine to chase away the chill and reorient my thoughts.

There was a long pause, and Roderick seemed to barely breathe. The skin under his inked runes started to flush red as if he was going to break out in hives.

That is not a good sign.

Finally, Roderick gritted his teeth slightly and sucked in a breath.

"My…*mate*." He said at last.

My heart stilled, and Rune's hand froze.

Air filled Rune's chest to bark out a retort but my shock coursing through our bond made him hold his tongue.

"Your…what?" The words felt like sandpaper in my mouth.

There were few religious concepts that I hated more than fated mates: A partner chosen by the gods to create a bond unlike any other. Some said it was for the betterment of the species, while others claimed it was divine pairing for a glorious purpose. The lack of autonomy in the matter was revolting. And Roderick had one, a *chosen by the gods* mate.

I felt nauseated.

Roderick and I had never been intimate, but it was not due to a lack of wanting to be that close. He had gone from being my guardian, to my close friend, to more than I knew how to describe, but the times we spent in this form had been limited. Life always seemed to get in the way.

Noticing my body go rigid, Roderick leaned forward.

"It is not what you think." He began, a hint of surprise in his eyes as he glanced between Rune and me.

"*Like fuck it isn't.*" Rune snapped in my mind.

"*This is enough to process without your commentary, asshat. Let me think.*" I bit back at Rune as I took the water from him to have something to fidget with in my hands. I needed to keep them from trembling.

"*Regardless of how you feel, having her as a mate will tie his allegiance to her. If she is digging around in your memories, for something about Yrsa, of all people, we need to be careful. That is all I am saying. We do not need to give him whatever she is looking for, fair?*" Rune's tone was gentle but firm in response to the tidal wave of emotions crashing over me.

"How many Blood Ravens have you heard of, Brynn?" Roderick inquired, his gaze transfixed on my expression.

"You, and now this Lerevna in my dreams, apparently. So, what, two?" I took a sip to try to wash down the boulder that felt lodged in my airways.

"Exactly. Two, in all of existence, we are the only two. As fated mates go, it is kind of a given when it comes to the gods picking out a match." Roderick exhaled heavily. "Lerevna and I were *made* into what we are now. I was not born a Blood Raven."

"Because you were…a White Raven of the North." I filled in from what little I knew about his complicated past.

The White Ravens were guards of the Old Gods' temples, mighty warriors who had answered only to the Old Gods themselves at the height of their reign. Skai, Hoflin's God of Death, had meticulously killed off the Guard, one by one…all except Roderick.

"Correct. Lerevna was the first Blood Raven created, made to serve directly at the right hand of the Old Gods. I was chosen to be her *sword* from the White Ravens' ranks." His eyes were trained on the cave wall, but his gaze was far away. "I did not know at the time what all it would entail."

He sucked in a deep breath to continue but winced. He cleared his throat and began again.

"When I transformed into *this*," He rustled his wings in emphasis, "I felt the mate bond just out of reach. She, however, rejected it, entirely. But, that was not before these took root."

He gestured to the exposed tattoos along his arms and torso.

"What do they all mean?" I asked as I studied the dark lines more intently. I would have liked to have had them all memorized by now, but these moments of stillness were not common enough.

"They are vows, layered into my skin, to her, to the gods, to Rhydar—my Master of War. There was a sacred…ritual that fashioned me into the weapon she deserved." He flexed his hands. "When I arose, I had been branded by these."

My eyes lingered on the black ink as my thoughts wandered. To have his bonds so publicly displayed seemed even more intimate of a connection, my heart sank.

"To mark you as hers?" My annoyance at my own insecurities made my cheeks flush.

Rune's presence in my mind nudged my subconsciousness in reprimand for condemning my natural feelings.

"To keep me in check." Roderick's chuckle was bitter. "I may have been known to bend rules within the White Raven's ranks. These ensured I remained…compliant. If I push the limits, they will activate."

"Activate?" I crawled closer to inspect them.

Roderick huffed a small laugh at my curiosity and took my hand in his to put it on his chest. Rune shifted his weight behind me but did not move to deter me from touching Roderick.

"There are things I am bound to not disclose to anyone. If I attempted to disobey direct orders or go against my *handlers*, these would heat to an unbearable degree, essentially burning me from the inside out." Roderick sighed and I felt his muscles tense in preparation. "For example, deep in the East, there is a—"

His voice cracked and he took a sharp breath. The sigils flared as his skin beneath them reddened.

I drew my hand back with a gasp; my magic recoiled from the searing contact of his designs. The type of magic woven into the cells of his body was old and dark. All the light in me flickered as power came to the surface of his skin.

I had felt the coldness of death, of gods and of wraiths, but *this* crept in like a frost over my very soul. I looked up at him horrified. Rune put a hand on my ankle in warning.

"Who bespelled these?" My voice trembled in awe of the magnitude of knowledge and skill it would have taken to hold such control over him. I stiffened in trepidation of his response.

What being from the Depths could conjure magic of this magnitude?

Rune flinched at the weight of such a possibility.

Roderick attempted to answer but he choked on the words. His neck muscles flexed as he strained to speak but was unable to make any intelligible sounds other than gurgling. The redness around the ink deepened and my magic sensed the severity of the burn penetrating his skin.

"Enough! I get it—I get it, enough!" I scooted away from him, into Rune's waiting embrace, worried my mere proximity would trigger a flare at this point.

Roderick expelled a ragged breath, his bonds finally allowing him to breathe fully. His shoulders slumped and his hands trembled slightly as he regained his composure.

"There are things I do not have the power to tell you. There is so much I wish I could explain, but I literally cannot voice the words." A deep exhaustion filled his gaze, and it caused an ache to swell within my chest at the hollowness that shone in his usually warm irises.

"Something I *can* say is that Lerevna is an independent minded warrior who detested the idea of some *god* making a choice for her heart, which sounds like someone else I know." He leaned forward and tapped the tip of my nose.

I relaxed slightly at his teasing tone. I did not need to look at Rune to know he was rolling his eyes.

"The fact remains," Roderick let his hand fall back into his lap. "She and I *are* mates, and have a connection even without the bond fully accepted and in place. I will not lie to you about that. I can speak to her, much like you can to Rune."

I studied Roderick, but Rune tensed behind me at the insinuation.

I trusted Roderick, with my life, but this was not something we ever truly discussed. He had never asked about my bond with Rune directly; it was an unspoken understanding that he never would either.

"How you two can…" Roderick evaluated Rune inquisitively; his head cocked slightly to the side like the raven that usually perched on my shoulder.

Rune gave Roderick nothing, but his presence entered my mind.

"We agreed from the start, Brynn. No one knows." Rune's voice was deep with seriousness.

"He would not betray us if we told him that it has nothing to do with mated nonsense. I do not doubt him, not for a moment." I retreated further into Rune's embrace slowly.

He was right, even if I did not like it. No one, not even Sif, knew the full truth behind Rune's and my connection; rumors abounded over the years since we were rarely apart, but *nothing* was ever confirmed nor denied, to protect us. People eventually lost interest when there was never any new tantalizing news about us.

"The truth of us not being mates would only invite more questions that you cannot answer—answers we cannot trust him with yet—not until we know more about this Lerevna. We have

not kept the truth of our existence secret this long, from those we have loved over the years and those we trust more thoroughly than him, just to risk the wrong person finding out now." Rune insisted as he took the water for another sip.

Roderick analyzed us, catching my slight squint and the twitch in the corner of Rune's mouth as our silent conversation concluded. He seemed resigned not to ask outright.

"I still struggle to understand, but wolf dynamics in the South are different than how life is in the East. I know when Lerevna is near, just how you can sense Rune. Yet, it did not bloom into anything romantic for her and I. If anything, it merely gave us a tactical advantage, which may have been what the gods intended all along." Roderick regarded Rune for a moment before heaving a sigh. "She is my superior, my general. I am her violent command in action. I do not know what she may be looking for in your dreams, Brynn, or why she chooses to walk through them unannounced. I will find out, for you, that I *can* promise."

There was a rawness in his eyes as he bared such vulnerable truths. I searched his face for the lie, a half-truth hiding in his expression, anything to give me reason to doubt him. I found nothing, just honesty and pain plastered over his features.

"When you can shift more freely out of your raven form during the solstice, we need to take a walk and discuss this further." I mused.

I needed more time to think this over, to come up with clarifying questions to ask, to allow myself time to feel angry or hurt if either emotion showed its face. Right now, I was purely startled, and annoyingly a little sad for him that he had been rejected.

Typical.

"You cannot be serious." Rune groaned internally.

"We need to find a way to understand this, Rune." I quipped back. *"You did not see how she watched me in that dream. Something is not right about this. I trust him but…there is something about her. This is bigger than just being mates."*

"Whatever you need." Roderick leaned against the stone wall with a sense of finality and stared into the dying embers of the fire. "Just know, no god can ever influence my heart."

There was a playful edge to his smirk, but it did not hide the sorrow lacing his words.

I ached to comfort him, to dispel all that brought him pain.

Rune's groan was audible this time as he opened his arms and motioned his chin to Roderick.

I crept over to Roderick's side, and he lifted his arm for me to sit next to him. Rune stretched out on the other side of me, his back leaning against my thigh. My body filled with warmth from both sides.

"If your feathers touch me while I sleep, I will bite them off in any form I take." Rune muttered as he settled into a more comfortable position.

"Fair." Roderick pulled me closer to nestle my head against his bare chest. He kissed my brow and rested his cheek against my hair. "I mean it, Brynn. The gods may have influence in a great many things in our lives right now, but not this…Enough of that for one night, though; you should rest, too. I will keep watch."

I threaded my arms around his waist and hugged him close, his feathers tickling my arm across his back.

He began to hum a deep, ancient melody. It was mournful in its tone. His smooth voice reverberated in his chest against my cheek, sending vibrations through my frame.

I had more questions now than answers but the two men I cared for most in this world were on either side of me. We were all safe and together; that was all I needed to know right now. With that comforting thought, I dared close my eyes again and let sleep take me to the sound of Roderick's lullaby.

Chapter 6

Brynn

Thunder rolled in early the next morning as we arrived at the outskirts of town. Rune shifted back into his human form after carrying me for the rest of the journey through the forest. He brushed back his wet coppery hair with light natural highlights that caught the rising sun as it peeked through the break in storm clouds. A streak of white hair started at his left eyebrow and ended at the back of his head. The rebellious streak made him stand out among the other wolves. Sif favored running her fingers through it on our usual outings together.

I tossed him a damp bag of herbs and berries that I had collected; I restocked my stores whenever I could, never knowing when I would be able to venture out that far again. He slung an arm over my shoulders. Warmth coursed through me from our bond biting back the chill that threatened to settle into my rain drenched bones; his joy of finally having me to himself for a moment was palpable.

The black fog would only ever escort us to the river and even Roderick had to return to roaming above the town in his raven form, gathering whispers to bring back to me. He would return to the border soon to report to his leadership before venturing through the rest of the kingdom like he normally did. Only now, I knew his leadership was *Lerevna*.

"How doomed are we?" Rune asked as he ruffled my soaked bangs plastered to my forehead. He had relaxed enough to speak out loud consistently now that we were back on familiar soil.

"The odds are not in our favor; but they haven't been since the beginning. This is nothing new." I tried to smile, but he knew it was hollow. Our childhood struggles had only been overshadowed by our present damnations. "I will spend the next few nights gathering what I need to make those vials last longer. We are going to need all the help we can get to keep these women alive."

"I have seen you use it before; Depths, you have even patched me up with it. I never knew it came from *him*…" He said, eying the bag I held closer to my frame than the rest.

I usually had an array of leather straps crisscrossing my hips; the various pouches of salves, tools, and bits of nature ready at a moment's notice helped the Night Wolf branded vial blend in with all the rest. He rarely saw me without sets of crossbody bags or one hanging from the crook of my arm. I frequently ran errands for others in town while I was out making house calls and would make deliveries on my way home.

Rune knew today was no exception and tried to lighten my load by shouldering another sack of rowan berries for my concoctions and sticks for him to carve for the mothers. He did not believe in the spirits or prayers, but he understood the value of having something to hold on to; he claimed he held on to me instead.

"What exactly is in those vials anyway? Or…do I want to know?" He shifted his weight into me in emphasis.

"You do not, which is why I never told you." I chuckled and leaned my head against his broad shoulder. "But, since you asked, it is Night Wolf saliva."

Rune stopped walking and turned me to face him. Faint steam rose from his frame as the rain evaporated from his hot core temperature.

"It is *what*? Tell me you are kidding." He balked. His eyes grew wider at my smirk. "Tell me you have not lathered my wounds in…Aksel's…spit."

Fueled by my exhaustion, laughter burst from my lips and rang out across the street of merchants setting out their covered carts. We received a few looks at the outburst, but the townsfolk paid us little attention.

"I have! It worked, didn't it? You did not need to know such details when your chest was split open last summer." I tapped the large scar hidden under his shirt. "You know as well as I that nature is always about *balance*. The saliva of Night Wolves has healing properties, some of the strongest I have ever seen. Their breed is so rare due to the forbidden blood rite it takes to curse them that it has not been thoroughly studied in the healer's texts yet. Their *spit* has yet to fail me and has brought back my worst patients from the brink. Roderick used it on me once and I have been researching it ever since."

A shadow passed across Rune's gaze for a moment at the mention of Sondre's attack but passed as he consciously fixed his face. Rune shook his head in disgust and led us onward, deeper into town.

"They are literal death, Regh." His eyes were transfixed straight ahead, focused on scanning each person coming in and out of the shops and taverns.

"Balance, Rune. From the mouth of death, comes life. Look at us, our start was just as dark as theirs." I reminded him.

He looked down at me with tender emerald eyes that were always ready to play, even when tiredness darkened the skin beneath them.

"I do look at us." He tapped the tip of my nose. "And we are way more attractive than those black lumps of angst."

"Speaking of attractive, be a good mutt, and run ahead to send Sif to me, won't you?" I asked, batting my eyelashes in mock pleading.

"Fine, but—" His strong hand clasped the back of my neck and pulled me close to plant a kiss on my forehead. "Halsten will be by tonight to debrief me on what they found yesterday while we were out. It may do you some good to *bathe* in case you two need to, you know..."

"That was one time, after a lot of mead, and it was Sif's idea..." I rolled my eyes as I pushed him away with an elbow. I did not have time for personal pleasures, regardless of how enjoyable his packmate Halsten was to watch in the Guard's training sessions.

"I hate to say it, Brynn. But as obnoxiously broody, and *suspicious as fuck*, as Roderick is, Sif thinks you would probably be much less grumpy and more pleasant to be around if that *capon* did us all a favor and released some of your tension—" Rune teased as he wiggled his eyebrows.

"Go!" I shoved his chest harder, and he laughed stumbling backwards. "And do not distract Sif from coming back here. You can have your *releasing* playtime later. I need her."

"Oh, I bet you do. *I* need her." He looked at me in feigned innocence and shock as he backed away. "And me? I would never distract her from you..."

He winked and jogged off in the other direction, oblivious to the growing tightness in my shoulders that I tried to keep at bay with our teasing. I scanned the alleyways but could not find the source of my dread. A shadow passed over my face, and I looked up to see Roderick flying above. My worry, and much of my frustrations, *would* dissipate if he could shift here and handle the growing ache for him settling into my hips.

The Blood Raven let out a loud croak as if in answer before banking to survey another part of town.

With a flustered sigh, I continued on my way through the town.

Dripping wet black drapes covered the windows to not call the attention of the arriving gods with a single reflective surface. Movement behind one made me pause. I gently pulled it back to see a young boy eating a scone he had snatched off a nearby cart. His yellow eyes went wide at being discovered. I recognized the baker Ivan's fresh treat in the boy's hands and knew a beating would be in his future if the little thief was caught. The boy was scrawny, his clothes sticking to his slight body, but the way light reflected in his eyes and the lean muscle hidden beneath his shivering frame told me he was a shifter.

"So, you must be the coyote who has been growling at everyone upstairs at Ahmila's, are you not?" I prodded as I crouched to his level, my skirt soaking up the water pooling on the cobblestones. "There is a girl in the room you are guarding, your sister, I presume?"

The boy blushed and nodded sheepishly as he wrapped the scone and placed it in his pocket.

"Yes, Healer. I'm—I'm Viggo. My sister is Freda. They have kept us in the kitchens, ma'am, and cleaning the rooms. That was until..." His voice faded as his face fell.

I could hear the apprehension in his chest building as it constricted his voice.

"Until her first bleed..." I sighed in understanding and rubbed my temple.

This was an all-too-common dilemma of the pleasure halls. Madame Ahmila took in orphans off the street, offering them shelter in exchange for labor. Stray children serviced the establishment by working with the cook or turning the rooms between clients in order to remain under Madame Ahmila's roof. Some of the stronger boys fetched the pails of water back and forth for the baths. The building, and women within it, were in constant need of cleansing. Girls were not forced to entertain clientele until they were of fertile age.

Asta's injured form left on the steps as a child flashed in my mind; that had been her introduction to this life, to womanhood, to be used and cast aside by the Guard. I had to do whatever I could to stop that from becoming this little girl's future too.

"It started a couple days ago." Viggo shook his head more frantically, droplets flying off his blonde hair. "They can't take her! I won't let them! The men already say things to her, nasty things, of what they will do once…but no one knows yet. But now…Ms. Ahmila can't let them touch her. I—I'll kill them all if I have to…I'll—"

Tears filled his pure eyes but did not fall as he searched for a plan, any solution to his nightmares. I reached out and took his face in my hands.

"Listen to me, they will not touch her, yet. And as much as they should be killed, you are not the one to do that. You hear me, boy?" I emphasized my question with a slight shake of his head that jostled his locks.

He nodded but could not find words.

"Do not go picking fights with the Guard;" I commanded, "Regardless of what form you are in—they will not think twice about killing you and then who will your sister have to guard her door, hmm?"

Viggo pressed his lips into a frown of determination and sniffed back his emotions.

I let my hands fall as his resolve grew.

"Here, take these to Ms. Thyra and go wait at your sister's door until I get there." I offered a half smile to encourage him. I handed him my last satchel of herbs to carry. "Do not let anyone in and tell *no one* we have spoken about this; you only came by to lighten my load on the way home, like the little gentleman you are."

He accepted it and took a deep breath to steady himself before he ran off to the brothel.

I assessed the magic within me and felt a deep-seated pain down to my bones protesting in return. I was approaching my limit, but one more favor would not be the death of me.

Most likely not, at least...

"Brynn Ulfhild, caretaker of runts and whores." A gruff voice sounded from the shop across the street, setting my teeth on edge. "Always such an inspiration how deep into the gutter you can go, you delicious street rat."

I did not have to turn to know the owner of that voice. A chill ran down my spine as every instinct told me to run. I brushed my skirts as I stood slowly.

Do not let him bait you, Sif is on her way.

"Oh, come now, *Healer*, I will walk with you." Commander Sondre said, falling in step with me.

His features were sharp, and his body was molded by years of combat. He was shorter in stature, but his muscular frame and brutality had more than made up for it over the years in the King's court. His black close-fitting uniform was sleeveless, exposing his arms covered in scars, the deepest of which were gifts from Gunnar and Roderick.

Sondre placed a hand firmly on my lower back and whispered in my ear, "Tell me, how fairs my boy?"

"*Asta* is resting." I replied without shifting away from him.

He often used his presence to intimidate others, but, today, I would not give him the satisfaction.

My fear battled against my indignation.

I saw Sif in the distance coming our way and knew I only needed to tolerate him for a short while, "She had a traumatic labor, to be sure."

"She is *alive*?" His voice dripped with disdain.

The audacity to sound disappointed!

I stopped and turned to face him directly, my rage getting the better of my trepidation. His hand slid from my back to my hip, refusing to break contact as I shifted. His thumb caressed the inside of my hipbone over my skirt and triggered a gag reflex that I forced myself to swallow. Now was not the time for my body to remember the pain he had inflicted.

I refuse to yield and cower like the rest of this damn town.

"Yes, she is *alive*. I know how much hope you had for that child; sadly, *it* did not make it." I spat. My frame shook and I did not know if it was from anger or from nervousness.

Probably both.

The Commander's eyes widened in pure outrage as he grabbed me by the throat and pulled me against him.

"You killed it?!" He accused, his breath hot against my face. "You cunt, if I find out you killed it out of some ritualistic healer *precaution*, I will—"

"No, Sondre." I croaked out between shallow breaths as his grip tightened. I winced in pain and knew his handprint would bruise. I took a hold of his wrist and tried to lean back enough to breathe deeply. "It died before birth. That was done by Valdis' hand, not mine. I can stop many things, but I cannot stop Death herself."

"I do not believe you. Where is it, you healer slut? Prove your innocence and show me how it died. Show me you did not slit its throat." He demanded as his hand on my hip dug into my flesh and shook me. I could see the vessels straining in his piercing amber eyes. "Give me my child, you useless—"

"It is here, Commander." Sif answered as she approached breathlessly. "I would appreciate if you unhanded my healer as she is needed at the brothel, preferably unharmed if she is to heal my women after time with your men."

Sondre lingered, holding me to him. His eyes raked over my frame held against his body. His gaze lingered on my chest rising and falling rapidly as I remained pinned against him. His arousal at my fear pressed against my inner thigh. He brushed his lower lip against my jaw with a low growl and breathed in my anxiety before releasing my throat to turn to Sif.

She offered him a glass jar full of ash as he blatantly adjusted his trousers.

"What kind of sick joke is this?" He sneered at Sif. He kept his other hand planted on my hip and did not motion to accept the bait.

"No joke, sir. As it was so young, the heart was offered to the Ever Pure One of Life Dahlia at the temple yesterday morning, right after the birth." I flashed a look at her, but she continued undeterred. "I saw to it myself as I do with all spiritual matters at our establishment. The mind and liver were given to Valdis, at her altar of the dead, the gateway of the Depths. The priest burned the rest, as custom, my Lord Commander. Since it was stillborn, the priest said it must be immediate to not spoil the offering, especially so close to the solstice. You know how the gods get picky around the Holy Days. I had searched for you yesterday, to see if you wished to accompany me to the temple, as I do with all the fathers of my courtesan's children, but, alas, I was unsuccessful. Yet, finally, here you are! These are your ashes, Good Sir."

Her voice was melodious, but the authority could not be missed in her tone. Before coming to Ahmila's, Sif had been a priestess in the temples and knew all the standards for each ritual. She left the temples when a priest took a liking to the worship practices of Herja, the darkest of all the Old Gods. He wanted to flay any living sacrifice brought to the altar, newborn Night Wolves included, to appease Valdis and end a sickness brought upon the kingdom; Sif refused and fled. Madame Ahmila's was the only place that would offer her shelter afterward. As with all the strays under her roof, Ahmila offered residency for service. Once favored by the goddess Dahlia, Sif knew all the ways one could worship with the body through passion and quickly became one of Ahmila's most valuable ladies.

The Commander took the jar from her, and I released a breath once his touch was gone. There was no compassion in his eyes as he looked it over. The glass clinked against the metal ring of the King's Guard on his finger.

"You will pay for this, Brynn." When his hateful gaze finally met mine, the wolf behind his eyes flashed, ready to hunt.

"It was the transition that killed him, Sondre. You only have yourself to blame." I gritted out the words, biting back my tempered fury; I knew I would never be able to win against him one on one. I wanted to scream at him for this, but my survival instincts knew to strangle my rage in front of such a mighty predator.

He caused this death, not me! I would have delivered his abomination safely, if it had remained alive, and would have risked my life to present the damned pup to Aksel for it to seek refuge in his pack.

Sondre raised his hand to strike me but someone across the way caught his attention and his arm fell. His expression broke into a fake smile, glistening in the sunlight.

"My lady, Bodhil! What a surprise!" His tone dripped with manufactured admiration.

A beautiful woman dressed in a cream flowing gown and a healer's apron tied around her waist walked over to us. The sun kissed her blonde hair loosely braided past her shoulders. She was the epitome of court elegance as she floated through the town square.

"Commander! Ah, Brynn, my girl, thank Dahlia you are here." She grasped the leather bracers on my forearms as she approached and pulled me close to kiss each cheek in greeting. "You're needed at the castle."

"The castle?!" Sondre exclaimed. "The King would never lower himself to see such a—"

"The *Queen*," Bodhil emphasized, finally looking to Sondre, "Has need of a specialized Healer. Do not delay her, Wolf, as it is the Queen's business, not to be questioned by someone in *either* of our positions. You are not Master of War, yet."

Bodhil did not break eye contact with the Commander. In addition to being the Queen's maid and Head Royal Healer,

Bodhil was married to my father, who was of the same rank as Sondre; it brought her closer to being Sondre's equal in influence in her own right. The men remained in competition for the position of Master of War after the previous' untimely death. As head healer, however, Bodhil answered only to the Queen, a status far above my own in the lower levels.

Sondre ground his teeth in his forced smile of fabricated court etiquette.

"We shall see." He bowed his head to her and raised a finger from his grip on the jar to point at me, as if I needed to be reminded that he was not through with me.

He never seems to be through with me.

He turned on his heel and walked toward the castle, surely to see how he could veto this request. Once he was further up the hill, he threw the jar against a nearby building, scattering ash and glass everywhere.

"Odious man." Bodhil murmured as we all watched him depart. She nodded her greeting to my closest friend and frequent lover, "Dearest Sif. You two go, see to your brothel, my lovelies. Sondre needn't know that the Queen is actually busy with the King right now until this evening, but, make haste once you are finished; she does indeed have herbal questions of what grows beyond our walls. I mentioned you have been to our borders with your father and your…with Rune. I meant it, Brynn, she calls on *you* for answers, we will not discuss it here."

Sif's side-eye was subtle, but I would feel the weight of her gaze, nonetheless.

"Yes, mother. I will check on Asta and the girls, then I will make my appearance." I assured her.

It was unlike Bodhil to mention my knowledge of outside our fortified city; I knew this had to be important. The Queen was a kind and curious woman, so I did not feel a threat on the horizon.

"Good girl, be safe you two." She gave my wrists a squeeze then brushed Sif's cheek with the back of her hand, before leaving to return to the castle.

I waited until Bodhil was out of earshot.

"Sif…" I began as I finally allowed myself to rub the growing ache around my neck from Sondre's grip.

"I spoke no lies." She raised her hands in mock surrender. Her hazel eyes danced, and a smirk played at the corners of her full lips.

So proud of herself.

"Whose heart, brain, and liver did you give to the priests then? Who was in that jar?" I lowered my voice as I linked arms with my friend.

"Shh. Not *who*, try *what* was in the jar. I never said it was the babe, I said *it*." She placed a hand on my knuckles at the crook of her elbow and chuckled as we walked back to the brothel. "You would be amazed how similar a little piglet's parts look like a human baby's parts."

"You did not!" I gasped and gaped at her in horror and astonishment.

"Oh, stop. Bo, the butcher, owed me from his last visit. I asked for a little extra when ordering the week's meat for Ahmila. Preferably, I said I need a piglet that passed this morning for a ritual. He didn't think anything of it; neither did the priest, when I presented the bloody bowl blessed with the finest of holy oils. Those truly were the ashes of the rest left over after I did some cutting. We are all meat once you chop us up fine enough. I am glad Sondre did not look too closely. Or worse yet, sniff it. Luckily, it was less of a risk with him in his human form, and worth that rage as he shattered it all the same. He destroyed any evidence that it wasn't his boy." She said quietly, her gaze radiant with mischief.

I tried and failed to contain my nervous laughter. The tension from having his hands on me again eased slightly with the release of the strained sound.

"You are brilliant, Sif." I leaned my head against her soft shoulder. "But what of the temple? Have you cursed yourself by bringing in false sacrifice, a pork one no less?"

"Dahlia always had a sense of humor when I tended to the offerings in her presence. She is delightful to those who actually get to meet her. Furthermore, I am pretty sure dear

Valdis on High hates Sondre and will not take offense; I did not tell her I was offering up a baby shifter. I simply said *it* had died this morning, and the priest *assumed* it was a child; not my fault he did not ask the proper questions. They have gotten lazy in the training of new priests. Plus, our holy ladies mainly just want a blood sacrifice, I just flirted with the truth of whose blood it was. I mixed in a little of mine so there was some human yumminess in it for them." Sif explained with a shake of her head.

As she motioned to a small bandage wrapped around her forearm, I scoffed and let a single golden tendril slip from my fingers, down her sun-kissed skin, and under the fabric. The cut was not deep, and my magic made quick work of the wound. I stumbled slightly, lightheaded at the effort.

"Bry…" Sif's grip tightened on my hand, but I shook my head to not deal with the reprimand for taking care of her, of all people.

If I cannot do that, what is even the point?

She cleared her throat and continued as if nothing transpired, "We broke no rules and harmed no oaths. There was no sin of ours to account for, it was Sondre who needed to repent for issuing the tonic early. He will need to bring an offering to stay Valdis' wrath as he killed an unborn child, a slight to both goddesses. The piglet was just a bonus treat for them in preparation for the solstice. Think of it as a holy snack."

"Rune told you our suspicions of the Commander's plan then?" I asked, not surprised.

I looked around at the busy street. Any woman here could be at risk of Sondre's schemes. Married or not, regardless of age, if the woman was fertile, Sondre could become so desperate that he would be willing to use anyone to get his pack. The wolf gene was dominant enough; therefore, any species of woman was in danger of being bred and killed to achieve his goal.

"Of course he did, that man cannot keep anything from me." Sif mused but slowed her stride as her voice grew softer. "There is something I wanted to tell you before I shared it with him, however. Once he knows, he will never let you out of his sight."

"Joy." I bemoaned as we reached the oak door of the brothel. "What are we dealing with *now*?"

Sif only shook her head, dropped my arm, and led me in by the hand. We weaved through the curtained rooms to the only space in the building with a door, containing the women's altar and dais. Sif closed the door and pulled a sleek blade from the garter on her thigh. She swiftly pricked her thumb and rubbed a streak of blood against my forehead and lower lip. I started to protest another fresh wound, but she cut me off.

"In case someone comes in, hush. Let this heal on its own." Sif whispered and wrapped her thumb in a piece of fabric tied to her leather belt for such occasions.

"Is this really that serious?" I asked, unable to resist brushing the tip of my tongue against the blood seeping into the corner of my mouth.

The rusty tang of her essence coated my tastebuds.

"He wants to kill you." Sif said in hushed tones. She brushed the ashes of notes to the deities aside for us to sit and pulled me down next to her on the edge of the stone dais.

"Sondre, kill me? No shit, Sif…That is not new. Ever since he attacked me years ago, he has threatened to finish what he started almost every day since." I said rubbing the fabric under my bracers that hid my scars from my violent encounter with the Commander.

The threat never lessened, but living in fear of him for years had made me slightly more callous to it. My body never felt like it fully relaxed, always hypervigilant, making a threat on my life part of my daily routine. If half the town knew what I was, they would help him get his way too. Harboring a witch was almost as bad as treason; townsfolk had been flogged, or killed, for less. I lived in this state of alert. One more threat blended in with the rest.

"It is more than that, Bry." Sif rested her hand against mine. "It isn't just about Sondre, either. You are a target, yes, but now your family is too. Clients have been complaining about your father's strictness lately. Ever since the pits were dissolved, the men have held a grudge against your father. They often remind those of us working here that they did not have to pay for services before your father's decrees. The last Master of War may have favored your father, but his men do not."

"They did not have to pay because they abducted women to be bred and raped in the pits, Sif." I said, my face flushed with fury at their insinuations.

"I know, I know. Many of them are not even old enough to remember those days, but they repeat what they hear from Sondre and the older packmates. The senior leaders claim the wolves in the ranks now are too soft from not fighting in the pits and learning how to *properly* claim a woman." Sif explained.

Yrsa's memories of being *properly claimed* flashed through my mind. I stood to keep myself from screaming in a deep-seated rage that was not only my own.

"And they want to kill *us* for it? As if that would make a difference: It was the King's own decree." My voice turned shrill as I began to pace.

"His Majesty's declaration was only made at the urging of the previous Master of War, Bry—Who met his untimely death soon after, I might add." Sif tsked in emphasis to draw my attention back to her face. "He favored your father as his successor and knew what the pits would mean for such a prized bloodline as yours. Once you showed magical favor with the healers, it was a given you would be bred if the pits stayed open. That was not a choice any father should have to make.”

I gritted my teeth, reliving the many times my father said otherwise when arguing about my *duty* to the pack. His greatest regret was that I had not yet born a litter for the crown. I felt the blood rush to my face and flush my complexion with indignation. If the previous Master of War had sired me, I would be able to believe her words. My father shared no such sympathies.

Sif shifted in her seat at the change in my expression.

“Regardless how he would have handled that, if your father was killed, Sondre would be appointed Master of War without competition. This is one of the first things he would change. It falls under the care and training of his troops; he does not need the crown’s permission to implement new tactics for the Guard. It would be a part of his title and role! He has even mentioned that this is how the Royal Guards conduct training and recruitment in other kingdoms, with success, I might add.” Sif said with a grimace.

“Where? In the North? Where they clip the wings of their men or execute them? I am sure this would go over *great* with their Queen; her Guard is the winged female shifters.” Sif raised an eyebrow at me as if I was confirming her point. “They do not have a breeding pit with *men* in it to be *mounted*. Sondre does not know what he is talking about."

"And you have been there to confirm this, have you?" Sif interjected.

I waved her off.

"Don't be ridiculous, those warriors have no use for men—" I began.

"Except for breeding." Sif interrupted again. She tilted her chin up at me defiantly, not willing to let this go. "Socially, they may not require a male's presence, but the same problem remains there as it does here. Soldiers, even for an all-female Guard, are *born*. The Hoflin Guard's stock is the finest in any kingdom, their breeding is *impeccable*. You really think that is by accident? Plus, you are telling me these warriors are forsaking their duties as Guard members for *love*, instead of to birth warriors? Bry, the men are studs; just like with livestock, they are chosen and kept separate. It may not be called a 'pit,' but Hoflin's practice is the same. Those men are kept alive for their *seed*, and their seed alone. Check your hatred."

I paused to look at her. I had to admit my bias. Yrsa's memories of the pits had haunted me after they started to trickle into my dreams, and even my waking moments. It was hard to imagine the male equivalent having to endure such horror, especially having healed so many winged warriors for prisoner exchanges. The women I had tended to reminded me nothing of the wolves in Yrsa's recollections.

Sif rested her chin on her knuckles.

"It is a coveted position for men in my livelihood. Some devote their lives to becoming the perfect specimen to be chosen to continue to Guard's lineage. But do not think for a moment that everyone is there willingly." Her warm gaze hardened. "Sondre will twist anything to gain the King's ear. Don't be naïve, he can manipulate the truth of Hoflin's customs to favor the pits here for breeding to compete with such an esteemed warrior class. What do you know of the other kingdoms?"

"The Kingdom of Arkanes barely has any wolves anymore; They were banished from the lands after the birth of the last set of Night Wolf twins which triggered Sverre's wrath. That was decades ago. There are no pits of any kind in the West at King Tytus' court; his Queen Ingrid would never condone that. Intimacy pools, maybe, but that is all consensual; they are renown for those. Arkanes' culture is weird like that, or 'free like that,' I should say." I continued to pace, attempting to keep my voice down as I flailed my hands in the air and struggled to collect my thoughts.

How amazing it would be to live in a land without this kind of daily fear…

"Bry, listen to me. Sondre is obsessed with the packs to the *East*. You have heard the stories of Reykia; the Night Wolves are known to take women captive in their caves to do the Depths know what." Sif insisted. "The women that go there are never heard from again. If Sondre is trying to make his own pack, you know he is going to present it in a way that is digestible to the King. He will frame it as the only way we can withstand more attacks from Hoflin is to be like the *only* Kingdom that has successfully kept the North at bay for centuries, Reykia, Night Wolf pack and all. He will not be able to create a pack quickly without the authority to control who lives *and dies* in a breeding pit."

"Out in town, that kind of murder will cause too much disruption, it already has, even on such a small scale with the recent deaths." I contested.

"He worships how King Torvald rules Reykia. There is no queen to keep him in line after he had Her Majesty executed. Torvald is more brutal than Sondre and his Guard combined; he keeps even his *gods* in check. Since Sondre will never be king as a wolf shifter, Prince Hurthur may very well give this desire to him if Hurthur takes the throne soon. The pits were filled with prisoners from the war camps and conquests of the time—yet another reason to take the fight North, to traffic more females into the pits to breed more soldiers for his army."

Sif reached out to get me to stop pacing.

With a groan, I came to stand before her as she took my hands. I could not deny the truth in her words. I chose not to believe Aksel committed all the atrocities the rumors suggested, but I did not put *anything* past King Torvald. He was a creature of nightmares; his skin was said to be like the crackling magma of his volcanic kingdom. Sulfuric gas steamed from his nostrils that misted up his massive horns. His eyes ever lustful for whatever he could claim—women, land, power; he stopped at nothing. He burned and consumed all that he touched, a walking emblem of death. Sondre craved that power, but it was destined by the gods to forever remain out of his grasp.

Kingdoms could never risk a royal heir to have wolf shifter genes and be born a Night Wolf; the devastation that would ensue from the gods would be catastrophic. Wolf shifters remained as the King's Guard in the South, or Death's vengeance in the East, always close to the thrones due to their mighty power but never on them to stay the gods' wrath.

"You are beloved down here and many of Sondre's men could be swayed by you against his schemes as you have healed them, their children, and most of this damn town at some point or another." Sif kissed my knuckles. Her soft lips pacified my rage into a simmer. "Sondre knows this. You would be a thorn in his side if he goes through with this; you are already. You are one of the few that can heal the mothers on the brink of death. If he throws you down into the pits as punishment, you will just foil his plans all the more by preventing the blood rites from occurring. He *needs* dead mothers' blood."

"There are more healers down here than just me." I deflected as she interlocked our fingers.

"That does not matter to Sondre. They cannot do what you do, we both know why, too." Sif's smile was weak as she pressed our hands against my waist in emphasis. "He knows Rune and Halsten will protect anyone in your family until death, especially you. If he had to go against both of them, he may not win. Add Roderick trying to peck out his eyes and, well, it's over. If he removes you, one by one, however, he can win. You are all at risk. If he goes after Rune first, you could bring Rune back from the edge. But, if he starts with *you*…With you gone, he could wipe out his opposition, your father included, and no one would be able to put them back together again, not even Bodhil."

I took a breath and let the warning sink in past my defenses. I could try to rationalize it all away but nothing about Sondre was rational.

"Okay, I hear you. Thank you, Sif—And for telling me before Rune. He would try to kill the Commander without a second thought if he knew things were progressing." Rune's protective streak ran deep, news like this was bound to set him off.

We cannot be reactive; we need to think this through.

"You know he could, too. Granted he would be hanged if he did so without the blessing of the crown, but he would still win." Sif said with a faintly proud smirk as she stood.

I hummed my agreement trying to think about what to do next with this information. I opened my mind to him in an attempt to see if he was trying to eavesdrop, but his presence was filled with the sounds of the training yard and the scent of Halsten as they sparred. I let him fade from my consciousness to find Sif's eyes aglow, as a taunting grin pulled at her inviting lips.

"Say, with that bond of yours," She tapped my chest just above my heart and raised her eyebrow playfully. "You ever peek down it when he is over here to see me through his eyes? Do I feel different under his strong hands than I do under yours?"

I scoffed at her change in topic in attempts to ease my tension.

"Sif, I have seen more of all the women in here than Rune ever could. I do not need to 'peek' to get under any skirts, especially not yours." I chuckled and shook my head. I had been the sole healer at the brothel for almost a decade; no one had been more intimately acquainted with all the women here than I, in far more ways than one in Sif's case.

"You know what I mean." Sif put an arm around my shoulders and held me close until our cheeks touched as we moved toward the door. "Just a peek every now and then, when he is with me? I know you can sense the things he feels. It would be like having you both inside me at the same time. You could taste me while on your errands..."

She hummed in my ear and kissed my neck teasingly.

The door swung open, revealing a startled Thyra holding a folded note in her hand.

"Healer! Sif! What are you two doing in here?" Thyra gasped in surprise.

I rarely visited the altar, but Thyra was one of the most devoted visitors to this room.

"Brynn wanted resolution from our beloved Dahlia after this morning." Sif answered and traced the dried blood across my forehead. "Although, to be fair, Dahlia prefers a sweatier, more passionate sacrifice."

Sif pulled my chin to her and licked her own blood off my lips before kissing me deeply. Her hand greedily started kneading my breast over my bodice.

"Oh, Sif! Bless the Depths! The rituals must always be so literal for you." Thyra said as she swatted Sif with her small branch of rowan.

"Dahlia is quite particular that to have a blessed life, the confessions of death are to be sealed with a kiss *that brings life*. We didn't get to the literal bringing about life part yet." She moaned in my mouth as she grabbed my hips and pulled me

131

flush against her. "A technicality when one of us does not have the right parts, but our High Lady Dahlia would honor the effort. And I would make it be a valiant effort indeed."

Sif straddled my thigh and grinded herself against my leg to distract Thyra further. It was rather effective and Thyra thrashed her rowan against Sif's arm.

"Those leaves won't ward you from the spirits in me." Sif laughed and leaned backwards to reach for Thyra mischievously.

I placed my hands on Sif's lower back to stabilize her stretch. Her leg cooked around my thigh for leverage as she committed to tormenting Thyra.

"Here, Ms. Thyra, fresh sprigs to beat away Sif's spirits." I chuckled as I reached over Sif's gyrating hips into my satchel under her leg and handed a bundle of sticks with red berries to Thyra. "Fresh from the outer banks this morning."

"Oh, Ms. Thyra, are you going use that switch to beat my spirits into submission? You know just how I like it." Sif cooed after the woman, removing herself from me and taking her heat with her. She wiggled her fingers after Thyra's skirts.

"Oh, you wicked thing." Thyra half chuckled, fully flustered, and shuffled past us to the dais.

Sif motioned for me to get upstairs while she knelt with Thyra to burn the prayer scribbled on the piece of paper. Sif's joking subsided as her priestess training took over and she hummed the beginning verse of Dahlia's favorite hymn.

"*Thank you.*" I mouthed silently to Sif and took the stairs two at a time. I dodged clients until I got to the courtesans' bedrooms.

Chapter 7

Brynn

Asta was asleep when I looked in on her. I hovered my hands over my friend to read how her body was accepting the healing. Everything was on the right course. On the desk, next to Rune's carving, I left a mixture of herbs and berries to be steeped into a tea later. I carefully took a set of sheets out of the dresser and left a purple bloom of lupine in its place for her to know it was from me. They were her favorite and any time I went into the forest, I tried to bring more back for her. As quietly as I could, I went up to another floor, avoiding the floorboards I knew would creak and give me away. I followed the sound of a soft growl until I saw a small coyote pup curled up at the foot of a doorway. Viggo issued a warning yip at the soft swish of my skirts but whimpered an apology once I came into view.

"Shift and come in to join us with a pail of water." I motioned toward the bundle of clothes on the floor next to the boy.

"Healer?" A small dainty voice called from inside the room.

I strode in to see a young blonde girl curled up in the bed, her eyes swollen and red from crying.

"Yes, it is just me. Freda, isn't it?" I asked gently as I came to stand at the corner of their shared cot.

"Yes ma'am." The petite girl breathed, eyes searching my face for hope.

"I am here to help. Your brother is getting a pail to wash up in, and I have a set of worn sheets that will not alarm any of the maids." I set Asta's sheets on the edge of the bed and sat. "This next bit will be a little scary, but I *can* stop the bleeding."

"Can you stop it forever? I don't want to be forced to work downstairs." She pleaded as tears filled her eyes again.

"You're not strong enough for that yet, that kind of magic takes a toll. I can, however, stop it for a few years. It will give us time to plan how to get the two of you out of here. How does that sound?" I offered.

Five years.

A five-year respite was all I could give the girls in the city before causing long-term issues within their bodies as their tissues rejected the magic. This was a natural process; to impede it too long would harm them and draw the unwanted attention of Dahlia.

The young girl nodded.

"I am nine." She whispered, fidgeting with the sheet.

I clenched my jaw. I was introduced to the pits at nine. I held Rune's bloody body at that age and was told to practice my healing magic on him. Asta had been near the same age when she was forcibly made to be bred. The children of this kingdom deserved better. Viggo walked in and set the pail down, stirring me from my thoughts. He immediately went to his sister's side to hold her hand.

"Alright. As your first bleed is a part of life, you two must both close your eyes and pray to Dahlia of Life with me for this to work. Do you know Dahlia's prayer?" I asked as positively as I could muster.

My bones ached and protested at the gathering power within me. I would not admit it to him, but Rune had been right; I was no longer flirting with the line of burnout, this would fling me so far beyond it. This little girl, however, was worth the price the magic would demand of me.

Both children nodded in agreement.

"Okay, quietly, Freda, you begin, but keep your eyes shut, so if Dahlia appears, we do not want to upset her by looking at her, uninvited." I coached.

I did not expect the deity to show, she never did. Their closed eyes were to shield them from me, and me from their unanswerable questions.

The two siblings held hands and began whispering in earnest.

I peered over my shoulder to ensure no one was waiting in the doorway and listened for any movement down the hall.

When I was certain we were alone, I let a subtle golden hue light up my hands. Whisps like smoke flowed from me toward Freda and mixed with new tendrils of pink. The magic covered the two on the bed and shifted to radiate only from the girl's skin as they prayed. My hands shook as the glow condensed into an orb at Freda's abdomen. Sweat beaded along my forehead as I reached out to fuel the transition. I pulled from the protective runes above several of the courtesans' door frames, a blessed talisman on Asta's dresser, the sprigs of rowan in Thyra's room—anything I could link to in order to ease the pull on my own body.

I was close but the spell could not yet take hold within her. As they neared the end of their prayer, I drew a small blade from my belt and cut across my palm. I dipped my fingers in the blood and traced a fertility stave upside-down across Freda's forehead. The magic emanating from it linked with my own upon completion and I felt her womb still. I released the breath I was holding, and the pink light dissipated; only the children's fervent whispers remained.

Viggo looked up at me at the sound of my sigh.

"Did she show up? Did Dahlia come to save Freda?" He reached a hand to his sister's damp forehead, examining the markings, bewildered.

"Dahlia approved our requests." I wiped the blood from her brow with a soft cloth from my belt. "Your sister will be just fine."

Freda dipped her hand under the covers and gasped.

"It stopped!" Freda exclaimed as she held up her hand in awe. There was no trace of blood on her fingertips.

"It did. And it will stay stopped for some time. It must come back eventually but nine is very early. We can delay it a few years without Madame asking questions. We will work on getting you into the kitchens instead. The cooks do not have to deal with the Guard." I chuckled at her glee and rose as Freda patted my hands repeatedly in excitement and agreement.

Every joint ached at the movement but I shoved down the fatigue. After all the stress the poor girl had gone through over the past several days, I refused to make Freda feel like her situation was a burden.

"Ask Ms. Thyra to let you bring the deliveries from Gro." I masked my wince with a stretch. "He will show you how he makes the stews with the meat Sif brings him. Freshen up with the pail and I will get these sheets switched out."

We each went to work. Freda cleaned herself up behind a small curtain tacked to the wall for makeshift privacy and I stripped off the bloodstained sheets. I bundled them up and put the fresh set on from Asta's room. These were pilling from years of use; however, they were clean and would not betray sweet Freda. I gathered up the bundle and bucket, then bid the two goodnight. Viggo pulled the wrapped scone out of his pocket and set it on the bed. Their giggles of delight followed me out the doorway.

As I made my way back to Asta's room, I attempted to catch my breath and collect myself. My hands trembled as chills coursed through me. This was far more magic than I usually would expend in such a short time, aside from days spent on the battlefield. The weight of culminating events started to catch up to me, but I shook my head and continued down the hallway just as a maid came up the steps.

"Oh, Eria, your timing is my saving grace. I just freshened up Asta's sheets and put on a new set. Will you bring these down to be washed? I wiped her down while finishing her healing; here is the pail I used, if you could throw it out too, I would appreciate it. The bleeding from the baby should have stopped by now." I lied gracefully as I handed Freda's soiled sheets to the maid.

"Of course, Healer. Terrible thing, losing that baby. Especially after dear Katla yesterday." Eria whispered as her eyes grew misty.

"Katla? The kitchen maid at Gro's?" I asked surprised.

I had just seen Katla earlier in the week and she had been perfectly healthy. I had cautioned against extra exertion in the kitchen without enough water as the baby could make her dizzy, but Katla had only missed her cycle by a few months. She was not even remotely close to when she would have been in danger of Sondre's tonic yet.

"Yes, Ma'am. Gro found her body yesterday when he went out to the chickens. She hadn't come in that morning with the eggs, like she normally does. He went to check on her, thinking a fox must have gotten into the hutch and startled her. That's when he found her… Another healer tried to help, but it looked like something tried crawling its way out of her, like an angry coon was caught in her belly. Both she and the little baby were dead. She wasn't as far along as little Miss Asta here, so the babe didn't look much like a baby at all. Pitiful thing." Eria stared past me as if the death scene was over my shoulder. Blinking quickly, she came back to herself and fiddled with the handle of the pail.

"Sad times," Eria murmured and took the bundle of linens downstairs.

"Sad times, indeed." I breathed after her in agreement and sank down onto the steps, my knees unable to bear the weight added to my shoulders.

I have failed one already.

Cold dread flowed through my veins and my face fell into my hands.

How am I going to fix this?

How can I save them if I cannot predict who Sondre may go after next?

A creature trying to crawl out of her stomach sounds like the tonic was drank too early again. Why would he try it on a mother not very far along and force a fatal transition on the child?

I tried to take a steadying breath, but the hallway felt like it was closing in around me.

I wasn't here. I cannot be everywhere at once; it is not like I am a god!

I lifted my head and looked at the ceiling.

"Why are you allowing this?!" I asked desperately. "Do something, for once!"

The hallway was eerily silent in reply. Neither of the Southern goddesses answered, again. It was up to me, *again,* to be the one to do something. My bones felt heavy, wanting to pull me into the ground and bury me under this pressure. I reached for my amulet of black garnet tucked secretly beneath my bodice and rubbed the stone before kissing it and holding it to my brow.

"Gods of Old—Tyr, Eir, or whoever chooses to listen—Forgive my impertinence and reward my boldness. Hear my plea." I stifled a sob that threatened to break my resolve in two. "I need you. I need help. Please, intervene and save your daughters."

Tears of exhaustion lined my eyes as I opened them. I rubbed the stone a moment longer before hiding it between my breasts once more. It warmed near my heart, and I chose to believe that as their reply.

I had to hold on to *something*.

I could not lose hope, not with so many counting on me to find a solution. With a deep breath, I gripped the banister and lifted myself to my feet. I wiped my eyes, careful not to smudge the kohl Sif always insisted on applying and brushed my skirts. I cleared my throat to release the tension that threatened to strangle me. I did not have time to wallow; the women of this town were running out of options. I looked at the ceiling once more and placed my hand on my bodice where my pendant hid before I was forced to face my bleak reality head-on.

"Mighty Tyr, give me the strength to do it *myself*."

Chapter 8

Roderick

I shifted once I reached the Cliffs of Tyr separating Reykia from the kingdoms beyond. I felt her before I saw the Blood Raven shifter sitting on the edge of the cliff with her leather boots dangling off the side. The morning light caught the silver charms decorating her interlacing braids, each marked with a different rune. The cherry at the base of her midnight black hair was more noticeable in this light as it draped across her strong exposed shoulders. From them sprouted two powerful feathered wings of ethereal darkness, some of the feathers were tipped in flecks of ruby just like my own. Whisps of shadows blurred the edges of her wings and pooled on the stones behind her.

Her off the shoulder dress revealed her inked collarbones and was cinched by a leather under bust bodice that accentuated the feminine curves of her muscular form. Her dress had slits up to her hips exposing the tattooed twisting braids and knots in the form of wings down her thighs, one inked set feathered, the other pair leathery. Her knees were decorated with protection staves surrounded by a braided pair of dragon heads on one side and a matching design of wolf heads on the other. Her boots were laced up her solid calves, covering the cord of runes interwoven through the ink all over her skin. Each piece symbolized the many oaths she was bound by, mirroring my own.

She did not lift her head as I drew near and sat next to her. Her chest rose and fell slowly as she looked out over the lands. Our check-ins were one of the few times I saw her out of her full body armor as her missions took her to Hoflin more often than not lately. We sat for a moment in complete stillness, watching the storm clouds gather over the neighboring kingdoms.

"Lerevna," I said, breaking the silence. "Brynn is noticing you in her dreams."

"I know," was her only reply. Her hand flexed as her sharp onyx nails scraped against the boulder beneath us.

"Have you found what you are looking for?" I dared to ask, not genuinely wanting to know the answer.

She sensed my hesitation.

I tried to block her out through the bond, but she saw right through me.

"I had to be sure. I am. Now I only need the spell." Her tone was colder than the Northern winds. "Have you lost sight of why I sent you to Vik? Have you forgotten your purpose in the last eight years of your flights South?"

"Lerevna," I started. "We go through this *every* week."

"And every week you fail to convince me. Have your affections for her clouded your judgement?" She turned to me and her reprimand cut to my core. "This is vastly bigger than your *feelings*, Roderick. I need to know if you can be trusted to do what is necessary or if I need to send someone else for the task."

"Stop." It was the only thing I could get out as frustration built within me.

Of course, my feelings affect my judgement, but it is not clouded!

The words spilled out of my mouth at the thought of being reassigned threatened to break something within me, "Brynn cannot be the one you are looking for, Lerevna. Yes, she has abilities, and, yes, her connection with Rune is unique, but something does not fit. You must have the wrong witch. Plus, she is from *Vik*, for Depths sake. He needs a *Reykian* witch. We are following the wrong lead. The other women with abilities I found in the kingdom are more promising to look into, if you would only—"

"What he *needs* is for you to return; Rhydar will not be kept waiting." Lerevna pushed off the ground and stood.

The scabbard at her hip scraped against the rock and set my teeth on edge.

"He what?" My voice was low as I slowly rose to face her. Standing, I towered over her, yet, somehow, she still managed to look down her nose at me, as if I was an insolent child afraid of losing a favored toy. "I need to be there, now more than ever. Lerevna, listen to me. Sondre is actively trying to make a Night Wolf pack. It could take years, but if left unchecked he could rival the pack in our kingdom. Brynn *and* Rune surely will die in the process; you cannot order me away from—"

"*Can I not?*" She asked as she took a step closer and raised her chin at me. Her wings brushed against mine and her indignation crackled around us. "I can, and I am, Roderick. Preventing a pack is not your mission, nor is it mine, lest you forget. Let the absent deities of the South handle their kingdom; that is not our concern. You were sent to search through Vik for the bloodline I need. Do not get distracted. We are bound to forces much bigger than our own desires. You *will* remain in Reykia, for one mission, then you will be allowed to return to your precious Brynn. This is about *Admund*, not a rumor of Night Wolves."

I leaned down into her rage.

"It is not my fault *you* lost the ward charged to you all those years ago; *I* will not lose the two entrusted unto me because of it." I snarled in her face.

Her blink was completely unfazed.

"You do not have a choice." She retorted, as the inked bonds on my neck were set ablaze with the finality of her words. "The sooner you follow the lead on Admund, the sooner you can return. Brynn's dream the other night confirmed Yrsa's connection to the warlock. I was finally able to dig deep enough to find the link. Yrsa knew him as a child. He's family, her brother, perhaps. It confirms Brynn is the witch Rhydar will need."

I shook my head in discomfort as the pressure from her words increased against my skull. It was a stretch to base such a decision on a dead woman's memories. The wind pushed against Lerevna's braids, and a stray strand brushed my cheek as we remained locked in a stalemate. She was my superior. The inked oaths to her on my chest burned as I wanted to go against her wishes, but they would not relent; I was bound to her. I gritted my teeth as it felt like a brand seared into my flesh.

"The solstice is in just a few days' time; this can wait one week. Allow me time to talk to Brynn about all of this, let her come to us willingly." I wanted it to be a demand, but it came out more as a plea.

"It cannot wait. Hoflin may very well attack. Their troops have been massing at the border. The solstice will be the perfect night to attack if Skai blesses it; you know that deity does not hold the Holy Days sacred. He is already in the South for the Council. It is likely he will make his move against Vik sooner rather than later. The moon is due to shine red, and his warriors will take that as a sign to attack. I need you to see whether or not they have Admund with them to ensure it is safe for our goddesses to cross the border. If Hoflin has a warlock with their war party, the risk is too great to travel." Her stoic expression eased slightly, a peace offering lingered on her lips if I took this mission without a fight. "If you can spot Admund in Skai's ranks, Brynn will no longer be a person of interest to me, or to Rhydar. *Admund will suffice.* Brynn could be free from having any part in our world; this could spare her from everything that will come with such a fate...Refuse, and I will drag you back to have Rhydar tell you himself, if I must."

"No," I sighed. I had no desire to speak with Reykia's Master of War over this. "No, if it means you could leave Brynn be, I will go look for Admund."

"Warn her if you must." Lerevna offered.

I looked at her in surprise, but she traced the runes on her chest. I put my hand on her sternum, and her inked oaths were painfully hot to the touch.

Her stoic expression gave nothing away, but from experience, I knew the pain she must have been enduring at this heat to be excruciating.

"You're bridled." My defensiveness ebbed.

She was not going against me on this of her own volition; she was under direct orders.

"What are your oaths keeping you from saying?" I insisted. "What does he not want you to tell me?"

A muscle in her jaw flexed repeatedly.

I took her face in both my hands and gave her a slight shake. The searing heat from her bonds radiated up into my grasp.

"What are you not telling me, Lerevna?" I asked, slight desperation edging my tone.

"The West." She breathed as if it took her great effort to speak. On the outside, she was a vision of calmness, conditioned by centuries of this kind of pain. "I have no business with the West. Brynn—"

She winced for the first time as the words refused to be uttered. The skin under her binding tattoos reddened as burns spread across her chest like lightning. She reframed her warning to be allowed to voice it as her chest flushed red.

"If Brynn ever found herself in Arkanes, she would be safe there. We—There is a Night Wolf in the Western Court, Njord, who can protect her and bring her to me if the need should arise in the future. Do what you will with that truth." Lerevna sighed as the tension in her chest eased.

I searched her eyes and found no deceit.

The crimson streaks spiderwebbing out from her tattoos dissipated to a faded pink. Whatever the order was, she was no longer fighting it.

"Roderick," Her blink was slower than normal and the only sign of her unease. "Rhydar will not tolerate a delay if we are *truly* this close to finding Admund. You must fly to the border. Rhydar still will not let you cross into Northern Territory, raven form or not, but I need your eyes as my scout. Troops have trespassed over the borders enough for you to remain in the other kingdoms. If you can get back in time, tell Brynn to go *West*."

Lerevna paused and my grip tightened around her head. Compared to the lingering heat from our bonds, the silver cuffs in her braids were cold to the touch.

"Am I released to take any form I wish for this mission?" I pressed.

Lerevna glared but begrudgingly nodded.

"Yes, for this mission, alone, you may remain in this form while you fly South. Only shift if necessary, though, we do not need *any* King asking questions why someone from our court is in his lands." Lerevna relented.

A tightness around my core eased slightly with her words as she loosened the magical leash. My wings stretched out further in response.

"Fail at this, Roderick, and I will have no choice but to move forward with what he has planned." Lerevna warned.

A new flair of warmth permeated my grasp. I searched her gaze but found no clue toward the orders that fueled her reluctance and filtered her words.

Given no other options, I hissed through my teeth and let go of her face.

There was no hiding the depth of the breath she took to steel herself for what was to come.

I turned and leapt from the cliff, beating my wings as fast as they could take me back to Brynn, to warn her.

"*West.*" Lerevna's voice echoed in my thoughts as I pushed myself to the limit to return.

I will not lose her.

Chapter 9

Brynn

The sun had descended past the mountain ridge in the distance, casting elongated shadows across my path by the time I walked through the castle gates. Although I did not treat patients often on this side of the city, it still brought a peaceful sense of familiarity as I had grown up within these walls. The scents of leather, steel, hay, and sweat permeated the air as I walked through the training grounds. The soft swish of arrows looking for a target, the grunting and cheering of men fighting, and the loud voice of Officer Magnus barking out orders were all a symphony of lethal productivity. A few faces lit up in recognition as I passed a group of trainees and earned a couple waves while others flexed then laughed. Many of them I had patched up after their last training session when they had come further into town to frequent the neighboring tavern. Bron, one of the sergeants Sondre kept on a tight leash, snarled while in wolf form at the lively group and their banter abruptly ended.

Briskly, I walked out of the training courtyard and through the halls toward the Queen's wing, nodding to the guards as I passed. Individual portraits of Dahlia, Valdis, and the Royal Family decorated the stone corridors. The ambiance of the passageway of gilded frames was a stark contrast to the environment I had just come from—a cot, desperation, fleas.

No, there are definitely fleas here too…

One painting made me pause. Each side of the canvas had a set of yellow eyes, always watching; regardless of where one stood, the glowing orbs held the observer's gaze. It was merely a talent of the artist, but believers thought it was the goddesses truly watching them through the art. One side represented the irises of Dahlia, shining bright like the sun's rays she was said to bless us with in the summer. Vines intertwined through waves of shadow to resemble her luscious hair and spiral horns. The other set of yellow eyes were that of the reptilian humanoids that roamed the forbidden forest. Valdis was whispered to have been a hybrid when she was a mortal, before achieving godhood. Holding her gaze in the painting was unsettling as the slitted irises followed my every move down the hall.

Maybe this is why they do not answer prayers; they are confined to this fucking canvas…

I rolled my eyes and scoffed at my own snideness.

Rune is rubbing off on me.

I increased my pace; the further I went into the castle, however, the gruffer the greetings I received. This was an unfortunate yet expected consequence of making an enemy out of one of their commanders. The nearer one got to the crown, the closer to Sondre the soldier had to be. Half of their noses were up his tail at this point. Two such guards stood watch in front of the room in which I could hear the light echo of Bodhil's voice. As I went to pass the burly men, an arm shot out to block the doorway.

"The Queen will not be sullied by your kind of trash. You can wait for the Royal Healer out in the stalls like the rest of the rabble." The guard barked.

My patience was even thinner than the thread that was holding the buttons on his shirt from popping off. By the way he stood, I could tell there had been a few knee injuries in the past, his weight shifted to alleviate the pain in his left joint. I paused to contemplate kicking out his foot ever so slightly to make that last connection of the tendon snap when I heard the merry tones of Bodhil's melodious cadence.

"There is my girl! You are just in time; the Queen only just arrived." Bodhil said from behind the guard. Her long, soft blonde hair was twisted in a loose braid. Her rosy cheeks were consistently rounded in a smile that accentuated her gentle, jade eyes. She patted the arm blocking the doorway. "Your commitment to the Queen is admirable, Finn, albeit misplaced today. Please step aside."

Finn looked at her, eyes wide in surprise at her scolding him, however politely, "Yes, my Lady. I was simply not made aware that—"

"Consider yourself now aware, dear boy." She interrupted and guided his arm back to his side. "Come, come, Brynn, right this way."

She waved me through the door and walked into a small, covered courtyard. I tried to stifle the chuckle rising in my throat.

Dumb oaf.

Most of the guard knew that I was the healer to the *rabble* in town yet often forgot I came from a notable family that resided near the throne. My separation from the castle to the other side of town had dimmed my significance in other people's eyes, just as Sondre had intended. If he could not attack me physically, he attempted to dismantle my reputation, brick by brick.

Not that my father had ever contradicted him either...

Sondre may have had sway in the Guard and the ear of the Prince, but Bodhil...Bodhil tended to the one who held the most sway in all the Kingdom: Queen Dagmar, herself. The radiant Queen sat on a large stone bench surrounded by plants with thick dense green leaves. Flowers blossomed in the trees above her, as occasional petals floated down to rest on the train of her cream gown. She cradled her hand in her lap with a wrapped bandage. The Queen looked up from the small caterpillar building a cocoon that held her attention in the lantern light. Her welcoming smile turned to surprise as the guard followed in after us.

"Finn, you have left your post." The Queen's brow furrowed as her lips pursed. Her gaze was quizzical, but her tone made it obvious this was a statement not a question.

"My Queen, I just wanted to be sure everything was alright as Commander Sondre had not informed us of a new healer." Finn answered quickly as he squared his shoulders.

My magic accessed his rapid heartbeat, and I saw a bead of sweat forming on his brow.

"And when has the Commander been in charge of *my care*?" Queen Dagmar inquired as she stood to walk over and stand at Bodhil's side.

"I beg your pardon; I meant no disrespect. No, I was just—" Finn stammered.

I tried to stifle a snort unsuccessfully.

Finn shot me a murderous glare as he tripped over his words.

"You were *just* interrupting the intimacy of your Queen and her most trusted healer." Queen Dagmar said, frowning. "In my personal garden, no less, that you had not been invited into…"

"My apologies, I—I know Bodhil is the head Royal Healer, Your Highness—I mean *Majesty*—It's the other one—" Finn searched for an explanation as his ears turned the darkest of reds.

"Fine, *Guard*, fetch me her father if you do not trust the young healer, that he may vouch for her. You are dismissed." Queen Dagmar waved her uninjured hand at him and turned to stroll back to her bench. She motioned for me to join by extending her finger toward the spot at her feet in invitation. The Queen sat back down as I knelt beside her and shrugged off my satchels.

Finn was frozen in place, staring in horror at the dusty bags that I set at the Queen's feet.

"Did you misunderstand me? Maybe this *dangerous* young healer should check your hearing, soldier. The girl's father. Her—" The Queen pointed to Bodhil, "Husband. Now, go!"

Queen Dagmar shooed him off as Bodhil leaned closer to Finn.

"Find Commander Ulfild, boy, before your stillness and foolishness cost you more than just your pride; neither the Queen *nor my husband* are in a forgiving mood today. Off you run!" Bodhil whispered.

Finn turned on his heel, wobbling slightly, and walked quickly out of the door. Once he was down the hall, we heard his walk break into a thunderous run as his heavy footfalls echoed off the stones.

The Queen chuckled mischievously.

"Men." She shook her head, her soft locks flowing like waterfalls down her shoulders. "Entering my chambers, and mentioning that loathsome Sondre around my *plants*, watch as they all wilt at the mention of him, the audacity...I dare say that tiff was worth the fear that will plague that silly boy for weeks around me now. Serves him right."

"Quite worth it." Bodhil said with a teasing twinkle in her eyes which faded as she took the Queen's injured hand. "Brynn, when I had first asked you to come, it was out of mere curiosity of herbs throughout the kingdoms as you travel more than any of our other healers. Since then, however, Queen Dagmar cut her hand on a broken piece of glass in Prince Hurthur's chambers. The wound will not heal with any of my usual treatments, and, then, this started."

Bodhil carefully unwrapped the Queen's dainty hand. Blue streaks snaked out of the open wound across the Queen's palm and slim wrist.

"Usual treatments. Do you specialize in the *unusual* treatments, dear girl?" Queen Dagmar asked me with a soft smile; pain limited the amusement in her warm tone.

"Yes, My Queen, I typically do." I offered her a sheepish grin. "Was there anything in the glass you may be sensitive to causing your body to reject treatment? May I?"

I reached for her hand and paused for approval to touch her, until Queen Dagmar nodded. I inspected the bloody wound and the wrappings for any signs of foreign materials.

"There was *something foreign* in the glass, I thought it merely to be wine. I knocked it over while looking for a book belonging to Hurthur to show Bodhil. The tome had a plant from the neighboring forest that I wanted in my garden; we were going to ask you to investigate it, as it is believed to have healing properties. Bodhil thought who better to discretely handle such a quest than her daughter, the traveling healer. When I picked up the shards of the wineglass in my haste, it burned so terribly. Once as a girl, in a moment of carelessness, I accidentally cut my hand on glass shards, but it never stung quite like this. I would have simply called for a maid to clean it, but I did not want Prince Hurthur to come in and step on it in the meantime. He can be rather reckless when he drinks…" Queen Dagmar's icy blue eyes narrowed as she pointed behind me. "The bottle of wine is just there."

I turned to peer at the stone pedestal. Atop it was an inconspicuous amber bottle of wine. My legs protested as I stood but the stiffness eased as I approached the pedestal.

"Are you sensitive to cinnamon? I know Prince Hurthur has been favoring a batch from one of the new vendors lately." I shifted the bottle in my hands to look at the labels. Sure enough, it was the mulled wine I had anticipated. Earlier in the week, I had inquired about the new vendor's trade and none of the spices the man mentioned seemed too out of the ordinary. Nothing naturally occurring in it could account for the blue streaks, but a random question such as this would keep the Queen talking to give me more time to think.

"That has never been an issue before." Bodhil offered, her tone strained. Her own training knew such a simple spice would not mar the Queen in such a way, but she graciously allowed me to continue to stall. "The Royal Family often has cinnamon in their desserts without any reaction in the past."

I lifted the neck of the bottle to my nose for a small whiff. Hints of oranges and cloves mixed with the sweet red wine greeted me first, followed by a scent I could not place. I hesitated but glanced back at the wound still slowly seeping blood on the apron Bodhil had placed into the Queen's lap. A typical allergic reaction would not look anything like that. If it had resisted Bodhil's healing magic and ointments, there had to be more to what the Prince was drinking.

The bell had not tolled that he was dead, unfortunately, so how bad could it be?

I scanned Bodhil's worried expression, her brow furrowed over her seafoam eyes and her lips quivered ever so slightly in anticipation. I knew her reaching out to me for this, to be asked to return to the palace, was an act of desperation, one I must honor.

For the Queen...For Bodhil's trust.

My magic stilled as my whole body tensed at the possible consequences of my next thought. With a sigh, I stoppered the neck of the bottle with the pad of my thumb and flipped it upside down. I winced as I waited for the potential burning pain that would accompany such a garish wound as the Queen's, once the wine hit my skin, but, to my surprise, none came. I lowered the bottle and examined my wet thumb, tacking my index finger against it. There were no granules scraping my skin, just smooth well fermented wine. I brought my hand to my face and cupped my nose to take a deep breath. There was that strange scent again. Unease crept into my bones.

What is that?

Tentatively, I dabbed my finger against my tongue to try to pinpoint the mystery ingredient to treat it properly.

Immediately, I grimaced and began coughing violently.

"Brynn!" Bodhil exclaimed and took a step towards me.

I raised my empty hand to keep Bodhil with the startled Queen and shook my head. Carefully, I placed the bottle down, still coughing, and fumbled for a leather pouch at my waist.

"Hexed." I choked out as I pulled out bay leaves, rosemary, chili flakes, and salt quickly from my belt, crushing them in my fist and sprinkling them around the bottle. I whacked the flint striker bracelet on my left wrist against the quartz bangle on my right wrist; sparks flew and ignited the herbs. As they burned, I fumbled on my belt until I felt glass and pulled it free. I unstopped the small vial of salt with my teeth and spit out the cork onto the floor. I gathered the smoldering mixture together and dropped to my knees at Dagmar's feet. Wheezing, I grasped the Queen's hand without permission and smeared the ashes and salt in with the blood in her hand.

Queen Dagmar leaned back aghast but did not object to the unapproved contact. She could have me killed for less, but I was seconds away from death at this point. She let out a small whimper as the mixture seeped into the wound, but the blue streaks retreated back toward the cut. Rasping, I rubbed the mixture onto my own face next as inky patterns quickly spread out from my lips; the tang of her royal blood seeped into my mouth. I reached for a knife at my ribs as spots formed in my vision and pulled a fresh lemon from my satchel at her feet. I sliced it in half and dragged it along the Queen's forearm.

"You are not welcome in this vessel. I bind and repel you. Leave this vessel. I bind and repel you." I ground out as my throat tightened with each word.

I squeezed the other half of the lemon against my cheeks down toward my mouth; repeating the command, I turned away from the Queen and stumbled back to the pedestal. The raw magic deep in my bones roiled against me when I reached for it; it was repulsed by the intrusion in my body. I unwrapped my own bandaged hand from healing Freda and reopened the wound, this time up toward my wrist for an immediate steady flow. My blood gushed out of one hand while I untied a drawstring coin purse full of fresh black salt from my belt with the other. I poured the salt around the bottle as I chanted my command on repeat and held my dripping hand above to fully saturate the spell with the undiluted power of blood magic.

"You are not welcome here, magic of old. I bind and repel you. You are not welcome, flee to the one who cast this evil intent." I dug in my satchel with my good hand before removing a small mirror bound in cloth. I bit at the string holding the protective padding together until it fell off. I lifted the bottle with my bloodied hand and set the reflective glass under it to mirror the hex from whence it came. "You are not welcome, return o' magic of old. Return."

My breathing began to steady as I drew runes in the salt, tapping my finger in the pooling blood of my palm for ink to write. I rolled my head back and sighed at the ceiling as the last of the blue and numbness left my lips. I repeated the words until the magic within me relaxed and coursed through my body without obstruction. The light around me shone a deep golden as my power released itself from the bounds of the hex. I felt the familiar caress of Bodhil's own power joining the space and tending to the Queen.

"Brynn?" A gravelly voice reverberated from the doorway as my light instinctively dissipated. "Valdis spare me, Brynn, what are you doing here?"

A man in a deep hunter green uniform with a gold sash walked into the courtyard. He ran his leathery hand through his thick white hair.

"Depths, your Majesty! Are you quite well?" He startled, as he took another step toward the scene of chaos.

The smoke from the herbs still hung in the air. I could only imagine how disheveled I looked to him, not to mention the Queen covered in lemon juice, ash, and blood.

"Father, lovely for you to stop by," I managed as I let my shoulders fall. I soon realized my face was still covered with my burnt concoction as he looked flabbergasted at my appearance then again to the Queen before letting his smoldering gaze settle on Bodhil.

"Ulfhild." The Queen breathed as she looked down at her hand that was already healing once nothing remained to resist Bodhil's golden tendrils. "Goddesses, your daughter is a credit to you, both."

His eyes now bore into me, he regarded me with astonishment, reprimand, and contempt. This opened a door into his life that the royal family has no business being aware of, for all our sakes.

It had been a risk—Bodhil deemed it necessary, otherwise she would have never summoned me.

If only I could explain all of this to him, but instead I lifted the edge of my apron to wipe off my face under his judgmental, glowering stare.

Respond to your Queen.

My lip instinctively curved in a challenge before I cleared my face of all expression.

He raised his chin slightly toward my bloody palm, and I wrapped it in my bandage from earlier without a word.

You honor me, My Queen. We are proud of our healer, who just so happens to know of the witches' ways. Nothing to look into, I assure you.

I caught my eyes midroll as my mind rattled off a response in my father's voice and turned back to Queen Dagmar and Bodhil.

Like he would ever speak so positively.

Queen Dagmar's keen blue eyes shifted from my father to myself, noticing the undertones of our relationship, without bringing further attention to it.

"You are most generous, Your Majesty. I can safely say that was a witch's toxin, in a bespelled bottle, no less." I brushed the remnants of the past few chaotic moments off my bodice. "A nasty one at that. I am honestly a bit impressed."

Queen Dagmar shook her head in shock.

"Your methods are peculiar, young one, peculiar yet effective. But there has not been a witch in this kingdom for decades." She regarded Bodhil for confirmation, who nodded with a fleeting glance at my father.

Bodhil gently wiped off the remnants of the mixture from the Queen's hands to reveal the fully healed skin, no scar to be seen.

"Dahlia, bless you, child. Unusual treatments, indeed. Where did you learn such things? The citadel does not teach counterspells." Queen Dagmar stated in wonderment.

I felt the heat rising up my neck and shot a look at my father and formed my answer carefully.

His wolf glowed behind his eyes in warning. Directly lying to royalty was unilaterally frowned upon but the truth would damn us all.

"When I would travel with Father and the Guard to the Northern battlefields, I tended to the enemy captives." I carefully explained.

Since I was deemed unfit to tend to our own officers after denying your piece of shit Commander Sondre.

"Some prisoners knew of spells that may harm us," I sprinkled in a half-truth. "The sedatives I used for amputations often loosened their tongues to mention all kinds of things. Most times, they were simply grateful for the pain to stop and would offer counterspells for the peace to continue. Not all were accurate, mind you, a mixture of rumors, lore, and wives' tales, but every now and again, I could come across something we could use."

"We are lucky you listened. Again, you should be proud of your daughter, Ulfhild." Queen Dagmar gave a half-smile, her eyes narrowing slightly at my father. Her wise gaze was edged with a knowing challenge at his silence.

Father refused to lie and confirm my story. His attention remained fixed on me as the rage within his wolf threatened to take control.

I curtsied to the Queen for her praise but tilted my head toward my father as he cautiously approached Bodhil. "Tell me, Father, when you closed the pits, where there any witches who remained?"

The deep-set lines of Ulfhild's brow intensified into crevasses for asking about the pits in front of the Queen.

Queen Dagmar, however, waved for him to answer, undeterred by such an indecent topic as she grew more impatient with his mute behavior than anything else.

"No. The few left alive fled North. Two went to Reykia, as well, to worship the Night Wolves. Why?" His deep brown eyes searched my face, curiosity finally winning over his need to chide my foolishness.

"Prince Hurthur seems to be acquainted with a witch, for ill or not." I motioned toward the smoldering mess on the pedestal. "It would not have been hexed by the vendor; that simple man was no warlock, I can assure you, a common merchant, at best."

"*Unless the cunt of a prince wanted a hexed bottle.*" Rune's voice rang out in my mind.

Notes of jasmine and vanilla filled my senses, and I knew he must have blocked out our connection to be intimate with Sif.

I hummed in response and I stared at the bottle.

"*I knew you could handle yourself long enough to go quiet. Be careful how you accuse royalty, but we both know that fucker is plotting something.*" Rune added.

I could hear Sif's faint laugh as his consciousness departed from mine again.

"Have you seen His Highness since cutting your hand, Your Majesty?" I prodded.

"No, child. He was to join the King and I on the terrace, but he did not show." She said as worry started to contort her features, and her eyes went wide in panic. "Oh, you do not think he drank it, do you? Ulfhild, find my boy Hurthur. Check his rooms, hurry!"

Father bowed and obeyed without another word.

"Try to breathe, My Queen." Bodhil soothed as she stroked the Queen's hand.

"You said there was already a glass poured when you knocked it over?" I asked, stepping closer as I adjusted my skirts from the commotion.

"Yes!" Queen Dagmar stood as she placed her hands on her ornate bodice in an attempt to ground her constricted breaths.

"Not to be crude, Your Majesty, but Prince Hurthur would not have made it out of the room alive if he drank anything from the glass." I surmised; I raised my hands as her face fell. "No, no, he was not on the floor when you went to get the book, right? The hex had to have been crafted with the potential for spilling without killing everything it came in contact with, to ensure the glass could be poured; the bespelled bottle sped up the effects and housed the magic to limit detection, which is why Bodhil could not sense it. The originating warlock must have used verbiage in the spell *to be drank* but his intention blurred the lines and shifted to any way the wine was absorbed. That is why it only marred your hand, slowly. You did not drink it, but it still absorbed it into your bloodstream. His Highness *couldn't* have drunk it and made it out of the room; since he was not passed out on the floor, he is likely alive and well."

The Queen frowned but nodded as she tried to calm herself. The fear of his fate ebbed from her picturesque face.

"Did he mention his plans for the wine?" I inquired as I returned to the pedestal to carefully put a cork into the bottle.

"*Let her make the conclusion on her own of her dear boy.*" Rune's voice was strained and bitter.

"He…Oh, Valdis, have mercy." The Queen gasped.

Bodhil's face turned to stone.

"He…Prince Hurthur was to toast the King with all his generals tonight, before they left for the Northern front in the morning. He said he wanted a special wine poured for everyone at the table, including the King…" Bodhil whispered, even repeating such things had treasonous undertones, and pointed to the bottle. "He requested the maid pour him a glass and set the table for the others. I was asked to join your father at dinner when the toast was given."

"*See, cunt. Only cowards use poison in a wolf kingdom.*" Rune seethed.

I felt a chill enter from his end of the bond and knew his time with Sif must have been interrupted for Guard business to already be patrolling the streets.

Queen Dagmar's worry instantly transformed into resignation as her dainty jaw flexed.

She knows Hurthur's true nature. Interesting…

"We can use this." Rune agreed before diverting his attention to a drunken believer in the tavern.

"I must see to His Majesty." Queen Dagmar stated solemnly as she gathered her gown and left the room in a hurry.

I bowed as she walked by and could feel the sense of dread and doom permeating from her frame as her heartbeat increased drastically.

Bodhil went to follow her but quickly grabbed my bandaged forearm and leaned close.

"Well done, Brynn. Your father will be furious, but we need that blessed woman alive if this Kingdom is to stand a chance. There have been whispers of dissension against the cause to go North. Reach out to Rune and have him escort you home. Do not leave this room until he arrives, do you hear me?" She tightened her grip as my eyes watered from exhaustion. Golden tendrils wisped between us as she healed from my palm up to my elbow. "The men are on edge, and Sondre is furious with you as it is. Now this."

"Prince Hurthur and Commander Sondre are in league on a great many things and are furious at more than just me. Have Father watch his back tonight, as well." I put my hand on my mother's grip. "*You* be careful, too."

"One night, we will have a normal dinner, as a family, without worrying of treachery and politics." Bodhil brushed my cheek with her free hand.

"Unusual dinners work for me too." I smiled.

Bodhil chuckled softly and let her hand fall to pat my arm and give me a final squeeze.

"Indeed, they do." She paused to look at my face, as if to memorize every detail before leaving the room. Her skirts whispered against the stone floor as she hurried after the Queen.

I closed my eyes and started to reach deep within and pulled at the cord that wove around my soul, connecting me to Rune. The bond already felt faint.

Rune must have closed me off and taken the brawler outside the gates to be dealt with properly.

The flutter of wings drew my attention away from our connection.

A raven flew through the small side window and shifted midflight. My heart stopped at Roderick's expression as he crossed the courtyard to me in two determined steps.

"Roderick," I breathed, my relief mixed with confusion. "*How are you like this?* The solstice is not for a couple of days. If someone catches you like this, in the castle—"

My protests were cut short as he grasped my face. He drew me to him as his lips claimed mine. Utter desperation lined his embrace, and his need drew a startled moan from my throat.

His scent overwhelmed my senses and heated my core. I opened my mouth and let his tongue enter me greedily. It felt as if he wanted every kiss we had missed over the years in that moment, and I craved to give them all to him. I threaded my fingers through his hair and pressed my body closer against him. His hand drifted to my neck, and I instinctively flinched at the tenderness left over from Sondre's grip. Roderick pulled his lips away immediately and I ached for him not to stop.

"What happened?" He asked breathlessly and he tilted my chin to look at my neck.

Faint purple fingerprints had started to become visible.

His gaze turned murderous. "Who did this to you?"

"Go back to what you were doing," I demanded and leaned forward to kiss him. I felt his lips pull up into a slight smile at my hunger for his touch.

"Wait," He managed in between kisses. "I don't have much time; I need you to listen to me."

I ground my hips against him the way Sif taught me, and he dropped his hand to my waist to still me. He rested his forehead against mine with a shuddered breath.

"There are not enough words in any language to describe how badly I want you." His lips brushed mine as the tightness between my legs increased. "But I need you to go home and pack a bag."

"*What?*" I leaned back enough to look at him fully. "Roderick. We have been through this. I am not running away, especially not now!"

"Listen to me you beautiful, stubborn woman." His dark eyes pleaded as they searched mine. "I *need* you to go West. There is a Night Wolf in King Tytus's court, Njord. Tell him I sent you. He will protect you until I can get there. Go with Rune, and whatever you do, *do not* get separated from him."

"Roderick." I was at a loss for words. "Where is this coming from?"

I could not leave now. Not with everything going on!

"Hoflin is coming. This is not about Sondre. We will deal with him, but, for now, please, *please* listen to me." The pain and desperation in his voice threatened to tear me in two.

I nodded, not trusting my own voice.

"Good girl." He whispered and kissed me again. His concern laced every movement of his lips against mine. "Call Rune and get out of here. Check on your girls, if you must, but leave soon."

The longing in his next kiss overtook me. His hand grasped my back and held me tightly against him as if it was his last chance to hold me. His fingertips pulled at my spine as his breath grew shaky.

I pulled back to see an unfallen tear rest against his lower eyelid. Questions flooded me as he lifted his lips to firmly kiss my forehead.

"Stay alive." He breathed against my brow before giving me one last gut-wrenching look. He released his hold on me and turned, shifting and flying out the window with a croak that split my heart.

I stood there, trembling in the Queen's garden for a moment. I took one breath followed by the next as I regained my senses.

Rune.

"I need you." I whispered.

Rune, come to the castle. We need to talk, now.

Heat rushed over me in a wave as I felt Rune shift into his wolf form. A howl sounded further out of town, echoed by another voice closer, in the castle. Soon there was a scuffling outside the garden as boots clicked in a salute.

"Sir!" Finn breathlessly called out but the only reply was a deep huff.

A head of curly brown hair peeked through the doorway. The man's tawny skin was tight against his muscular frame and emanated warmth as he strolled over to me barefoot. He had not bothered with a shirt, and his trousers were torn at the bottom.

"Hey, Little Pup. Heard you needed a ride," He said with a wink.

"Halsten." I tried to smile at Rune's littermate, but a hollowness in me threatened to take hold. The adrenaline from the day had started to wear off, and my knees buckled.

Halsten was at my side in an instant with an arm around my waist to steady me.

"Easy there, Regh." His breath was warm against my cheek. "Rune warned me you might be spent, but he did not say how bad you were this time. You deserve to be brought home by the scruff of your neck for overdoing it this much. Here, up you go."

Without giving me time to refuse him, he lifted me up into his arms and held me close.

"We need to leave." I muttered.

I rested my head against the familiar chest of my childhood friend as the world around me started to fade. For a moment, in the safety of his arms, my magic let me feel how tired I truly was. I dozed in and out of consciousness as he carried me all the way to our shared cabin on the outskirts of town.

Chapter 10

Brynn

Howls filled the crisp night air as I sprinted for my life. Holding tight to the baby wrapped in my arms, I prayed to any god who would listen. The forest floor was slick as I ran, but the bed of leaves muffled my escape. Deep hunter green tendrils of magic swirled around my waist as I tried to knit myself back together, pulling from the wildlife in the forest. I would not let them take this child; they had sentenced too many to a life of misery and death already. The sounds of snarls and hungry jaws snapping, frothing with rage, grew louder as my pursuers closed in around me. The light of a solitary window glimmered from a cabin in the distance. I had to make it there before they reached me.

Flinging myself up the steps, I slammed my fist against the door. I tried to catch my ragged breath and soothe the child in my embrace when it hit me...I recognized the tattoos on my arms and the bronze bangles that clanged together as I pounded against the wood. Dread coursed through my veins as I realized I was stuck in another memory of Yrsa's, one I knew all too well. My fist raised of its own volition and banged against the door again. Recognition fractured my heart, this was Rune's and my cabin, but it was missing the shutters that he installed last summer. There were different pots set about, none of my usual herbs. The light flickered under the door as a shadow passed in front of the threshold, I half expected Rune to open it with an expression as confused as I was. The door opened to reveal a shocked woman in her night dress carrying a small candle. There were no laugh lines around her mouth, and her temples did not have grey highlights yet in her blonde hair.

"Bodhil! You must take her; they are after me." The words wheezed out of my mouth as I pressed the baby into Bodhil's arms.

"How did you get out? It has been years!" Young Bodhil sobbed as she took the child and pressed it protectively against her nightdress.

"You cannot let them find her. Promise me, Bodhil, they must not find her. Train her as Father wanted for me." I grasped Bodhil's arm with bloodied hands. I was a passenger in Yrsa's body, able to feel every ounce of urgency as I tightened my grip.

"I promise, but come inside, let me tend to your wounds, quick." Bodhil insisted, taking a step back to let me through the doorway.

Tears filled my eyes.

"They cannot find her; they cannot find my Brynn. I love you." The words spilled out as I turned away.

Horror strangled the shouts in Bodhil's throat as I fled off the porch. I was already running through the trees by the time the door closed. I had to lead the pack away from the cabin; it was the only hope for the child to survive. Branches reached out and tore at my face as I ran. Icy dread sunk its talons into my heart and I glanced over my shoulder to see the woods darker than the previous times I had this dream. Hidden in the shadows, I saw her. Lerevna. She leaned against a tree studying me. The wolves' howls were closing in; I did not have time to stop and confront her. Stumbling over roots, I orientated toward the sound of the river. It was a risk, but it had not rained in weeks; the river might be low enough to cross before it reached the waterfalls and rapids. Yrsa knew that even if she slipped into the glacier run-off, freezing or drowning would be a better way to die than what the pack would do once they found her.

I thanked the Old Gods above and below when I arrived at the river and saw the boulders to cross were dry at the tops. I leapt onto the first, scraping my bare feet. Onward I pushed, slipping on the second and opening a fresh wound on my knee. I could not stop and register the pain. A howl further behind sounded. The wind that bit my skin had shifted and led the pack in the wrong direction, but they had just caught my fresh scent again as I bled. I reached the soil of Reykia and continued running. The downy birch brush ripped my already tattered clothes and tore at my arms and exposed shins.

A loud caw sounded in alarm and a shadow flew out of the brush next to me. The moonlight caught a warm hue of red on the raven's large wings. The omen of a bloody death took to the skies. There was no sense of familiarity when I watched the bird take flight. The coloration was wrong; unease settled into my bones. As it banked, I got a better look and knew deep in my heart, that was not my Roderick. The details became clearer as I watched Yrsa's memory of Lerevna's Blood Raven form soar above and nausea struck me; Lerevna had been there that night all those years ago. I gritted my teeth and pushed onwards.

If the pack followed me onto Reykian soil, it would be more than just my death tonight. The Night Wolves patrolled these woods and could end those pursuing me. I could only hope. A stream babbled ahead, and I rushed towards it hoping to mask my scent. The forest grew silent around me, and I knew nature was aware of the hunters behind me. There were more nightmares than just wolves in this forest, and I was prey to them all.

I splashed into the water but heard a branch snap close by, too close. I crawled against the river rock to hide behind a black boulder nestled in the center of the stream. I shivered as the icy water chilled my bones. A low growl sounded from the bank. I closed my eyes and reached down to the bond I had long kept hidden.

"Find them, Admund." I pleaded in my mind, forcing my words through the void within myself. "Find my children."

I felt the wolf's hot breath against my ear before pain seared through my neck.

I awoke with a gasp and reached for my throat. Nausea filled me as I looked around the room frantically for my attacker. A wolf of warm pecan coloring rested near my feet on the oversized straw mattress taking up much of the living room floor. The light of a dying fire filled the room with gentle orange hues. Another wolf was staring out the window with his back to me. The copper fur on his neck was raised, and his ears were pinned to the back of his head. Rune turned to face me with sadness and rage battling in his emerald eyes. I got up from the floor and went to him, stepping around Halsten's sleeping wolf form. I buried my face in Rune's warm fur and cried. Regardless of how many times the nightmare plagued me over the years, it never grew easier to watch Yrsa die, to feel it in my soul as she was torn apart and defiled.

"I could not wake you." Rune said quietly and he stroked the bond to soothe the frantic thoughts in my mind.

"I know you tried." I whispered into his chest.

He always tried.

He draped his heavy head across my shoulder and pushed me closer against himself. I welcomed the heat that filled my trembling frame. The chill eventually subsided, and I was able to catch my breath. As I took a step back, he gave me a little nudge with his muzzle.

"Let me shift back, I will make us some tea." Rune offered gently.

I ran my hands through the fur between his ears then agreed. I shuffled back over to Halsten and sat with my back against his curled form. A soft hum came from him as he brushed his nose against my leg and fell back to sleep. The room was still as Rune picked tea from the cabinet full of glass jars filled with different dried flowers and herbs. I stared out the window at the branch Roderick often frequented, but he was not there. He regularly had to fly away on missions around the kingdom, but this felt different. I had never seen him in such a state when he had appeared at the castle.

Rune came back with a mug of tea in each hand and under his arm was a leather-bound notepad stuffed with extra crumbled sheets of paper. He passed me a delicious smelling cup and spread out his papers on the bed sewn and stuffed to accommodate multiple wolves.

"I figured we could start going over what Halsten and I have discovered since neither of us will likely be able to get to sleep for a while," Rune began. "Before we do, however, tell me about the dream. It was not like times in the past when you had this nightmare."

He rested his hand on my knee, and I sensed the depth of his concern through the bond; I let the comfort in it wash over me and mute the horrors still raging in my mind.

"Lerevna, the dream walker Roderick mentioned, whoever she *really* is, she is searching for something. My dreams of late do not feel like how they usually do when I stumble my way through Yrsa's memories. They are increasingly vivid." I stared into the fire in the hearth. "There is a sense of urgency."

Rune's gaze scanned my face as he tilted his head.

"As if you're approaching the end of something?" Rune asked softly, already assessing the emotions I did not voice. "You think this is what the Witch alluded to with Aksel, that someone is coming for you?"

"Yes." I breathed as a chill crept down my spine. "I am, or Lerevna is, I cannot tell. This is all so much more…desperate. The dreams are building to *something*, running out of time maybe, but I don't know what exactly."

I looked up to his warm eyes shadowed by his furrowed brow. The deep green mirrored my own.

"As much as I don't like it, we should cross the border soon to speak to Roderick directly about this. We need to know more about what this Lerevna is looking for and why." He nodded toward the windowsill. "Especially since he is not in his usual perch *preening* for your attention."

I let out a soft chuckle before looking at his various notes.

"And what of going West like he suggested?" I asked.

As I read over all the names of the at-risk mothers in Rune and Halsten's handwriting, I knew I could not leave them all here. Rune was silent as he too examined the sheer number of pregnant women counting on us to help them, to save them.

"If an attack is imminent as he says…" He began.

I felt the battle within him churn like a storm. The desire to protect me and to send Sif away with me weighed heavily on his heart. But the undeniable fact that we were needed here stared us in the face. His gaze stilled on a sheet that listed some of our youngest mothers yet. I rested my hand on his.

"If Roderick is right and Hoflin is coming, these women will all be in danger, not just me." I countered as I leaned forward to kiss his cheek. "They will need your protection even more, plus healers during an attack will be in short supply."

"I cannot risk you and Sif." His voice cracked.

"We stay." I resolved. "Sif will not leave her girls, regardless of how much she loves either of us. Honestly, neither will I."

Rune lifted his hand to the back of my neck and pulled me close until our temples touched.

"We will figure this out." He promised.

I cleared my throat and sat up straight.

Solution mode.

"Okay, tell me what we know…" I took a sip of my tea and steeled myself for what was to come.

Chapter 11

Brynn

It had been Halsten's bright idea to spend our morning at Gro's tavern as payback for *disturbing his slumber* all night talking, when the wolf had been snoring through most of my conversation with Rune. My spot in the curved horseshoe-shaped wooden booth was toasty as sitting next to Halsten was like curling up next to a blazing wood stove. His muscular thigh against mine felt like the hot stones Sif would massage my sore muscles with whenever I had time to visit her, when we were not both drowning with work.

I need to stop by soon.

The sense of longing in my thoughts caused Rune to case a side glance at me. I waved him off as he returned to surveying the room. Halsten's attention was on his plate as he devoured the meat and steaming potatoes after finishing his eggs. He spoke of

Guard business to Rune while I tuned them out and scanned the patrons around us.

Many of the guests had yet to go to sleep after the night's festivities. Scents of pungent incense and body oils used in the pleasure rituals at Dahlia's temple filled the air; others carried the potency of smoke and sorrow of Valdis' offerings with them like weighted robes. Rune's lip curled slightly from where he sat at the table across from me each time our space was infected with the scents of religious devotion.

Luckily, none of Sondre's men were in the tavern with us. Rune evaluated each person in the crowd instinctively as well. He leaned against the back of his side of the booth with his arm outstretched across the top. To the untrained eye, he looked relaxed, calm even. I, however, noticed his middle finger digging into the nailbed of his thumb from where his hand rested on the wood. His knee bounced slightly under the table, and he would routinely flex his shoulders as if to force down the tension growing in his traps. His gaze trailed after a wolf shifter before flicking back to another patron. Visitors came from all over the kingdom for the yearly pilgrimage whenever Vik hosted the Council of the Gods; new faces brought new threats and set Rune on edge this time every year.

His focus landed back on me as he sensed my assessment of him through the bond.

"I'm fine." He assured me internally with an unconvincing grin.

A drunken satyr stumbled into the side of our table as he walked passed. Halsten barked with his mouth full at the patron to watch where he cantered.

Rune's expression went deadpan as he raised an eyebrow. *"See, I haven't tried to eat him. I am fine."*

"Right." I replied as I leaned into Halsten's shoulder until the grip on his fork and knife loosened slightly. I did not want to waste any of my recovering magic reserves on needing to heal a satyr with a fork lodged into his throat.

Rune huffed in amusement at the image my thoughts presented while Halsten continued with his report on the new litter of troops to enter training.

Rune's searching gaze landed behind me and his tension melted in an instant as a smile lit up his face. I looked back to see Sif walking in, her silhouette unmistakable in the doorway.

"There she is." Rune interrupted Halsten in the middle of his sentence. Rune's voice was low, but the joy in his tone was obvious.

Halsten glanced at me before catching sight of Sif.

"He will not hear anything I have to say now." Halsten rolled his eyes.

"Nope." I chuckled and patted his knee.

"Neither will you." Halsten tilted his head with a smirk before going back to his breakfast.

I scrunched my nose at him and gave his thigh a squeeze in confirmation. Rune and I shared countless qualities; our mutual adoration of Sif was paramount. Jealousy never entered our relationship as we were both secure in how much she loved each of us in return.

Patrons and staff alike greeted her enthusiastically as she made her way to our table. Rune reached for her as she came to sit next to him in the booth. Rune buried his face in her neck and groaned with contentment as he wrapped her up in his strong arms. She let out a soft giggle as his scruff tickled her throat while he kissed his greeting into her skin.

"Halsten." Sif chimed as she slid a sandaled foot up his calf under the table.

Halsten only grunted in response and took a swig of his ale. He fished out an orange slice floating on the top and handed it to Sif. She beamed and accepted the citrus offering. Rune begrudgingly leaned back as she reached for it. Sif sucked the rind before giving Rune a pacifying kiss on the lips.

She hummed as she pulled away enough to ask, "How fares our fearless protectors?"

"Tired. Thanks to the terror here." Halsten nudged me with his elbow lightly.

"You got the most sleep out of all of us, you whiny pup." Rune mocked as he leaned forward and plucked a chunk of potato off Halsten's plate. He popped it into his mouth before pointing at Halsten. "Every creature in the forbidden forest could hear this oaf snoring while Brynn and I tried to figure shit out."

Sif melted into Rune's side as she relaxed into their joking. Her gaze, however, settled on me with all too familiar concern.

"The nightmares again?" She asked.

I simply nodded as Liv arrived with our plates from the kitchen. Liv was filling in after Katla's murder until Asta could make it to Gro's. She set down another plate in front of Halsten with a wink before heading back.

Sif took a fork and helped herself to Rune's breakfast. "Oh, do you have the good salt?"

With a laugh, I unwound a leather pouch from my belt. I loosened the string before setting it on the table.

"Holding out on me." Halsten scoffed in mock insult as he sprinkled some on my plate before seasoning his own.

"It usually isn't used for food." I murmured as I watched Sif help herself and wink at me gleefully.

Rune waved his hand from around Sif's shoulder at Liv before pointing to a bowl of fruit at the end of the bar. Liv quickly grabbed a red apple with yellow streaks on it and came close enough to toss it to him. Rune caught it effortlessly and took the first bite. Juice still streaming down his chin, he handed me the rest of it. Ever since a wounded shifter had caught me in the jaw with her wing in the medic tents, Rune had started taking the first bite of my apples to make them easier for me to eat. Even with my bones long since healed, he still continued the endearing morning routine.

"But, to answer your question, yes, Sif. Brynn's nightmares have been more livid lately." Rune answered as I bit into the sweet fruit.

I chose to enjoy my apple instead of adding anything further, as we all had known each other since childhood; my visions were not new information.

"Have you heard of a dream walker in your priestess trainings?" Halsten asked Sif nonchalantly.

Rune coughed midchew.

"*Halsten.*" I whispered as I crushed his foot with my heel. "This is not the place to discuss it."

"No one here gives a fuck." He replied casually, undeterred. He motioned his fork to the rest of the tavern before using it to point at us with each word he emphasized, "Plus, *we* are the only sober ones here. *They* have all been drunk since the feasts started last night for Dahlia. *I,* on the other hand, had to listen to *you two* nitwits argue about it half the night. I want to sleep tonight; talk now so *we* can sleep later."

He circled his fork around the table before stabbing a piece of potato and shoving it into his mouth.

Sif chewed on her lip but raised her brows to signal Halsten had a point.

I regarded Rune as he frowned slightly.

"*Your call.*" Rune offered down the bond.

Sif glanced between Rune and I as if to not interrupt our inner dialogue.

"Have you?" I relented with a sigh.

"I have…" Sif began tentatively. "But some heavy rituals must take place first before someone is capable of that. It is rumored to only be allowed if the behavior is ordained by a god or that it is a skill belonging to a *particular* community…Why?"

Sif scrutinized Halsten but he only bit into his pork and tilted his chin toward me. Sif peered at me in return as I stared at the apple in my hand, avoiding her gaze.

"*This is not the time nor place.*" I directed toward Rune.

"*You are the one who wanted to get involved with a headstrong, holy priestess.*" He countered.

"*Why*, Brynn?" Sif repeated as she lowered her voice and leaned her elbows on the table. Her cleavage heaving from her loose neckline.

I gestured to her full bosom with my apple.

"That's cheating," I deflected.

Sif rolled her shoulders and crossed her arms under her chest. She practically spilled out of her dress now, in defiance, earning a chuckle from each of us.

"Fine, you win—" I started to admit as I put down my crispy diversion.

"I think we all just won," Rune mused as he beheld Sif with heat filling his green irises. He pulled her back and dragged his finger along her collarbone and down her sternum.

Sif tilted her head up to kiss him and bit his lip in a gentle reprimand.

"You will get your time later," Sif's sultry tone scolded. "For now, though, tell me about this dream walking business."

Rune raised his lip in a mock growl before kissing her nose and turning to face me.

"The *winged bastard* that you two ladies giggle over has a friend apparently." Rune divulged and Sif snapped her head at me.

"A *mate.*" Halsten corrected.

"*Depths!*" I covered my face with my hands. "How much were you awake for?"

"Like I have been saying *all morning*, enough to not sleep worth shit!" Halsten added more salt to his plate and mumbled, "Now, talk."

I reluctantly filled Sif in on all the new information I was still trying to process myself. Her expression shifted from frowning in concentration, to nodding in agreement, and raising her brows in surprise but she did not interrupt. I felt more comfortable as Rune shifted in the bond and removed himself from the conversation; he devoted all of his attention to the tavern around us to ensure no unwanted ears were heeding us. His presence was supportive but mentally distant. No one paid us any attention as the drunken commotion continued around us. I picked at my plate when she asked questions and shared my drink when it was her turn to listen. Sif's face grew grave as I concluded with Lerevna's recent presence in my dreams and Roderick's connection to her. The dream of Yrsa's death removed all the color from Sif's face.

"Brynn," Sif began carefully as she swirled my mug of water with lemon and ginger slices in it.

Halsten reached over and put his hand on Sif's. The gesture seemed innocent enough to anyone who may have noticed but it silenced Sif instantly.

A wolf shifter walked by our table while Rune had been surveying the other side of the room. The young man had a brand on his neck from a pack along the southern coastline. He nodded to Rune and Halsten before approaching Liv at the bar. Rune observed the man before subtly gesturing for Halsten to check the newcomer out. Halsten let go of Sif's drink with a casual stretched before dropping his hand under the table to squeeze my knee.

"Don't let Rune eat my food." Halsten murmured as he leaned in close to kiss my cheek before standing. He rubbed his stomach contently and took his ale to the bar. He clasped the new wolf on the shoulder and Halsten's charismatic energy shone in his wolfy grin.

Rune brushed Sif's shoulder to continue once Halsten's loud voice drowned out any possibility of us being overheard.

"Do you remember anything of that night? Have you dreamt of it and relived *your own memories* of it?" Sif whispered.

"I was a literal newborn." I answered, exasperated. "Fleeting moments in the past but nothing of any substance. Why?"

Sif searched my face; pain settled in her eyes before she spoke.

"There are a great number of things that can be accomplished through a blood rite, in and out of the temple." Sif's tone was weary. "There has been death in each of the dreams Lerevna has visited?"

"Of her father and village, then of Yrsa herself, yes." I claimed softly.

"And…" She leaned closer, this time with no ulterior motive. "Magic? …not the gold kind?"

I bit my lip and nodded.

Magic had held Yrsa in place during the forest raid nightmare and Yrsa had used it to heal herself as she fled in the woods in last night's dream. Sif's gaze flicked to the amulet of black garnet resting under my bodice.

"Did this Lerevna see that Yrsa wore one those too?" Sif asked.

The question about my necklace was vague, but Rune and I locked eyes. Bodhil had given me Yrsa's amulet, and I never took it off growing up. That was until it had been ripped from my neck during a struggle with a Northern patient when working at the frontlines. Rune had made this one for me as a replacement. The stone was almost identical to Yrsa's and eased some of the pain with the loss. It was my connection to the past and the only gods who seemed to listen.

Our exchange was confirmation enough as Sif's face fell at the realization.

"That complicates things..." Her voice dropped in seriousness as she continued, "Blood rites need a *grounding element*, often a crystal. The priests initiate blood offerings with a black garnet blade and have been since the Great War against the Old Gods. It is one of the few practices kept from the foregone beliefs in Vik. If using a metal blade, the blood is poured onto the black garnet slab in Valdis' temple to ground the rite or sacrifice. If Lerevna is looking into deaths while a token like *that and magic* is present, she may be trying to pinpoint a ritual."

"Because the bloodline is known for having so many priests in it?" Rune tone took a sharp edge with his rhetorical question.

He has a point.

My family rarely frequented any temple except for pack related business that father had to preside over. The Reykian temple for Tyr, where Rune and I rendezvoused with Aksel, was the only religious place that ever saw our regular attendance.

"Priests are not the only ones with rites," Sif mused.

She moved back gracefully as Halsten's laugh grew closer. She turned in her seat to whisper into Rune's ear. She stared at him and nodded at me before directing her attention to the approaching wolves with a radiant smile.

Halsten sat back down and scooted me further into the booth closer to Rune to make room for the coastal wolf. Under the table, Halsten rubbed my knee and glanced at my food for approval.

I motioned slightly with my chin in agreement to his diversion. He handed the newcomer my barely touched plate and made a remark about the long journey to get here for the festivals. Sif flicked her hair over her shoulder at the prospect of another devotee; she made distracting conversation with them as I subconsciously turned my attention to Rune.

"Who else would conduct rites that Lerevna may be looking into?" I inquired through the bond as I pinched a piece of meat off Rune's plate and popped it into my mouth as indifferently as I could.

Rune stretched his other arm along the curved booth behind me as he reclined against the wood backing. His fingers grazed against my spine to chase away the chill that slithered down my back. The comfortable movement was at odds with the storm that brewed in his eyes.

"Witches." He replied.

Chapter 12

Brynn

I collapsed onto Sif's bed with a groan. Her room was much larger than the other girl's, second only to Madame Ahmila's. The four-poster bed felt like lying on a luscious cloud, nothing like my straw filled mattress poking my back. Her exotic silk sheets were gentle against my skin. I did not want to move; for a moment, I did not want to exist.

I had spent the last two days since our breakfast together checking on the women Halsten and Rune believed to be at risk. I added my own list of mothers with questionable origins of their pregnancies, just in case the child was sired by one of the Guard. Thirty-seven women, in various stages of development, could be Sondre's next victims of ingesting the shifter's tonic too soon. I had inventoried the healer's central infirmary in town, while

Bodhil verified the castle's counts, and took stock of the vials of the tonic.

When Bodhil met me in the town square to inform me of her findings, we spoke about what to anticipate the next time I saw my father. He was livid with me for using spell work within the castle and apparently had yet to calm down. I would add that to the bottom of my list of things to be concerned about at present. Four vials from the castle had been unaccounted for as of yet, eleven from in town; fifteen vials to trigger fifteen potential deaths, at any moment.

Fuck.

Since it was midway through the birthing season, I could not lock the vials away; there were too many consensual births happening naturally to well-intended shifter couples throughout the city to put those under lock and key. It was law for every healer to have access to the means necessary to help the public. Sondre knew this and was using it to his advantage.

The bastard.

But I could keep track and remind the mothers when reviewing their birthing plans to not ingest the tonic until nursing their child. It would not make a difference if he forced them to take it, like Asta, but they now knew how to send for me immediately if anything like that happened.

I pulled one of Sif's silky pillows over my face and screamed into it. Once I finally stopped to take a breath, I continued to hold the pillow over my face. My life was far more suffocating than this smooth fabric against my skin. I let it drown out the sounds of the brothel and the light shining in from Sif's open balcony door. The breeze that blew the curtains tickled my skin and I allowed myself to close my eyes.

Just for a moment.

The promise to myself was weak as I let the temptation of sleep take me.

I opened my eyes slowly to find that I was swaying in a pair of arms as a chill bit at the exposed skin of my face. For a moment, I wondered if I held the pillow too tightly and a god had come to escort me to the Depths, but the touch was too tender for any deity. The forest above me was dark, clouds hiding the stars and any hope of light. A lantern swung from my escort's hand and lit the swirls of breath coming from us both. Rapids roared behind us and a stream babbled up ahead. A raven flew into view and croaked at us repeatedly as it circled the stream. A cry came from the chest I was held tightly against.

"No. No. My sweet little sister, no," The melodious voice wept. "What have they done to you?"

My heart broke as I recalled this distant suppressed moment. It was not Yrsa's memory, but my own, long hidden in the deepest parts of my mind. My escort set down the lantern and splashed into the water. I felt the spray of cold glacier run off. The woman holding me dropped to her knees in the water. I turned my head away from the warmth of her chest to see a black stone parting the flow of water. The shredded woman's form was wrapped around the small boulder; before us, Yrsa lay face-down in the water, her long red hair flowed downstream with the gentle current. The woman holding me wept; her sobs shook us both, and, for a while, her sorrow was the only haunting melody in the night, as even the forest around us went silent in reverence.

"All the gods above and below, forgive me." The woman sobbed as she started to unravel the wrappings around my face.

Once I could see clearly, I welcomed the sight of Bodhil, although her eyes were full of tears; I had memorized the wrinkles from laughter that would have accented her long lashes, but none were on this youthful face. This version of Bodhil was so much younger than when I last saw her in the town square. Bodhil gently pulled the dirty swaddling cloth off me, and the cold air hurt my delicate skin.

"They took your youth, my beloved sister, Yrsa. They took your innocence. And now, they have taken your life. But they will not take this last gift from you." Bodhil shuddered as she dipped me into the icy water, cradling me with one arm. With the other, she gently pulled a black garnet amulet loose from Yrsa's wet hair. "As was the way of your mother's mother, let it be so with you. Forgive me for this, my darling Brynn."

I wailed as the frozen claws of the stream dug into me.

The water was red with blood that coated my skin as Bodhil held me downstream of Yrsa until the glacier runoff licked up to my neck. Bodhil, the gentlest of healers, voiced a spell from the witches of old, long since forbidden in Vik.

I had since heard whispers of it from Hoflin's Guard in the prisoner tent and recognition of the magnitude of such a spell she cast settled into my core. The Queen's Guard had learned it from the witches who had escaped the pits and used it to preserve the memories of battle tactics between the elite officers. It was never meant for a baby born on such a fateful night.

My gaze fluttered behind Bodhil to see the darkness take shape.

Lerevna stood on the riverbank as her wings pulled in tight behind her. Her coloration was slightly off compared to the dream around her as she walked into my consciousness. She surveyed the stream and surroundings as if she was trying to gain her bearings. Her steely gaze narrowed as she scrutinized Bodhil holding me in the stream below Yrsa's body. Lerevna remained silent, watching, listening.

"Brynn!!" Rune's voice boomed in the sky around us.

Lerevna startled at the noise and hissed in frustration.

"Brynn! Damn it all, wake up!" Rune bellowed and the world began to shake.

No, I was shaking.

Lerevna cursed and took to the skies, her wings a blur of shadows.

"You stubborn woman, for once, listen to me!" Rune was shouting as my eyes flickered open. Relief washed over his face as he came into focus, and he released his grip from my shoulders.

"Who are you calling stubborn, wolf?" I grimaced and swatted at him. "What in the Depths was that for?"

Rune collapsed on the bed next to me.

"I felt your panic across town and rushed over." He panted. He ran his fingers through his coppery hair, utterly exasperated.

I raised an eyebrow at him.

It was not hard to discover where the other was with the bond, but I could not have been out *that* long for him to pinpoint where I was so fast.

He huffed at the speculation working its way across my features, "No, you were not in the nightmare for long. Your terror was so overwhelming, regardless. Caraway was leaving Officer Magnus' quarters when I went to speak with him, and she said she saw you on your way here. She wanted to meet at the tavern later since the visiting patrons are a little rowdy at night. I saw Sif in the market earlier this morning and she said you were going to freshen up here after your rounds, so I knew where to find you. But for Depth's sake, I thought you had run into Sondre here with how intense it all felt. Liv rushed up to me when I got here claiming she heard screams coming from Sif's room."

"You got more gossip today than I do all week and I have a winged whisperer collecting peoples' whereabouts for me." I released a half-hearted laugh as I rubbed the sleep out of my eyes.

Rune propped himself on his elbow, his brow furrowed with concern.

"Do not deflect," He chided.

I focused on my heartbeat instead of answering him; jokes aside, it was thundering in my ears still from the shock of the icy river and realization of the magnitude of Bodhil's actions.

"Brynn, where were you in that dream?" He asked firmly. "The dreams have always stopped at Yrsa's death. We have never been there like this before."

I sighed and stared up at sheer fabric that draped between Sif's bedposts. My nightmares often bled into his consciousness, but this memory had been buried for decades.

"*I have.*" I sent through the bond as I could not muster the strength to admit it.

Rune reached his hand over to brush the hair from my forehead.

"You were not sleeping as deeply as you normally do when you have these visions," Rune mused as he rubbed his thumb against my temple. "I think that is why I could wake you."

"I could hear you, not how it is through the bond, but as if I was not really asleep. Like you were calling me out of a daydream." I answered. "I do not think Lerevna picked the dream to search through as she has been with Yrsa's memories. This was *mine,* Rune. She seemed surprised, and curious about what was happening. She was so angry when you woke me, like…"

"Like that is what she was looking for?" Rune's voice was thick with dread.

I merely nodded and rolled closer to him.

He wrapped his arm around me and let his heat chase away the chill every nightmare brought with it. Sif's mention of blood rites must have triggered this to surface, as if my mind knew I would finally be ready to face it after all these years.

"Normally when I have two people in my bed, they are far more lively." Sif's voice greeted us as she entered the room.

I only grunted in response. Out of the million things whirling around in my brain, wit was not one of them.

Rune chuckled and kissed my forehead before releasing me. He stood and crossed the room to Sif.

"I think she needs your love more than I do tonight." Rune admitted. He squeezed her hand before closing the door on his way out.

"Ah. I know what you need." Sif mused as she set her knee next to my hip and lifted herself onto the bed to straddle me.

I rested my hands against her thighs and raised an eyebrow at her.

"Pray tell, oh mighty priestess, what is it I *need*?" I asked sarcastically.

I needed a way to fully embrace the power available to me without being found out as a witch and chained to a breeding bed.

I needed Night Wolf saliva on tap if I was going to save thirty-seven women.

I needed the crown to care about what was happening to the women in town instead of being focused on country barriers in regions that are entirely uninhabitable anyway.

I needed Sondre's heart to rupture so he would finally just fucking die, or a vessel in his brain to pop; I had no preference.

I needed the gods to intervene and display that illusive wrath the priests all whisper about in their cautionary tales.

I needed time away, with no one demanding something from me, for me to have a day to myself, with a book and a certain attractive Blood Raven shifter in my bed. All day... Repeatedly... While Lerevna explodes into a cloud of feathers, instead of haunting every moment I dare to close my eyes.

Sif leaned down and placed her forearms on either side of my head. She watched as my unspoken responses triggered micro expressions across my face and smiled. She brushed her lips against mine to silence the thoughts before kissing me languidly. Her full lips were soft and attentive as she took her time. She grazed the tip of her tongue along each lip before sucking on the lower one.

My grip tightened on her thighs, but she sensed my exhaustion.

She kissed along my jaw before tracing her mouth up the side of my ear, sending a shiver down my spine.

"A bath," She whispered and sat up. She rocked her hips against mine playfully. "Come, the boys have already drawn the hot water. Let me take care of you, I have no clients today."

"The bath was drawn for you to be able to rest." I halfheartedly protested.

That actually sounds amazing.

"I will be able to rest when I know you are not half dead, are actually *clean*, and ready to face whatever is to come next." She tapped my nose and climbed off the bed.

If only she knew.

Grabbing my hands, she pulled me up after her like a limp doll. A triumphant smile graced her face as she quickly added, "Then you will come to the temple with me!"

"Sif!" I groaned. "I have far too much to do, I—"

"Always make excuses." She interrupted as she pulled me toward her bathing chambers.

My feet felt like they were made of lead as I trudged after her.

My excuse for being stressed out of my mind was that Yrsa's memories did not simply haunt my evenings, they were given to me though a blood rite passed down through witch lines, no big deal.

Fuck me...

"It is Solstice week, Bry!" Sif chimed as she led me forward. "The streets are full of the fear and gloom of Valdis, let us go see the wonders of Dahlia instead. The impending doom of Sondre's plans will be here when we get back. As your best friend, I demand it. Hret and Sverre, beloved gods of the West, have already arrived for the Solstice Council of the Deities. Reykia's brilliant goddesses are not far behind; we may even be able to get a fleeting glance from the divines. Say yes, my lovely, *please*."

The steam in the bathing chamber melted away all resolve against her reasonings. The scent of fresh jasmine and coco butter filled the space, cleansing my mind. The large copper clawfoot tub in the center of the room beckoned for me to let my troubles be washed away. She knew her plan was working as she stared at me with her gorgeous pleading eyes.

"I can feel your worry from here." Rune reprimanded in my mind. *"Be present or I will march back there and steal Sif all to myself."*

"Alright, alright. Shoo. It is girl time." I scolded, and felt him leave my consciousness with amusement.

"Fine." I conceded. "You win. One hour, then I have to get back to work."

"Mm. I knew you loved me." Sif crooned and pranced behind me to unlace my bodice.

I scoffed my agreement.

Her deft fingers made quick work of my belts of potions and elixirs. She was careful to set them aside where the pouches of herbs would not get wet. She was well versed at removing my clothing after years of practice. I had my share of sexual encounters with men, but Sif was the one who had taught me the body was not just a conglomeration of muscles and bones to be healed; it was a vessel designed to experience such pleasure that even the gods considered it worship. Her fingertips grazed my shoulder blades as she guided off my chemise. She kissed the back of my neck as she navigated my dress past my waist. I felt the weight of the last few days fall to the floor with it. She ushered me to lean against the edge of the tub while she knelt in front of me to untie my boots. I ran my fingers through her soft hair as she pulled them off with my wool socks. Her fingers dragged up my thighs as she stood.

"In you go," She gently demanded and I obeyed.

The warmth enveloped my aching muscles, and a suppressed groan escaped my lips as I lowered myself into the water.

"Now, the Commander's name is not to leave your lips while you are in this tub, do you understand? Nor that winged woman's." Sif instructed.

A smirk pulled at the corner of my lips as her tone took a lightly authoritative edge.

"Understood." I leaned my head back against the side of the tub.

She dipped a cloth in the water and rubbed her bar of jasmine soap against it until it lathered. Starting with my hand, she massaged up my arm slowly.

I stared at the ceiling painted to resemble clouds at sunset, a surprise gift from Rune several years ago. The blending pinks and reds fit Sif, her warmth and tranquility. But the clouds were not calm, they bellowed with the threat of a storm under the stunning colors, much like the tempest next to me. She could open up the heavens and bring down a rage unlike any other. I lulled my head over to the side to look at her with the thought.

"Sif." I started, unsure how to frame my question.

"Yes?" She did not stall her work as she rubbed the cloth in circles over my collar bone.

"How are your gods not enraged?" I asked hesitantly. "By everything that is going on, I mean, with…the beast I will not mention by name."

"I often forget that your father usually kept you out of the temples growing up. You are one of the few people here in the South that call them *my* gods, instead of *the* gods." Her eyes drifted over my face until she held my gaze. She did not pause her scrubbing as she educated me. "Every deity has a different approach with those under their domain. Some are more hands-on like Skai, Hoflin's God of Death. He does not have many wraiths under him to collect souls as he prefers to do that himself, especially on the battlefields. It makes him a frightful sight to behold as he may only be visiting you to take you to the Depths. Hret of Arkanes takes his role of God of Life to a literal degree and shares in the lives of his worshippers. He is accessible in the temple and is often seen milling around with the townsfolk, listening, answering prayers, or taking stock of the quality of life in the kingdom. We may even see him *participating* in the festivities at the temple with worshippers today."

"I cannot imagine what that would be like, to see a deity on my way to my house calls." I mused; it *would* make them more personable.

"And that is because our deities are the opposite side of the spectrum, they are not integrated in our daily life in Vik.

There is structure here, not personality. We have our laws and either the rewards for following them, or the consequences for breaking them." Sif caressed my breasts and ribs, giving my nipples a light pinch that elicited a playfully sharp look in her direction.

"What *consequences* are at play here?" I scoffed but could not suppress the smirk as I batted her hand away.

"The better question is, what laws have been broken?" Sif retorted.

I opened my mouth to argue about the morality of it, but closed it when I realized she was right. There were rules set by the crown on how to conduct yourself around others to keep the peace within the kingdom, to not steal, rape, or maim, but they were not religiously based laws. I frowned at this conclusion.

"But it's…wrong!" I blurted out. It was not a well-honed debate point but an undeniable fact.

"It is. But our goddesses are not parents holding a switch ready to correct our wrong doings." Sif rubbed the inside of my thighs with the rag, putting the sensations at odds with the protests building up in my throat. "You forget, these deities were once mortal before being raised to godhood, some of their mortal traits still remain. Think of Dahlia and Valdis as our absent mothers. They give us the means for life, the quality of it is up to us. Dahlia gives us the midnight sun during summer, to be able to work the land in preparation for our hard winters. She sends the rains for the crops to grow, and gives us the breath in our lungs."

Sif grazed her fingers at the apex of my thighs teasingly.

I shifted my hips to feel more of her which brought a taunting smile to her lips.

"If we use that breath to curse one another or to make the sounds of passion," She slid a finger into my entrance and rocked it back and forth. "It is *our choice*."

I shivered as she slipped it back out and my core clenched at the aching void she left behind. I shook my head at her teasing and rested back against the tub. She sounded so sure in her beliefs, a certainty I craved in this turmoil.

"The Old Gods were different before they were forced from the Kingdoms in the Great War." Her brow furrowed pensively as she massaged down my legs. "This would not have continued if Tyr still roamed our lands. The Guard would be reduced to ash under his just reign."

"Do you think they will ever return?" I inquired.

Bodhil was taught in the Citadel for Healers which prayed to the majestic white dragon Eir and her descendants. I had heard whispers of the mighty being growing up. Eir and Tyr were the only two of the five Old Gods who were typically spoken of in Vik.

"Someday. I believe once you get a taste of worship, it is hard to let it go. Especially if the gods who replaced you are not tending to your followers as well as you would have. Even gods can become jealous." Sif chuckled as she rubbed my sore feet. "Dahlia often was when Vik had to host the Councils; she was not one to share, not like you and Rune."

"Hmm…" I hummed as I melted at her touch. I was the one who took care of people, it was rare for me to be on the receiving end of such care.

As if reading my thoughts Sif stood and pulled off her own dress. She had not bothered with a chemise, choosing to bask in the confidence of her naked curves. I took a moment to relish her beauty. As if she enjoyed her own taste of worship in my stare, she beamed and motioned for me to scoot forward in the tub. She stepped in behind me and pulled me back against her torso. She tilted my head against her shoulder, opening my neck up as her kisses took on a firmer edge.

"Speaking of jealous," She murmured against my skin, "It has been too long since I have had you all to myself. I have missed your whimpers of worship."

She wrapped her arms around me and trailed her hands down to spread my legs for her. I sank into her as she massaged my entrance, teasing as she went around and around without entering me. I gripped her wrist to try to end my torture and a reprimanding nip to my collar released an obedient chuckle and my grip.

With her thumb, she exposed my clitoris and began rubbing it with her middle finger while her other hand pressed against my opening. I whimpered under her touch, starving for more.

"There they are, your sweet sounds of ecstasy. Now, do you choose to use your breath for passion or curses?" She whispered tauntingly in my ear.

"Passion." I gasped as she entered me.

She gripped within me, expertly pinning my nerves under her fingers as she rocked them back and forth. My legs instinctively started to close as the tightening ache built within my core, but she wrapped her legs around mine and pinned me open to her stroking.

"Keep being good for me." She breathed against my ear.

I arched my back against her, gasping as her speed increased against my clitoris.

"I love the sounds you make," She praised.

A moan from deep within me broke free as she bit down at the nape of my neck sending chills down my spine. Goosebumps coursed over my skin. I felt like willing clay in her hands that she molded into whatever she desired. I came undone at her touch, released from worry, from fear, from anger. It was just heat and pure undiluted pleasure coursing through my body. It felt as if every muscle in my torso was being pulled down into my core as I began to tremble. Sif did not ease up as she slid an additional finger into me, stretching me further to accommodate her.

"Fuck, Sif." I groaned as I rocked my hips against her grip.

"You are not allowed release yet." Sif ordered against my skin. "Not until you're ready to break for me."

I moaned at her instruction as she increased her force. I tried to slide my hand behind me to please her in return, but she bit down again on my neck in correction.

"You do enough, just take this pleasure. Take all of it." She eased a third finger inside me, carefully straddling the line of pleasure and pain. "Touch yourself for me like the good girl you are."

I immediately obeyed as my fingers took over for hers on my clitoris, freeing her hand to knead my breasts.

"That's my girl." She moaned into the crook of my neck between biting and sucking her way down my throat. "I feel how ready you are for release. I am not done with you yet."

She let go of my breast to reach to the small table at the side of the tub. Hidden under the towel was a thick rose quartz wand like the ones she used for pleasure rituals, but this one was only for me. The light reflected off the well-polished ridges. I whimpered in growing anticipation of the curved stone filling me.

"Sit on the edge of the tub," She instructed.

I obliged and sat on the rim to face her, my insides protesting at the removal of attention. She coated the smooth stone with the tin of salve resting next it. She kissed my thighs as water dripped off of me and began sucking against my clit. I moaned at the presence of her mouth on my most sensitive of places. I ran my fingers through her hair and pulled my hips against her mouth. She pressed the slick quartz against me but did not let it fully slide into me yet; she looked up at me, damp hair clinging to her face, waiting for my agreement.

"Please, let me take all of it inside me." I pleaded, "Fill me with it, Sif, *please*."

Needing no further instruction, she slid it into me as I was warm, ready, and dying for release. I stretched around the firm girth of the wand as my legs began to shake. Her movements started out slow as she plunged it fully into me before pulling back. Her thrusts with the stone were deep, hitting every spot I needed for my pleasure to build to an excruciating level. Everything in me tightened as I neared my limit. Sif pressed on, coaxing every second of pleasure out of my body.

"You deserve this." She breathed against my inner thigh. "You deserve to feel this good, to be taken care of, to be devoured. Tell me you deserve this."

"I deserve this," My breathing increased to desperate rasps.

She looked up to watch me squirm in ecstasy as she railed my core.

"I wish you could see how good you look." She moaned as her thumb took over for her tongue. "You're so pretty. Say it back to me."

She bit lightly on my thigh.

"I am pretty." My voice waivered in response as I groaned.

"You can do better than that, come on." Sif bit slightly harder in reprimand. "Be my good girl, and tell me how pretty you are, or I won't let you finish."

"Oh, fuck, Sif." I was on the edge of oblivion, but she slowed enough to keep me from falling. "I am pretty, beautiful, gods; I am stunning."

"There you go, that's my girl." Sif put her lips back on my clitoris and sucked harder in praise.

It was my undoing; *she* was my undoing.

Any ounce of control left in my body shattered as I climaxed. It felt like I was drifting out to sea and the waves of pleasure crashing over me brought me back to shore. Heat pulsated between my legs with each release.

She kept her pace, making the pleasure last, determined to draw out every contraction of my core.

I felt lightheaded as a tingly sensation coursed over my body.

Sif kissed up along my hipbone, her warm breath caressing my skin.

"Well done, my love." She murmured as she kissed her way back up, pausing to lightly suck and bite each of my nipples. "You came so well for me. But, you are not finished."

I lost track of time as she proceeded to coax another two orgasms from my willing body until the water began to cool around us.

I took her face in my hands and kissed her deeply. My magic, always feeling refreshed by her touch, now burned within me anew. I pulled back to gaze into her mesmerizing hazel eyes.

"That was…" All words and thought evacuated from my brain, leaving a happy humming sound to echo off the empty space where my mind used to be.

"Not something they teach you in the Healer's Citadel." Sif chuckled as she pulled me down into the water to straddle her lap. Slowly, she eased the quartz wand from within me and massaged my entrance.

I wrapped my arms around her shoulders as I nestled into the crook of her neck, utterly content.

"One day," She murmured into my skin in between kisses along my exposed neck, "We will live far from here and can have a bath every evening, in one of those hot springs in the East; there will be no boys needed to fetch the pails of water. Just us. Our own salt cave to soothe away the aches, then I can have my fill of your sweetness on the banks of it, in the moonlight.”

I let out a soft moan in agreement.

“Just us?” I grinned against her shoulder, knowing the half-truth in her words.

“Well, fine. *And Rune*. I need that man inside me far more than a wand.” She giggled.

Sif peppered my shoulder with light kisses.

“Once you catch your breath, I have a stunning black dress for you to wear to the temple,” She crooned, victory now lacing her tone.

“After that, I will wear whatever you want me to,” I mumbled with my eyes shut.

“You may regret saying that.” Sif laughed, the sound light and airy, a melody my soul could sing to whenever she was near.

Chapter 13

Brynn

Sif was right; I immediately regretted my words. She traded my hunter green dress with layered skirts and leather bodice for a sheer black chiffon gown cinched at my waist with a girdle of silver discs, each with a rune inscribed in them. Sif tied a corset under my bust, but I felt bare without all of my usual concoctions weighing down my hips. The black was meant to honor Valdis, but it mirrored the darkness stirring within me as thoughts of Sondre's plans bled back into my mind. Sif was adorned in a white rendition of the same dress with flowers etched in her silver girdle in homage to Dahlia. Each had a slit up our thighs and the light breeze friskily tugged at the strips of fabric as we walked up the steps of the temple carved into the side of a cliff.

"You checked on them all?" Sif asked quietly not to be overheard by the crowd as we approached, sensing my growing apprehension of not devoting every moment to finding impossible answers.

I let loose a forced sigh in attempts to relieve the pressure growing in my chest.

"All but Asta, since she has already given birth. She should be in the clear now. I went to her room this morning, but she was not there. The maid Eria said she saw Asta leaving to trade out with Liv and help Gro in the kitchens since Katla died." I squared my shoulders, "Since Katla was murdered."

Sif took my hand and brought my knuckles to her lips. Her kiss was firm like her support.

"We *will* figure this out, Bry." She promised against my skin before sealing it with another kiss. "But for now, be present. Do not let Sondre steal your life while you still breathe."

I simply nodded my agreement and tried to focus on our surroundings.

The entire temple was divided down the center by a waterfall. White marble softly reflected the sunlight on one side for Dahlia. A seam separated the black onyx floors for Valdis that lead to the back side of the falls. Sif and I stood on either side of the line, holding hands over the division, our dresses blending with each side's worshippers, as shifters and various creatures of all kinds from every corner of our kingdom made their pilgrimage for Vik's solstice celebrations. Unfamiliar reptilian eyes scanned over our frames before turning to join the crowds of furs, scales, and differing hues of flesh.

Dahlia's division was open to the sun and elements; priests and priestesses in flowing robes mingled with the worshippers like light whisps of smoke. A dais was situated above the commotion, and atop it sat a magnificent marble throne; flowers of all seasons were carved into the ornate seat. New mothers with their children for dedication rocked their babes, the cries drowned out by the falls and rhythmic drumbeats from deep within the temple, echoing off the stones. Incense burned as small offerings from the first fruits of the townsfolk's harvests were brought to the throne.

Fauna, their species predominately reserved to work in the temples of Dahlia throughout Vik, milled around with pitchers of blessed wine. Their hoofbeats were a soft melody against the stone floor. Each wore a chiffon skirt like Sif's dress, their exposed ample breasts unrestricted. Their human torsos were lathered in holy oil, an invitation to any follower that desired to express their worship in the throes of passion. We walked past two fauna assisting a patron reach such divine extasy. One straddled his face while the other rode his cock, his moans were muffled against the fauna's fur but were no less an offering to Dahlia.

He has chosen to use his breath for passion as well.

I smirked at my own cleverness and cast a look at Sif. She was like a statue of the divine, like those surrounding us on pillars, her skin practically glowed as she soaked in her element. I knew it was the simmering oils I had rubbed into her skin before we left, but the sight was no less ethereal.

She belongs here.

I soaked in her beauty before gazing toward the darkness behind the falls.

Valdis' half of the temple was in stark contrast to the celebrations of life next to it. The floor gave way to the steps of a deep amphitheater, the water of the falls running through a channel in the center. The sunlight did not reach far into the cave and torches flickered from the dark pillars. The air was damp and moss grew on the slick stones. Wolves mingled through the crowds, coming to pay their respects to the Goddess of Death. Priests wore heavy grey robes that dragged across the floor as they walked, the hems saturated; their hoods hid all their expressions in shadow, kohl streaked across their eyes deepening their dark features.

Valdis' throne was at the base of the amphitheater with a trench encircling it, separating the seat from the rest of the worshippers. The altar next to it had a carved channel that led to the shallow moat that ran a river of blood from the sacrifices into the trench. The drumbeats reverberated in my bones as I saw the three massive minotaurs tirelessly filling the space with the sound of ominous power. It was all rather overwhelming to witness. Wails from grieving widows and mothers echoed off the stone as they rocked to the rhythm of the beat near the base of the amphitheater.

Sif squeezed my hand bringing my attention back to her.

"Come away from the dark," She coaxed.

As we strolled through Dahlia's side, fauna and priestesses greeted Sif with affectionate embraces and kisses to each cheek. The older priests nodded in her direction while the younger ones offered her a genuine smile. One such priest started walking toward us when his face fell abruptly and he stood frozen. Terror filled his eyes as his gaze was transfixed behind us.

"I remember you," A silky male voice sounded behind us.

Every instinct of mine screamed to flee as it felt like all the air was sucked out of the room. Devotees around us quickly bowed their heads and scurried away in fear, all muttering apologies as they brought their fingers to their foreheads then to their navels in their sign of prayer. Sif turned us slowly around and attempted to pull me down with her to the floor as she knelt in a fluid motion. I had no such grace and remained standing, transfixed by the shifter now in front of me. Every sense went on alert as I stared at the elite predator.

"You honor me, Your Holiness." Sif said in reverence with her head bowed, familiar enough with the voice to know its owner.

The only movement my petrified body allowed was the widening of my eyes as I took in his majestic wingspan. Rivaling the size of Roderick's, this being's wings were various shades of brown with white flecks, like the hawks that dared to nest in the forbidden forests. They protruded from his muscular bare shoulders. His chiseled chest shone from obvious run ins with the oiled fauna around the temple. He wore plain brown trousers tucked into his leather boots. His belt had an array of daggers, a sword, and a coiled whip. He was an unusual sight in the weapon free temple with the exception of the knives for blood sacrifices. My gaze ventured back to his face where his grey eyes stared back at me. His short beard and mustache were a darker blonde that matched his wind tousled locks. His lips curved faintly into an amused expression.

"One of Dahlia's favored brought an *unbeliever.* Things have changed since the last Council of the Deities I bothered to attend here." The man stated as he looked me over in turn.

It felt like he could see through me, piercing through every pretense and barrier I had *ever* erected in protection. Power radiated from him and glued me to the stone. His eyes rested on one of Roderick's feathers I had braided into my hair.

My muscles were too locked to even flinch as he reached out and stroked it thoughtfully. His forearm rested against my chest as it rose and fell in trembling breaths, pinning my amulet firmly against my skin. My fear seemed to please him.

He withdrew and looked back to Sif, "Your devout soul smells as sweet as I remembered. I knew it had to be you as soon as you two entered; it is the rarest of treats that I allow myself to indulge enjoying when visiting Vik. The truly devoted are scarce in these parts."

The scent of her soul?!

I looked at Sif incredulously as she gracefully rose to her feet.

"You bless me with your kind words, Exalted One." Sif lifted her head, and a gentle smile warmed her features. She squeezed my hand tightly, her nails digging into my skin. "Brynn, this is His Eminence, the Glorious Skai, God of Death in the North, gracing us with his presence from Hoflin."

I blinked rapidly at the realization that I had just looked a *god* up and down in shocked assessment and bowed my head.

"Of course, my apologies, Sir—Your Holiness? I meant no disrespect." I blurted out and waited to be struck down as befitting the whispers of this ruthless deity.

"Your soul, however," Skai tucked a finger under my chin to raise my head to meet his piercing gaze, "…is unlike any in this room."

My magic retreated deep within me at his words.

He knows.

"Brynn is our healer on the lower levels. On the battlefields, she is confined to the prisoners' healing tents. She has saved the lives of many of your kingdom's flyers." There was no pleading tone in Sif's voice, but I knew she was trying to persuade him from harming me.

As if one could persuade these deities if our unanswered prayers were any inclination.

Skai raised an eyebrow, and I wondered if it was due to Sif's words or my thoughts.

Can the gods read minds?

Of course they can, we pray with our thoughts.

Or did they only heed the ones spoken out loud, and that is why there has been no justice in this kingdom as of late.

Skai's lips ticked up into a slight smirk as my thoughts unraveled.

Oh, Depths, I am so fucked.

"Has she now? Idonea will be pleased to hear it." Skai mused as his eyes traveled up and down my frame again, as if reading my works written on my skin.

Idonea, Hoflin's goddess of Life, I had often heard of in the healing tents as warriors prayed to her for deliverance and safe passage back to their lands. They prayed Skai would not come for their souls as they were brought to me bleeding.

His thumb brushed my lips before resting on my chin, "You do not pray to Dahlia or Valdis. Their worship does not taint your lips."

My eyes flicked to Sif, but his grip tightened as he turned my attention back to him.

"It was not a question." Skai stated firmly.

His gaze burrowed deep into my being and to the many secrets within it. He brushed the knuckles of his left hand against my exposed sternum and amulet resting against my skin.

"To Tyr," I whispered. "I pray to Tyr."

"A Southerner holding to the Old Gods?" Skai mused as his right hand moved from my chin and drifted to my throat. His grip did not tighten, but it triggered a slight tremble throughout my frame. It did not go unnoticed by him as he narrowed his eyes slightly at the movement. "Interesting."

He took a deep breath and removed his hands, along with the invisible weight that had been crushing my chest. He nodded to Sif.

"Enjoy the festivities, Delectable Soul, maybe *your* deities will show up for them." Skai motioned to the empty throne with his chin before walking past us.

Sif's earlier words of every deity having their own approach rattled through my mind.

He does not approve of their absence…

My whole body began to tingle as I leaned into Sif, realizing at some point I had begun holding my breath. People fell to their knees as Skai walked past them, some prostrated themselves before him.

And I had just stood here, like an ignorant fool!

"Only you would look upon the most vicious of all the deities of death and remain standing." Sif whispered into my ear, her breath warm against my chilled flesh.

All the blood had to have drained from my face and seemed to have pooled in my leaden feet.

"Fuck me." I managed with a nervous chuckle, my body unable to process what had happened in any other way.

"Happily." Sif kissed my cheek and tugged at my arm. "Come, let us go down to Valdis' altar. With death so often at your heels, a little blood offering to her would not be such a bad idea."

We made our way down the many steps to the bottom of the amphitheater. From here, the drums rattled the thoughts out of my mind and vibrated my bones. Patrons sat on the descending levels, some observing while others knelt. There was no sunlight or teeming energy of life as we descended. The air was damp and heavy with the sorrow and fear of those who made the pilgrimage to come here.

Among the crowd, I saw a man leaning against the far wall, wreathed in shadows. His wavey black hair tapered short at the sides contrasted with his fair skin with cool undertones. His keen blue eyes surveyed the temple under his stern brow. Stubble trimmed short accentuated his strong jawline and cleft chin. My gaze landed on the open maw of a dragon tattooed on his neck, all its teeth bared as it spewed black flames and smoke inked down his chest. The sleeves of his soft black tunic were rolled up exposing his corded forearms. The designs of two pairs of wings, one set feathered, the other leathery, matched the ink decorating Roderick and Lerevna's skin. Atop his trousers was a thick belt housing his sword and scabbard, with an assortment of daggers. Strength radiated off him into the shadows that emanated from his frame. The corner of his mouth quirked up as he met my gaze. He raised his chin slightly in greeting.

Sif's face immediately blocked my view of him as she planted herself in front of me.

"Brynn Ulfhild," She whispered, her rosy complexion, usually kissed by the sun, was drained of all color. "How is it you draw the attention of those who could smite you down without even blinking?"

It was I who blinked repeatedly as I tried to process her reprimand.

"Goddesses, help you," She tightened her grip and led us deeper down into the ominous temple.

A commotion brewing in front of us drew my attention away from the handsome stranger and started to compete with the music as worshippers closed in around us.

Maybe Valdis is going to show.

Sif's hand was torn from my grip as a reptilian male from the southern coast stumbled into us. Sif called out something about meeting after we were bled for penance, but her words were drowned out by the raising voices. A wolf stepped on the edge of my dress, causing me to lose my balance and stumble into the lady next to me. She barely noticed me as she looked up to the dais at the priest escorting a robed figure to the altar. Onlookers crowded around me from all sides as I was pushed closer to the front. The deeper the masses went down the steps, the darker the room became. The cave grew pitch black, save for the light flickering from the torches and the freshly lit fire in front of the altar.

"Behold!" A priest's voice rang out, silencing the drums. "Before you, I present a blasphemer!"

The crowd jeered; the voices were a conglomeration of human and animalistic grunts.

"Caught in treasonous actions against Valdis and our kingdom, punishable by death. Let us flow their blood to Death Herself!" Exclaimed the priest as he brought the hooded being forward.

Shadows danced across people's faces as they looked at the altar, thirsty for blood to their deity. From the corner of my eye, I could see Skai's wings above the worshippers as he stepped across the bloody moat to the place reserved only for the gods themselves. He did not sit upon the dark throne, but he watched the priest with subtle interest as he folded his arms.

"What is their crime?" Called a boy, holding his mother's skirts.

She immediately placed her hand over his mouth and shushed him.

Skai glanced down at the boy as the child quickly hid behind the mother before peering back out to see the god. Skai was slow to return his focus to the priest, who seemed all the more emboldened now that he had the attention of the Northern Death himself.

"Their crime, dear boy, is subverting the very laws of nature! They schemed to break one of our most sacred religious edicts in the Kingdom!" The priest's eyes were wide with indignation as he waved his hand theatrically. "They are guilty of a plot to attempt to sire *Night Wolves*!"

The crowd erupted in chaos. Snarls from nearby wolves cut through the air as they frothed at the mouth for violence. My gaze whipped to the cloaked figure.

Did they catch Sondre? Are the gods truly intervening?

Hope swelled in my chest as the figure stumbled out of the shadows and as the priest readied his blade. I had seen the priests offer many animals to Valdis over the years at Sif's side, but to sacrifice a living person was rare. I squared my shoulders at the rising dissonance this brought to my spirit as it contradicted all of my healer training to stand by and watch an execution; yet, for Sondre's death, I would be willing to make an exception and not interfere. My heart stilled as I got a better look at the bound offering. Although hidden by the thick cloak, the individual's stature was too small to match Sondre's broad shoulders, the steps forward were too light.

Something is not right.

The priest lifted the hood to reveal the treasonous sinner.

No!

Asta's bruised face shone under the torchlight. She looked confused as she scanned the crowd. She was gagged by a braided leather belt, pulled tight between her teeth; it muffled her words as she pleaded with the priest. Her cheeks were wet with tears that ran rivers through her dried blood from a wound across her temple.

"No!" I pushed the man in front of me to get closer to the front. "No, she is innocent!"

I wedged past a satyr and bumped into the wolf next to him who bit my skirt in irritation, the thin fabric tearing. In my blind need to get to Asta, I punched the wolf in the maw and ripped my dress from his teeth. I stumbled into another worshiper and shoved past them as the wolf retaliated against the satyr in his confusion. Asta, too far ahead of me, was grabbed by the back of the neck and forced to bend over the altar.

"Commander of the Guard, Valdis blesses you for bringing forward such a sinner that sought to harm our kingdom by instigating such holy wrath upon us all!" The priest called out into the crowd.

That was when I saw him, appearing from the darkness, before the altar.

Sondre's blood stained face was smug in the firelight, with fresh nail marks across his cheek where Asta must have fought back.

"Bastard!" I screamed. "You liar!"

Sondre turned at the sound of my voice, just one of many in the throng. He searched the crowd of faces until he locked eyes with me, and smiled.

Smiled.

My blood boiled. My magic snapped a barrier within me, flared to the surface, I felt the power coursing through the temple around me. The blade in the priest's hand sang to me, as did the sacrificial blood pooling in the trench; the presence of so many worshippers believing together for one purpose made the air buzz with power. I let it all soak into my bones as I threw my weight into the last person separating me and the trench.

If I can just cross, it is a straight shot to the altar.

Sondre's smug smile turned into a sneer as Sif's voice echoed in the crowd. He turned to face her and navigated his way from the front.

He will not even stay to watch his actions unfold, coward!

"She is innocent!" I bellowed at the priest as I finally reached the edge. "Stop!"

The priest looked to me as he brought the knife to Asta's throat. The kohl lined stare was full of blind rage and righteous indignation.

Asta's frantic gaze found mine as she tried to yell out my name past the braided leather belt gagging her.

"No!" I went to step over the trench as my magic coiled in my hand ready to snap like a whip around the priest's wrist.

A large hand grabbed my wrist just as it reached the threshold of the holy space and pinned it to my side. A strong chest slammed into mine and caused me to lose my footing, stumbling backwards. I thrashed against the being in my way, but the firm grip did not relent. My magic recoiled from the contact, attempting to flee from any physical connection. I looked up to see Skai staring down at me.

"It is immediate death for a mortal to cross the sacred blood barrier of Death." His voice was low, but it drowned out all other noise in my head.

Terror filled my core, yet I still tried to pull away.

"He has the wrong person." I rasped.

Skai only shook his head.

Yet another god unwilling to do what is needed?!

"No, you must stop this!" I begged, my pride long since gone in his grasp.

"This is Valdis' temple, not mine; *she* must intervene." Skai claimed as he pinned my wrists behind my back with one hand and moved to stand behind me, pulling me against him. His breath was warm against the back of my ear as he dipped his head to whisper as we watched the priest. "Valdis knows the ramifications of each death in her kingdom. Some she will allow, others she will prevent. Tell me, does she still tend to her flock with such intention, or will this lamb die unnoticed?"

I trembled under his grasp and tried to twist a hand free. My body, my mind, and my magic were all frozen under his might.

His power spread from him and stilled me like one of the statues in the temple. His callous hand grazed over the chiffon on my chest and slid up my throat to grip my jaw, holding my head in place to gaze at the horror before me.

"Does Valdis *deserve* to be god over this kingdom?" He breathed into my hair. "Will she allow such blasphemy of a Night Wolf pack to develop in her kingdom, or worse yet, will she allow the false offering of an innocent girl's blood to mar her altar? A *worthy* deity would never. Let *her* stop her holy man of the cloth before he commits the unforgivable."

As if in response, the chaos around me came to a crescendo.

Skai allowed my head to shift enough to peer into one of the dark alcoves behind the throne. It remained empty, devoid of this *just* goddess he taunted.

Do something. Show up, for Depths sake, stop him, for once!

My entire body started to tremble in anticipation. I tried to will Valdis' presence into being. The shadows only seemed to deepen as the hollowness of the alcove filled my frame. I looked to the priest in hopes she would speak directly to her servant to stop.

Something. Anything.

The priest took a deep breath.

Please.

He let it out as he slit Asta's throat, spilling a waterfall of fresh blood to flow down the altar.

A sound erupted through my throat from my shattering heart.

I tried to send tendrils out to heal her neck, but Skai's arm resting on my chest held me to him. My magic halted under his divine grasp. I tried to fight it, but his power overshadowed my own, pressing my tendrils back to coil deep within my core. I shuddered as I watched Asta choke and sputter out blood past the leather between her teeth. I tried to shake him off and go to her, but his grip remained firm. My darling girl writhed against the stone.

"Asta." I shook, in rage, in sadness, in disbelief.

The light faded from her fearful eyes and her body went limp as I could only repeat her name in agony.

"Asta!" I cried.

I would never hear her laugh again as she struck Rune's arm for teasing her. She would never sit at the edge of my bed, listening to Halsten tell stories as I braided her hair.

"No, no, not my Asta." I screamed and thrashed against his grip.

I had kissed her brow and heard her whisper, *I love you, Bry*, as I closed her bedroom door at night for the last time, without knowing it.

"Asta…" My voice cracked.

I would never hear her sweet voice again; my sister had been forever silenced. The ache in me threatened to shatter me into a million pieces, fractures splitting through my resolve, my mind, my very being.

Her body was unceremoniously slid to the side of the stone slab to continue draining as another priest brought a devoted follower up to the altar. A bowl was placed in Asta's pooling blood, and the priest cut a small slit into the fresh worshiper's hand. Droplets fell into the bowl as a blessing was spoken over it before the next person stepped up to do the same; a line forming behind them as it had been before the commotion. All as if my friend, my sweet, caring, innocent little sister, was not bleeding out next to them.

Deep hatred burned through my veins as I watched them all do nothing. No one reached out to her, no one tried to stop the bleeding, no one shifted the robe to cover her terror-stricken face. A wolf shifted into his human form to offer his blood atonement and spat in Asta's hair as he walked past. My magic lifted its head like a snake ready to strike, but the deep disappointment in Skai's voice retracted my tendrils' fangs.

"Mm. Disappointing. So, this is how she cares for her people…" Skai's voice had shifted; it was smooth and gentle in contrast to his unrelenting grip. He spun me around to face him, and it took everything in me to not crumble at how he looked at me, like a wounded animal, not a healer, not a person, but an abandoned pet without a present master.

I felt so small in his hands, and the feeling turned to bile in my gut.

His grey eyes pierced through any defenses my raw soul had left, "As Valdis has not shown up to claim this lamb's soul yet, I will bring your sister to the Depths to find her peace."

"You could have saved her." I gritted through my teeth.

I mustered all the strength I did not feel and shoved his strong chest with all my pain, my hatred, my anguish, but he did not move. The sorrow was tearing me apart; I heaved myself into him again as hard as I could as a sob ripped itself free from my lips.

He grabbed my arms and pulled me close to his face.

"She was not *mine* to *save*. That responsibility belongs to Valdis." He said simply, his gaze wandering over my tear-stricken face. "After death, however, souls are not bound by kingdom distinctions. I can and will put her to rest."

I trembled from the onslaught of emotions raging within me.

"*I* could have saved her. She was *mine*. My responsibility!" I shakily ground out as I struggled for an even breath. "Why stop *me*?"

"Your soul—Hmm…" He raised a hand to brush the tears from my cheek with his thumb. He looked down at the wet droplets as he rubbed them against his fingertip in thought. "Your death is not meant to be over something as trivial as stepping across a holy barrier and falling over dead due to the old magic written into the walls of this temple. No…*your* death…"

He brought his fingers to his lips and sucked my tears off his skin. He closed his eyes for a moment as if relishing something sweet. When his eyes fluttered open, something dark lurked within his gaze.

"Mm. No, your death will be much grander, meant for a glorious purpose. I hope that day *I* will be there to carry your soul to the Depths, but I doubt it." He stared at me a moment longer before brushing his knuckles against the feather in my hair. "Do give our dear boy Roderick my regards."

I choked on the question rising in my throat, but he released me.

He shifted past me before I could respond and stepped over the trench. His power anchored me in place when I tried to follow after him on instinct alone. As he strode over to the altar, the priests and believers stumbled back in reverence and trepidation. Skai unbound Asta's wrists and removed the leather from her mouth. He lingered his hand over her blood as if it spoke to him and confirmed my insistence of her innocence; he met my gaze once more. He offered me a curt nod, and, in a fluid motion, he removed a dagger from his belt and plunged it into the priest's heart. Onlookers gasped and hurried away from the deity, trampling over each other. Skai twisted the blade without remorse and removed it from the shocked priest.

"No deity of Death will accept false sacrifices. You will pay for your deceit with your life. *Your blood* is demanded to wash away this *stain* from the altar." Skai seethed at the man of the temple.

A coin purse levitated from inside the folds of the priest's robes and landed in Skai's outstretched hand. Skai raised his lip in disgust and slit the priest's throat.

The God of Death pivoted on his heel, picked up Asta's frail body in his arms, and made his way back to the barrier.

The priest collapsed against the altar, gurgling on his own blood and holding his chest. He reached for me, having once been a patient of mine, like so many others in the temple around me.

I felt Skai release my magic in its entirety, but it remained still within me as I watched the priest suffer. In his last moments, confusion etched itself into his expression as he stared at me, gargling and choking on his treacherous blood. For the first time since becoming a healer, I did not try to save the person before me; I let him suffocate.

I willingly watched the useless waste of the man die in his oversized grey robes. The life left his kohl covered eyes. I felt no remorse, no loss, only a gaping hole in my heart where Asta's love had once filled.

Skai motioned for me to come to him and gently set Asta's still, warm body into my arms. He placed the coin purse in her lap.

"For any debts she may have had in this life. The North does not kill our women for sport or politics. Remember that next time you pray, Little Soul." He brushed Asta's blood-soaked hair off her shoulder. "She is with me now. I will guide her home."

His gaze lingered on me, but I had no words.

I rested my forehead to Asta's and sank to my knees. People murmured behind me as Sif pushed her way through the crowd and dropped down next to me. I looked up to find Sif's eyes were red and the kohl lining them streaked down her face. She placed her palm on Asta's cheek, and the tears threatened to flow again. Her attention drifted over my shoulder to the opening of the cave at the top of the amphitheater.

"A group of Sondre's men have arrived. We need to get the two of you out of here." Sif urged. She grabbed my face as it hardened and gave me a light shake. "This is *not* the time to fight, Bry, my love. We need to go. Call for Rune to meet us—I know a way out."

She stood and helped me to my feet as I held Asta close. Sif turned to Skai who remained watching us and bowed her head whispering her thanks. He nodded to an alcove before directing his attention toward the pack of wolves descending the stairs. Sif took my arm and guided me through the crowd. We entered the dark archway which lead to a set of stairs to the surface.

Screams erupted behind us, but Sif pulled me deeper into the darkness without looking back.

I felt Skai's breath on the shell of my ear as we departed.

"The time will come very soon for your enemy to be dragged to the Depths to atone for his crimes." His low tone promised.

I turned expecting to see him directly behind me again; the god had remained near the throne, yet I was surrounded by the magnitude of his presence.

The torch light flickering off his wings casting shadows dancing through his feathers that now dripped crimson. A wolf lunged toward the alcove but burst into a cloud of red mist. A flick of Skai's wrist manifested a brisk wind to carry the droplets into the trench. Utter chaos had ensued in a red haze of destruction as Sondre's men fell one by one to the floor writhing in pain before bursting in a spray of blood and bone. Deeper in the chaos, the man with the dragon throat tattoo pushed off the wall and walked toward the Northern Death, undeterred by the violence and gore of his surroundings.

Skai angled his head slightly in my direction and the corner of his lips curled, his voice a terrifyingly warm caress of a predator right before devouring his prey.

"Just as Death will come for you, Little Soul."

Chapter 14

Brynn

Rune was waiting for us as the tunnel widened slowly before opening into an abandoned courtyard not far from Madame Ahmila's. The rage and despair I felt deep in my chest reflected back in his face. He rubbed the leather reins in his hand as the horse next to him jerked its head in apprehension. The anxious clopping of its hooves echoes off the short stone walls of the perimeter. Horses always knew when a deity of death was near, their snorts and whines would sound the alarm at any war camp.

"I cannot let you go into that damned forest alone, not this close to solstice, Regh." Rune started as soon as we were within earshot. He had not taken kindly to Sif's and my plan that I had relayed down the bond on our way here. "I am going with you."

"No." Sif answered for me, still breathless from the temple. "We need you here, Rune. If Sondre is willing to kill Asta in front of everyone, *even the gods*, all the other mothers are at risk. My girls need you here, Rune."

Sif crossed the expanse and clasped his face in her hands to kiss him tearfully.

"You have to trust Brynn's judgement on this." She whispered against his lips. "We need you *here*."

Her voice cracked as she stifled a sob.

"*I* need you." She admitted as the facade of strength fell and she melted into his arms.

Rune held her close but did not break his gaze as it burrowed into me. His fear for my safety turned my insides to ice.

I tried to push his emotions back down the bond, but they flooded me.

"Rune, Sif is right. Help me lift Asta onto the horse." I urged as I reached their embrace.

The gut-wrenching pain in his eyes magnified as he looked to the bloody frame in my arms. Her pale skin and limp body broke all resolve in him. Sif felt the shift within him and gently released her hold on him. He carefully transitioned Asta out of my arms and into the saddle. He gently let her rest against the horse's neck before boosting me up into the saddle behind her.

"Sondre did this to get to *me*." I explained hurriedly. I removed the rope from the horn of the saddle and tied Asta's body snuggly against my chest. "His men are either dead or dying in the temple thanks to Skai seeming to favor our cause. You know this will enrage Sondre all the more. He *will* come after me, *tonight*. He will not let this rest. He will conjure up some lie to get the crown's approval to enact any justice he wants upon us, and anyone harboring us, be it that we are Northern sympathizers, or have offended the gods. We cannot hide from this in town."

"And how the fuck is going into the woods going to help anything?" Rune snapped as Sif put her hand on his chest in an attempt to steady him.

"Roderick will be on his way back from his weekly check-ins at the border. He can shift this close to the solstice to escort Reykia's goddesses to the Council of the Deities at the main temple. Aksel and his pack will likely be with them, as they have been in years past. I just have to lead Sondre away, away from anyone who might meet the same fate as Asta." My voice hitched at her name, but I swallowed the rising lump in my throat. "If *Skai*, of all the deities, is willing to stand up to Sondre's men, maybe Reykia's goddesses will too. That is half the Council. They could force Valdis and Dahlia back into action. This has to end."

The horse pranced out of Rune's grip and tugged on my hold of the reins. Rune looked to Sif as if to gauge the plausibility of my desperate plan.

Sif pursed her lips but nodded.

"It is risky, but we must provoke them out of their inaction. They were not even present for the offerings today. It has never been this bad for them to be so withdrawn. At least, at previous solstices, they were more invested and presided over the festivities when Vik hosted. Skai…" Sif shook her head in shock of her own admittance, "Skai was unchecked in the temple. A wolf lunged at him, Rune, *at Skai*. The fear of the gods has become so trivial that a wolf lunged at the *Northern God of Death*. That is unheard of…Skai will not stand for it. He will demand Valdis and Dahlia are stripped of their godhood for letting the people forget the true power of Death. He will send the goddesses to the Isle of the Gods, if they are lucky. After today, he may even try to kill them, himself."

"If Skai takes aim to do the worst, to kill them for such incompetence, there would be no war with Hoflin; our kingdom will fall if he slays the very gods our people believe in…" Rune's voice drifted at the ramifications of it all.

"Another reason to get to Roderick and Aksel. Reykia would never allow Hoflin to do that." Sif insisted. "Reykia's goddesses Braxcia and Terōta will stop him."

"We must find a way, Rune." I turned the horse toward the woods on the edge of town.

"Fuck." Rune relented as he ran his fingers through his hair. "Hurry, and do not stop until that horse's heart is ready to give out, you hear me? Then, you heal the beast and keep riding until you get there. Do not stop for anything. I will send Halsten to you as soon as I can. Find your way back to me, Brynn."

My eyes locked with his in promise.

"I always will, to the Depths." I swore, and looked to the woman we both loved so dearly. "Keep Sif safe."

"To the Depths." Rune vowed in return.

Chapter 15

Roderick

Unease grew in my gut as I flew. I scoured the landscape, searching while in raven form this close to the border to remain undetected.

Had Brynn listened and gone to Arkanes?

Is she safe?

I knew the answer deep down but tried to deny it. I beat my wings harder as I scanned the encampment for the warlock vital to Brynn's salvation. Brynn was far too honor bound to leave the women in her care unprotected against Sondre's schemes. She lacked any self-preservation instinct, as if she was expendable.

Expendable!

"Are you on a reconnaissance mission or on a date with yourself, discussing a woman over tea?" Lerevna's dry voice resounded in my mind.

"Both." I replied with a squawk. *"Tea would be delightful right now."*

"Have you found him?" Lerevna's annoyance was palpable, warming me slightly on the inside.

Better than tea.

"No. I do not believe he is here. There are no enclosures big enough to contain him, so far." I admitted. I wanted desperately for him to be here to divert Lerevna's attention away from Brynn, but there had been no signs of Admund or anything that could conceal and restrain the powerful warlock. *"Do you think Skai is keeping him on a tight leash close by?"*

"No." Frustration laced her tone. *"Skai is already in Vik, and we would have discovered if Admund was with him. He is not."*

"How can you be sure without being there yourself?" I dared to hope she would send me back to check in-person.

Silence.

A searing heat filled my core in warning as I neared the Hoflin border and banked to remain on Vik's side. Even in my raven form, the bindings of my inked commands to not enter the northern lands held firm. Small campfires dotted the ground below me as winged female shifters mingled through the crowds of foot soldiers standing around the flames for the warmth. The air bit this deep inland as the winds came down from the perpetually snowy mountains.

I dove abruptly and dropped below the tree line. Near the ground, I shifted forms and jogged to a stop to keep my footfalls light. The ground was disturbed with countless footprints leading toward Vik. It was no surprise with the current tensions that they were pushing South for the solstice, but that was not why I was here.

"*Lerevna.*" I called. "*Again, how can you be sure Admund is not there? There are enough wheel tracks and hoofprints left behind for him to have been carted in, bound in hexed chains if they truly wanted to go that route. Unlikely, but worth looking into at least.*"

Silence. This time, it was intentional.

"*Lerev—*" I began.

"*Rhydar is there.*" Lerevna finally answered and my blood ran cold.

"*With our deities?*" I asked slowly, my heart started to thunder in my chest.

"*No.*" She admitted. "*Things have…progressed. Skai massacred wolves in the temple. Worshippers and guards alike were slain by his hand.*"

The dryness of her voice was like a millstone crushing any peace in my mind as my thoughts turned frantic.

"The river to the Depths runs red as in the times of old." She concluded. *"Our goddesses Braxcia and Terōta have not crossed our border into Vik out of caution; the Council is cancelled."*

A chill skittered down my spine. The carnage would be great, but Skai would be found undeniably within his right to enact such justice. Skai killed mercilessly, but could always justify his actions to the Council. Valdis was unlikely to retaliate against him for undermining her in such a way as that would take actual effort.

Depths forbid she was ever guilty of that.

"How did Aksel respond?" I inquired.

The wolf presided over the Councils in the past to keep the deities in check and avoid outbursts like this. Gunnar, Aksel's second in command, was known as the *God Killer* and he had earned the title well, brute as he was. I released my jaw in an attempt to alleviate the pressure growing in my head.

"He…also is still here in Reykia." Her tone was thick with her distaste, the order to remain was obviously not her own then. *"Rhydar went alone. The pack is here."*

There it was.

Brynn was out there, with no one to stand between her and a bloodthirsty god of death, and to make matters worse, Rhydar, of all people, was the only representation of Reykia present.

Fuck.

"There really is no trace of the warlock, is there?" She asked, her defeated sigh rang in my ears.

"No." I conceded.

"Go, Roderick," She commanded. *"See that she is safe. Without Admund...I* will *need the girl. I will not be far behind. I have almost everything we need."*

Relief and dread battled within me as I turned and flew South as fast as my wings could take me. I prayed to the Old Gods that I was not too late.

Chapter 16

Brynn

The stallion galloped beneath me, ears pinned back as it huffed. Its ribs were slimmer than a wolf shifter's back that I had grown accustomed to and we sprinted closer to the ground. Asta's lifeless form pressed against me, her remaining blood soaking into my thin dress and the leather of the saddle. I nudged my heel into the beast's side and hissed. He found his reservoir of energy and increased speed. I let my magic seep into his body to ease whatever tension and exhaustion I could. I felt my own limits fast approaching but we could not stop; I would not stop. I could not kill Sondre and all his men myself, but the creatures in this forest certainly could.

The water in the river separating the kingdoms had risen since the last time Rune and I crossed into Reykia. I urged the horse forward, and we plunged into the icy waters. The current was gentle enough for us to tread across without being swept away. The horse snorted in protest against the cold, and I could not agree more with the sentiment. The chiffon dress was useless against the cold and now clung to my skin, drenched in blood and glacier run-off. Luckily, the stallion soon found purchase on the bank and lifted us out of the water. After a shake mid-step, he returned to a gallop. Howls of a hunting party sounded behind us as we crossed the border.

"Roderick!" I screamed into the night.

All the monstrous creatures in the woods already knew we were there by the thunderous galloping hooves and the aroma of Asta's blood; there was no use in being quiet and small now. Rune's usual protection as he masked my scent when we travelled was not here to save me.

Let the monsters come.

"Aksel! Roderick!"

I searched for the glorious Blood Raven's dark wings in the sky above me, but the tree canopy grew too thick to see the stars starting to grace the heavens.

Where are you, Roderick?

Skittering in the leaves behind us was the only reply. Pairs of glossy red eyes reflected in the moonlight as beasts above gave chase. Their shrieks pierced the night as their rows upon rows of teeth caught the little bit of light filtering through the trees like glimmering promises of death. The dense forest tore at our legs as the horse ran; his chest now lathered in sweat.

I reached out to the power around us to fuel the tendrils of magic healing the stallion's cuts. I dared to look back and saw one of the creatures drop from the canopy; its long black tongue licked across the trail of blood on the leaves in our wake. Another dropped from the trees next to it. The freakishly humanoid head jerked up as its blank stare locked with mine. The creatures' multiple limps bent at unsettling angles as they crouched and lurched into the brush after us with a resounding screech.

I turned forward and urged the horse onward.

An answering howl sounded in the distance as the hunting pack drew closer.

Eat them, not me!

As if in response to my thought, the howl was strangled by sounds of pain. This did not deter the creatures pursuing us, but it meant one less of Sondre's wolves were on our tail. From the corner of my eye, I could see a mouth full of fangs in the center of the monster's palm as it reached for me from a nearby tree. I yanked on the reins and squeezed my thighs against the stallion's ribs; he obeyed and bolted to the left, leaping over a fallen tree. A hiss in annoyance sounded behind us before a thud as the creature missed us, colliding with the log. I could see the meadow in the distance, usually the sight filled me with dread, but, tonight, I was relieved.

At least they will not attack from above there.

I steered us toward the clearing. One beast leapt from the bushes next to us, aiming for the horse's legs. The stallion faltered and stumbled as we collided with it. I shot my hand out as deep blue tendrils of protection coated the steed's legs and the creature's fangs did not puncture the skin beneath. A tremor shot through my body at the effort, but I gripped the saddle as my mount regained his footing. A hoof to the face of the beast between his legs derailed the attack. Snorting, the horse pushed on, although his strength was waning, even with my help.

Midstride, the stallion's ear shot forward. The other ear cocked to the side as apprehension filled his frame.

"We cannot stop." I gave him another nudge with my heel, but I felt every muscle in his body tense.

Something reflected the moonlight as it fell to the ground in front of him and he reared back on his hind legs. Asta's weight against my chest threw off my balance and I was unable to recover. I slid off the back of the stallion, powerless to catch myself, with Asta's lifeless form landing on top of me. All the air rushed from my lungs. I tried to cover my face as the beast bolted in a fury of hooves.

"Cowardly fuck!" I groaned as I untied the rope holding Asta's frame to my own. I sensed a fracture in my rib, but nothing was broken as I rolled onto my side.

I had never been bucked off a wolf, useless beast.

Panting, I pushed myself up onto my hands and knees to assess my surroundings. Across the way, freshly trampled by the fleeing horse, the monster started to rise. From here, I could better see the almost humanoid shape albeit its multiple arms were too long to be confused for a person. Where each palm would be, the flesh splayed open to reveal rows of teeth. They closed into a tight ball as the beast pushed off the dirt to right itself. Dark green blood slipped from its haunting face where the horse kicked it. It opened its large mouth to unleash an earsplitting scream that echoed through the trees. As it was disorientated and not facing me yet, I slowly moved to Asta and prepared myself to lift her from the ground. The film on its translucent skin glimmered in the shadows as it jerked its head to listen for me. I stilled as my arms reached under Asta.

If it can outrun a horse, it will be able to outrun me.

Abruptly, it spun to face me and shrieked.

This sound, however, was not out of aggression, but fear. It backed away as it released another high-pitched wail.

Please be Roderick.

The forest floor went dark as the little bit of moonlight peeking through the leaves was blocked. The monster now fled, faster than it had chased me here. Something large and glistening fell from the canopy.

I froze.

Before me, on the damp forest floor was a signal to the object of the monster's fright. Shining in the darkness, a thick droplet of saliva pooled in the moss.

Fuck, not Roderick.

A billow of hot breath blew against the back of my neck. I wanted to run, to turn and fight screaming, but I remained planted, my body still leaned over Asta's. The ground shuddered from the impact of something massive landing from the canopy. Moonlight now streamed in and I realized how gigantic it must be to have blocked out so much light. The fresh moonbeams reflected against something within the saliva.

There, within the blob, glimmered a single bronze bangle.

Bronze is a warning.

I slowly lifted my head and turned to see six amber eyes staring back at me. The lindworm clicked its maw as it slowly lowered its head. Momentary relief flooded my core, but was quickly dashed away as the colossal beast took a step toward me. We had a transactional relationship, but never a physically close one. I let my waning magic reach out to it, but the lindworm clicked and bit at the tendrils with a huff. They dissolved instantly as my magic retreated within me. The being sniffed the blood on my dress before turning its attention to Asta.

"No." I whispered.

I knew I could not get away while carrying her; I knew she was dead. But I was not ready for her to be taken from me yet. Grief threatened to consume me. The last piece of my heart broke as the giant creature brushed me to the side with its snout and gingerly scooped up her limp body in one claw.

"No!" I shoved all my weight against its maw, but it barely flinched.

The lindworm assessed me with its ageless knowing gaze. It nudged the bangle of warning with its snout and peered behind me.

The hunting party's howls grew closer.

I was trapped at an impossible impasse. I would not leave her to be devoured by the wolves chasing us, but I could not carry her without the horse and still hope to get away.

"No." My voice cracked this time as I fell to my knees and reached for her in its claw.

The lindworm put its mouth around my extended arm in a warning but did not bite down. I retracted it as heat increased in the back of the beast's throat. It lifted its head and let out a small puff of ethereal blue flames that warmed the air around us. It looked back to me before nuzzling Asta in its grasp.

"Burn him…" Asta's request for her boy rang through my thoughts. *"Valdis and Dahlia don't deserve my baby boy. They did not intervene; they did not stop Sondre…They did nothing. Will you bring him to your deity in the forest?"*

They did not stop Sondre, again.

I stared up at the pensive creature.

This was the nearest thing to an answered prayer any of us had ever had, from a creature close enough to a deity in this forest.

"Burn her?" My voice trembled.

The lindworm let out a warm breath as if to agree to my request.

I stood and took a step back, my legs weak beneath me.

I whispered the prayer I had spoken from her doorway almost every night since she was a little girl, "Asta, May Tyr, Your Protector, watch over you. May his wings shield you, and may the light from his fires burn away your fears, my sweet sister."

A sob escaped my throat as I tried to stifle the pain that threatened to shatter me again. The lindworm offered a final click before returning to the tree canopy with Asta's body in tow. The leaves rustled under its scales as they disappeared into the darkness.

I wanted to scream. I wanted to dissolve into the dirt and die. I wanted to explode in a burst of magic and kill everything in a near radius. My depleted reserve of magic recoiled at the thought.

Too burnt out for that, fine.

I reached down to find any morsel of courage I had left to continue, just as I heard a twig snap behind me. My mind recalled Yrsa's memories while dying not far from here.

This forest had enough of my family's blood soaked into its cursed ground, no more.

Chapter 17

Brynn

I turned, ready to fight with what little I had within me. A wolf across from me slowly rose from the ground. His pecan fur blended with the soaked terrain as the wolf stood taller than even the stallion. Relief escaped my lungs as the beast shifted and Halsten jogged towards me.

"Depths, Regh." He lifted me in an embrace and held me tight. "I came as fast as I could when Rune told me what happened. Sondre's men are not far behind me. They blame you for what happened in the temple, saying it was *you* who disrespected Skai. People saw you shoving him, then he wiped out the worshippers because of it."

"What?!" I exclaimed as I leaned away from him. "You cannot believe that."

"I don't. Well, the shoving part I do, because, well, it is you." He cupped my cheek with his warm hand. "But Rune filled me in on what Sif saw, about Asta, and a wolf charging the god. We have to get ahead of their narrative, but, first, we need to get you the fuck out of here."

A long throaty howl sounded from deep in the distance at the castle.

Halsten turned his head at the sound, confusion filling his face.

"That is Officer Magnus." He breathed as he listened. His head tilted in focus. Confusion gave way to surprise, then rage. "That is Magnus' call to arms. We are under attack; the North is at the castle gates."

"*West!*" Rune yelled in my mind, causing me to jump. "*Fuck the plan! Go West to the sea, like Roderick said; it is not safe for you here. I will meet you there with Sif.*"

"Rune!" I gasped.

Halsten's grip tightened in concern.

"*Stay with Halsten. I cannot risk linking to you and draining you of any more power. I can feel you depleting. You have done too much magic lately; you will burn from the inside out.*" Rune cautioned.

I felt the bond grow cold.

"*No. Don't you dare!*" I pleaded.

He was right; if he drew from me in a fight, I probably would not survive it. Regardless, I could not stand the thought of being disconnected now, not with the lindworm taking Asta from me too.

"*I love you. Stay alive, Brynn. I will find you when this is over,*" He promised.

Tears filled my eyes.

"*Never apart.*" I whispered down the bond.

"*Never apart, to the Depths.*" Determination laced his tone.

For a moment, heat filled my frame as he shifted into wolf form then the bond went cold as he shut me out.

Halsten's jaw set as he concluded that the conversation was over.

"I was afraid of that." He sighed. The resignation in my features was enough for him to know Rune blocked the connection. He forced a half-smile. "Stay close and keep up, Little Pup. We will stop to rest once we know Sondre's men are no longer on our tail."

"Arkanes." I choked out. "We need to make for Arkanes. I will explain on the way."

Halsten assessed me.

Finally, he nodded; the furrow in his brow told me he was doubtful but willing to take direction on this. He grabbed my hand to help me step up onto a thick nearby root jutting out of the ground. He shifted into his wolf form, and I hoisted myself onto his back. His muzzle pressed against my thigh to help me up. I tried to muster an encouraging word but we both knew how hollow it would be.

It was going to be a long night.

After trudging through the forest, dipping in and out of streams to mask our scent, Halsten finally resolved that we had travelled far enough without sight of Sondre's wolves to be able to stop. We both hoped the creatures of the night had found the hunting party and devoured them whole. Halsten shifted back to huddle down on a small patch of grass; an oak trunk protected us from behind as Halsten let me curl against his back for warmth. I dreaded what may await me once I closed my eyes, but I knew we needed to sleep before continuing through the night.

"Rest." Halsten said. He looked over his shoulder to see the apprehension on my face. "If that winged bitch shows up, I will wake you. Get some sleep."

I nodded and nestled my forehead between his strong shoulder blades. The moment my eyes closed, I felt cold water rushing up to my neck.

No, no, no.

I shot my eyes open, but it was too late. Lerevna drew me back into the memory. I thrashed against Bodhil's hold on me in the river, but it was no use; I was only a newborn here. I screamed for her to stop, to not say the words Lerevna desired to hear, but it only came out as a baby wailing. Lerevna was already on the bank of the river, as if she had been waiting for me to fall asleep. She crossed her arms and tilted her head toward me.

Oblivious, Bodhil began the blood rite that would stain my life forever.

"Wake up, soul of Yrsa, Wake up. Awaken from the doors of the dead." Bodhil started to chant.

Lerevna sighed as if in relief and lifted her chin to the sky. For the first time, there was a sense of sorrow in her eyes as she looked at the stars and waited for Bodhil to recite my damnation. I wondered if the Blood Raven's search was finally at an end.

"The way ahead is long. Guide, Guide your daughter. Cast your spells, release your memories, to lead her, though the way ahead is long." Bodhil's hauntingly smooth voice called out into the void as she dipped me in the last blood of Yrsa, of my birth mother.

The forbidden blood rite began, darker than any Night Wolf birth. As the last of Yrsa's lifeblood washed over me, her past intertwined with my future.

"Keep her along the road. Wake up, oh, soul of Yrsa. Wake up. Your daughter calls to you. Imbue her with your knowledge of the road, for the way ahead is long. Cast your spells. Release your memories. She takes your blood. May you

ever slumber in her." Bodhil wept as her shaky voice began to chant the final dooming verse, linking Yrsa's memories to my consciousness. She did not know the nightmares she unleashed to forever plague my slumber.

I wanted to make her stop, to beg her not to finish, but the babe in her arms only cried.

"Wake up, oh, soul of Yrsa. Wake up. I bring Brynn to the doors, to the doors of the dead. She claims your memories. I release you now, rest in the Depths, oh, soul of Yrsa." Bodhil sobbed as she lifted my trembling infant body out of the water, sealing my fate.

I felt the heat of the amulet as she pressed it to my chest.

"My precious niece." Bodhil whispered to me as she cradled me back against her body to soothe my cries and warm my fridged skin. "I promise to love you as my own. To love you the way Yrsa would have. To teach you my sister's ways and mine, and to protect you with my life."

My gaze stayed fixed on the sky above, as Lerevna shifted and her Blood Raven form circled above us. There flew the omen of death.

Her croak pierced the night.

My eyes opened slowly. Dismay threatened to swallow me whole as I resigned myself to the knowledge that Lerevna had been searching my slumber for *that dream.*

She had found it.

Halsten's face filled my vision as I blinked, waking up. It was not sorrow that was crushing me, it was his body that was pressed on top of mine. One of his hands was over my mouth while the other gently brushed back my hair.

"Sorry, Pup," He whispered. "I could not let the whole forest know where we were with your hollering. I will remove my hand if you promise to neither yell, nor bite me, fair?"

I smirked at his insinuation and slowly nodded my agreement.

He had been present for many nights in the cabin when Rune had tried to wake me during my night terrors and had suffered my unintentional wrath. To be fair, I had only bitten him *once* and that had been years ago.

Halsten removed his hand and let his forearms rest on either side of my face.

"I wanted to let you rest as long as I could, but we need to get going if we are going to stay ahead of the pack. Once you started thrashing, however, I knew I needed to get you away from that raven woman. Are you alright?" He asked as he brushed his thumbs against my temples.

I simply shrugged and raised my eyebrows. It meant nothing, because deep down I felt nothing. I was numb with the shock from the day.

Why did Lerevna need that spell?

I leaned my head into his shoulder to avoid his discerning gaze. Halsten's body was warm, and I knew as soon as he moved, I would be hit by the cool night air. I let out a quiet grunt in acknowledgement.

"There are creatures far bigger than any pack not far from here; they will make that lindworm look like a garden snake." Halsten's wit always tried to lighten any mood.

I could hear the grin in his voice as he continued, "I cannot blend our scents the way Rune does to protect you, so we need to be careful. I will stay in this form to not be a more tempting meal, as a wolf will not scare anything we may come across. This time of night, *I* prefer to be the one doing the *eating*, I don't want to become some other beast's late-night snack, okay?"

A tired huff was the closest I could get to a laugh.

He pulled back enough to kiss the tip of my nose before lifting himself off of me. I sighed as I propped myself up on my elbows. Halsten reached down to offer me a hand, as I took it, he lifted me up with ease. He kept a hold of my hand as he guided us toward Arkanes.

For a while, we walked in silence, but I noticed Halsten chewing on a thought.

"What is it, Halsten?" I quietly voiced, keeping my eyes on the dark terrain to not fall.

"We may very well not get out of this alive, Pup, so there…there is something I think you should know." The slowness of his delivery confirmed that he had been rehearsing each word in our silence.

"Now is not the time to admit undying devotion, Hals." I smirked. When I dared let my gaze drift from the path, I was surprised to see him simply shaking his head.

"I am serious, Regh. It is not often our world falls apart—" He began as he checked over his shoulder in his routine sweep of our surroundings.

I scoffed.

When is our world ever not in shambles?

"*And* you are separated from Rune." He finished as he raised a brow. "I don't ever have time for these thoughts when we are handling things all together."

Okay, fair.

"You have my attention. What are these thoughts tumbling around up there?" I waved a hand toward his head, which was substantially higher than mine even in his human form. "Confessions?"

"Yes." He admitted.

This time I held my retort and waited for him to continue. The roots beneath my feet were slippery with moss and I reflexively squeezed his hand each time I caught my balance.

He called no attention to it, nor did he let go as we trudged onward.

Halsten's long exhale informed me he was ready to disclose whatever had been weighing on his mind.

"I heard you discussing with Rune, about that night in the caves, when you two were with that Roderick fellow. I heard more than I led on at breakfast…" Halsten finally confessed.

I chewed on the inside of my lip but only nodded for him to continue.

"He is wrong." Halsten slowed his steps slightly. "I know he is. And if this could be the end of all of us, I want you to know that I have known for a long time."

"You have known Rune was wrong about what?" I pondered. There had been a plethora of things Rune and I had debated that night—on a great number of topics, I had thought Rune was wrong.

"No, Roderick…was wrong." He claimed. "I know…I know you and Rune are not mates."

His declaration caused me to cough in surprise and stumble. The air felt thin as I sucked in a shaky breath.

"How do you figure?" I managed as he helped me regain my footing, his grip strong and consistent in contrast to my clumsy movements in the dark.

Shifter vision would be beneficial right about now.

This was not the direction I assumed his thoughts had been headed.

"Back when we were young, when your father first put us on the detail to protect you and Bodhil, we started staying overnight at the cabin. You and your father got into a big fight about who you should marry to strengthen the pack." His voice tightened with anger at the memory.

It had been a screaming match, fracturing an already tense relationship with the ever-practical Commander Ulfhild. He had even recommended Sondre to ease the growing rift between the two leaders and that we could sire a litter of powerful breeding.

Breeding.

My jaw locked at the thought.

"Mm." Was all I could grit out.

"After Ulfhild left and we were all talking, you snapped that whatever Rune had joked about was not funny. The part that I could never get out of my mind though, was that he had not *said* anything. Not aloud, at least." He explained as I felt the closeness of his damning conclusion reach its tendrils out into my chest and constrict me. "You two had not slipped up like that before. You knew things about each other that were hard to believe, sure, or said things at the same time, or maybe finished each other's sentences, but had not responded to the other's mere *thoughts.*"

"No?" My tongue felt like it would stick to the roof of my mouth with how dry everything became.

"Which is not abnormal for *mates*," Halsten stopped and pulled me to face him. "But, that bond does not form until a pup becomes a wolf, if ever. It is once we reach adulthood when the gods make such a match. We were just kids, Regh. You heard him in here, as a kid…"

He placed his other hand against my cheek and cradled my face.

Tears pricked my eyes as the relief of no longer needing to keep this a secret from every living soul was finally in my reach, after all this time.

"Not to mention, we all have fallen asleep on that bed together for years, but *I* am the one who has been intimate with you, not him, even if it was only the one time." His smile was warm and safe.

I chuckled as the tension loosened its grip around my heart.

"Plus," He added with an amused glint in his eyes, "Even Sif has said it can feel like fucking the same person with you two."

"No, she has not." I shoved him lightly as my shoulders released.

His grin widened and he wrapped an arm around me to pull me close.

"You can breathe, Little Pup, your secret is safe, and it has been for a long time. Just thought you should know, you have another shoulder to carry that burden. Neither of you have been alone in this, not since we were kids." He leaned in to plant a kiss on my forehead, and the warmth of his breath let my guard fall.

His lips, however, did not reach my skin as he froze. His grip on me tightened as his muscles flexed.

A branch faintly snapped in the trees behind us, and he kicked my feet out from under me.

"Stay down." He barked and turned toward the threat, but it was no use.

A thick arrow whizzed at us, piercing through Halsten's brown eye, the metal tip breaking through the back of his skull. I screamed and shot my power towards him as a shield, but I was too late. Four additional arrows followed, puncturing his chest, abdomen, and legs. Another shot passed him and struck me in the shoulder. The sheer force pinned me back to the ground as Halsten landed on top of me. I roared in pain and pushed with all my might to roll him off and scramble backward. Cloaked figures dismounted off wolves hidden in the shadows and walked past my downed protector. One took out a sword and swung at Halsten's neck to ensure he was dead.

"No!" My cry echoed into the night.

Grief and rage erupted from me, and I broke open a part of myself long since hidden.

No one will know my secrets if none of us leave this forest alive.

I drew from the magic within the woods, the holy solstice moon, and any reservoir I had left within me. Tendrils of magic shot from the ground like roots and wove around the man over Halsten. My magic compressed from every direction; once used to stop bleeding and heal, now crushed every bone in the soldier's body as he fell in a clump on the ground. The forest was filled with screams, both from the figures and from myself. Violet power radiated out of me and fractured, shooting across the air in shards, catching two of the beings unaware. They grasped their chests as blood spurted out. I felt my body immediately weaken from the blast and I reached down the bond for Rune's help.

The utter void in its place was quiet and cold.

"No," I whispered.

I stumbled in shock and pushed further down the bond to find him.

Rune!

Empty silence filled the space of our connection. He had blocked me out in the past, but this was not a wall separating us; it was an abyss. I could not feel him at all. I could not sense his heartbeat.

Rune!

A wolf approached as I hesitated, and a form barreled into me from above. Cold metal began striking the back of my head, and the world went dark.

READER DISCRETION IS ADVISED

Chapter 18

Brynn

I stirred. My body was riddled with pain. As I moved my hand, familiar fur brushed through my fingertips, and I breathed deep. A woodsy scent with hints of vanilla and jasmine from Sif's chambers filled my lungs.

"Rune," I whispered in relief.

He had found me.

Depths, you scared me.

As I flexed my hand, I paused. There was something wrong, his fur felt cold, stiff. The rusty tang of blood mingled with his familiar smell. The sharp cracking of a tent flap rustling in the wind outside our space pressed in on my ears.

Soldiers.

I could hear soldiers outside calling to each other. My eyes flickered open, and I realized we were lying on the dirt floor of a tent. A pair of black boots filled my vision as they stepped onto the fur before me; confusion laced my senses, distorting my thoughts.

"I always knew that vermin would be useful, who knew it would be as a rug?" Sondre's voice broke through the ringing in my mind.

I shuffled back to see Rune's wolf coat beneath me, but nothing registered as I began to hyperventilate. The honey brown and copper hues were dull against the dirt. Fresh blood marred the white streaks across his shoulders. Holes from arrows pierced through the sides and slashes from teeth and claws racked across the rest of his fur that laid *flat* in the dirt.

"A tattered rug, mind you, but, oh, how good it feels to wipe my boots on his pelt." The Commander taunted as he scuffed his boot against Rune's hide.

I started shaking violently and tried backing away from the sight. As I turned away in shock, I saw a red blur in the corner of my vision. There, hung Rune, bound by his paws to the ceiling, *skinned*. A tub was beneath his frame, collecting the blood that still dripped from his raw body. I lunged forward and vomited at the sight, my body rejecting food, reality, everything. The edges of my vision darkened as I reached down the bond. I hoped against hope that this could not be real. It had to be another one of my nightmares. Rune would wake me up.

Rune.

A subtle flicker lit at the other side of the bond and my head shot up. It was coming from the bloody form. I crawled toward the table between us to get to the basin and the flicker grew slightly in strength.

"So, you *can* feel him. I always wondered about that. The way he would annoyingly show up whenever I got you alone, there had to be something. Do not fret, I could not let him die, not yet." Sondre said and waved his hand to another form in the room.

I followed his gesture to see a woman in chains. The protective runes tattooed on her ivory skin were slashed open. Her face was swollen and covered in blood and dirt, but I could still recognize the Witch of the Night Wolves. The whites of her yellow eyes were red from tears and strain; they were glazed over as she stared fixated at the pool of blood, running her fingers through it in circles. Cracked, bruised lips whispered a spell repeatedly.

"I had her keep him alive, for you, in case I had to lure you back here after sprinting off with little Asta. But it seems Valdis smiled upon me, once again, as you were brought to me as a gift instead. Lucky me. You were a present from Prince Hurthur's personal men. This delightful spell will keep Rune alive until the last drop of blood is leeched from his carcass." Sondre gloated.

"I will kill you for this." I rasped as I attempted to get to my feet.

"I am sure one day you could have, if I did not have other plans for you *tonight*." Sondre snarled as he grasped my hair and dragged me up to the table next to us.

"You see, girl." He slammed my head against the table before throwing me against it.

My body did not respond to any commands to flee as it went into shock. The edge of the table bit into my hips as he bent me over and pressed my face against the blood-saturated wood. Rune's blood, Sondre had cut him open here. The same knife slid down the lacing of my corset, slicing it free while cutting into my back. He leaned over me and pinned my hands to the table. My body reflexively recoiled from his closeness. He held a braided leather belt in his hand that pressed against my skin as he tightened his grip around my wrist and groaned in sick delight.

"I had my suspicions you were a witch since you were a child, but that show in the forest, oh, that confirmed it. I saw your pretty purple light show from here as I cut into that miserable excuse for a wolf. It took twenty of my men to subdue him when he saw that burst of light and knew you were in trouble, but, without the extra juice from your powers, he inevitably fell." Sondre pushed himself off me and cracked the belt against my back.

I cried out in pain and my legs gave out. I tried to brace myself against the table, nails digging into it to keep me from falling back onto the pelt below us. His calloused hand grabbed the back of my dress and tore a strip free. I attempted to turn to face him but a firm grip on the back of my neck sent me back to the table.

"Hold her still, Bron." Sondre ordered his second in command who had just entered the tent.

Bron already had leather straps pulled taut in his hands to cinch my wrists down to the table legs. Bron's thick hand slid up my forearms greedily after tying the knots tight. The pinched nerves in my wrists felt electric as sensations pulsed down my fingers. Sondre wound up again and brought the braided belt down as it cracked against my exposed skin, drawing blood.

"Look at him, Brynn. Look at your dear Rune." Sondre hissed and he whipped me with more force.

I reached for my magic, but inside, I was raw. Pain numbed my concentration, and all I could focus on was the *drip, drip, drip* of Rune's blood. Darkness emanated from the belt that Sondre struck against my skin; not a simple hex to counteract, this leather was cursed.

Fuck.

"I followed your scent into the woods after you took off on that horse. To my delight, I found this witch running to your aid aside a Night Wolf." Sondre growled. "I lost even more men to him than I did Rune, but it was worth seeing how formidable my new Guard will become when they are Night Wolves themselves. In the end, she was his undoing; he hesitated when I went to slit her throat to keep her from chanting. I hear that is why you fell too. Your love for another made you stall, made you *weak*."

My skin split open under the force of another crack. I could barely distinguish the heat of my own blood trickling down my back over the overwhelming stinging pain that felt like fire under my skin.

"She put up a fight, but, you forget, that bitch came from my pit. I had years of learning how to cancel out her tantrums, to bend her to my will, as I bent her over a table just like this one, in the pits night after night." Sondre pressed his hips against mine in emphasis, earning a huffed laugh from Bron.

Crack.

"I would hang her up with a braided belt like this, for example." Sondre leaned over me, his chest against my bloodied flesh. His breath was hot on my ear as he brought the dripping leather belt to my face. "It pays to know a warlock with the same hatred for your kind as I have. Each of these are spelled to weaken you filthy wretches, block you from channeling."

His heat left me in time for another crack against my back. The flow of blood streaming down my ribs turned to rivulets, soaking the thin chiffon he had left on me.

"Each of the witches in the pit had a belt that we used to bind them with when it was their turn to be mounted and raped. It made for more entertainment if they struggled but could never get free. Will you struggle for me?" He grunted and I heard fabric fall to the floor before another crack.

I could hear screaming and it took me a moment to register it came from my voice. The pain, it was becoming too much, then…I felt him. His skin pressed against my back as I bled onto his chest. His hands travelled down to my hips and pulled at my skirt. I tried to lift a leg to kick the bastard; at the sign of movement, Sondre slid a finger into one of the slashes across my back and my body convulsed as he dug around.

"What do you think, Bron? Will my fingers be this wet when I plunge them into her? The witches said they hated it, but their bodies dripped like I am sure you will. Fight me or not, you will be slick with cum and blood. Just how I like it." Sondre removed his finger from my back, and I could hear him sucking the blood off his hand with a groan.

Bron rubbed his own erection against my pinned hand in agreement.

"You know," Sondre triumphed, "Some of the whores you heal still have leather belts taken from the pits. My men pay extra to use those and to get the same feeling as fucking a witch. Their thrashing makes us harder, but there is nothing quite like the taste of a wet, angry witch."

Crack.

The sound got slicker with each strike as my back flayed open before him.

"When they disobeyed, it would be used to remind them how worthless they are, like you are now. Worth only the sweet blood you spill." He licked his lips.

Crack.

Wordless sounds of agony escaped my lips, and I looked to the Witch. A worn black braided belt was still tied around her waist covered in dried blood.

She had received the same treatment.

"She will not help you. She is conditioned to the screams when her sisters were punished. Some witches tried to hang themselves with the belts." He leaned across my bloodied form to whisper into my ear. "Do you want to hang yourself with it? Let it all fade to black as I use up your limp body for what it is worth?"

He slid the belt against the back of my neck slowly, lathering my throat in my own blood.

"I am afraid it will not end for you that quickly. You were meant to be bred in my pits. You have years of catching up to do. This would have gone so much easier for you, if you had let me put a wolf in you all those years ago…Flip her, Bron, I want to watch the pain in her face as I fill her."

Bron was quick as he unbound my wrists and forced me to my back to face Sondre. Torch light flickered across Sondre's face, and he looked up to the tent flap opening. In walked Bron's older brother Alaris, grinning as he took one of my wrists from Bron's grasp and tied it down as well.

"It feels like an age since we shared a witch. I could hear her screams from across the camp and knew it could only be your work, Sondre." Alaris chuckled darkly. He bent closer to lick the blood from my neck. "Mm. Something is off with this one, though."

Sondre laid the bloody belt across my neck and used his hands to rip away the rest of my corset. He exposed my usually hidden line of tattoos on my lower abdomen that the Witch inked in my skin after his first attack. Bron and Alaris both reached for a breast with a grunt.

"Protection staves, you clever bitch. I knew your blood tasted different from last time. Bind her tighter." Sondre mused and Bron wrapped the belt around my neck. Sondre unsheathed a knife from the scabbard at his hip and slowly dragged it across the inked skin.

"Your witch friend thought hers would save her too. They do not work once they have been broken though, do they?" He pressed on the knife, and it cut through one of the inked lines.

Bron and Alaris both growled hungrily at the unmasked scent of my blood pooling around the blade.

"One to keep us from scenting you properly as a witch." Alaris hummed and Sondre offered the blade for him to lick off the blood. An animalistic moan emanated from Alaris as his pupils dilated at the true taste of me. "That is more like it."

"Now you finally taste like the witch you truly are." Sondre bowed his head to murmur into my skin before biting down on my hipbone and sucking.

I cried out and tried to kick him as hard as I could. Sondre put a strong hand against my knee to stop the blow with ease. Bron pulled down on the belt causing my head to slam down against the table. I gasped for breathe but Sondre only laughed.

"Feisty. Just the way I like them. Fight me, Brynn. Fight as hard as you can." Sondre said as he grazed his mouth against my skin, up my ribs, and to my neck to pull the bloody belt off with his teeth.

"Fight me like your dear Yrsa did in the pits." Sondre groaned.

I felt his hands exploring my waist as I struggled but he cut into another tattoo, the upside-down fertility stave.

"Mother dearest always put up quite a fight before your father took her for himself." He pushed a finger into the fresh wound. "She was one of our favorite witches, that Yrsa. Will your fear taste just as sweet?"

"No!" I screamed and tried to get a hand free.

Alaris' grip on my breast tightened and he pressed down his weight to keep me on the table. The fractured rib, from falling off the horse, fully broke under the force, causing me to scream. Alaris' hips slammed against my hand with a pleased grunt in response, pinning it to the edge of the table.

"Naughty thing." Alaris ground out, his claws shifting slightly into his wolf form to penetrate my skin. "You thought a little bit of ink could keep us from putting a wolf in you?"

"Stop, Sondre." I rasped; the pain darkened my vision. I had to make it stop; I had to give myself enough time to think and get out of this. "I will give you whatever you want if you stop this. I will help you make your pack, just stop!"

Sondre dipped his thumb in the blood pooling at my hips and ran it across my lips. He leaned in close, pressing his body against mine. I felt the hard length of him now pressing against the side of my thigh.

"This *is* what I want." Sondre growled deeply. He brought his lips to mine and licked off the blood. "*This* is what I have wanted since you fought me off last time and got sent out of the castle to tend to the whores. Did you learn anything from them? Let's see if they taught you how to take every bit of a wolf."

Sondre reached up to hand Bron the blade and took a handful of my hair. I screamed as he bit down on my neck tearing through the skin; his canines transformed mid bite and elongated into my flesh. I felt Alaris shift around the side of the table and grab my knee, opening my thighs up to Sondre. Sondre's other hand reached for the buttons on his trousers as he drank in the taste of my blood, my fear, my hatred. I could already feel him ready to take me, and his erection grew harder with every swallow of blood. I thrashed, kicked, and tried to inch myself further up the table away from him with the little strength I had left. Sondre thrust his fingers between my legs, sinking deep into me to pull me back down to him. He gripped so hard that I bled into his hand.

"Now that pussy is slick for me. There is no escaping me this time." Sondre taunted as he pulled back to look at me. He withdrew his hand to rub my blood against his exposed cock.

Bron and Alaris turned frenzied at my struggling.

With tears in my eyes, I looked at Rune's bloodied form hanging there and reached out with any magic I had left before closing my eyes. I felt tearing in my center, then nothing.

Chapter 19

Brynn

I opened my eyes to find myself looking down at Sondre hunched over my physical body. I gazed upon my own face; my throat was wrapped in the belt that Bron had pulled taut. My eyes were glazed over as my body rocked under Sondre. I could feel a distant aching as they ravaged my still body, but nothing else. I tore my attention away and surveyed the room. Red tendrils of magic emanated from where the Witch once had been kneeling under Rune, but neither of them were anywhere to be seen. Dream walking was one thing, but spirit walking was a spell reserved for the Witches of Old.

Did she cast this spell on me?

As if in answer, the tendrils faintly trailed away, out of the tent. A gentle tug down the bond pulled me toward the magic and a warm protective golden hue glowed from my ethereal skin. Hope sparked in my chest.

Rune?

Leaving my body behind, I followed the pull. I peered out of the tent to see wolves and soldiers alike walking through the snow in between rows of tents. There was yelling and screaming from different tents that echoed my own struggles. No one turned to look at me as I walked through the encampment to the source of the pull.

A sob escaped my lips as I turned the corner. Next to a campfire, a metal rod stuck out of the cold ground with a body skewered upon it. Caraway's face was frozen in terror with the metal protruding out of her mouth. Her blonde curls were matted and sticking to her temple, caked in dried blood and mud. The armed soldiers around the fire cheered as a man groped her corpse and a wolf bit into her calf, shaking his head back and forth until part of her ripped free. I turned from the sight and hurried past. I could not help her now that she was dead.

Am I dead too?

Wiping my tears, I pushed on, past piles of corpses, toward the edge of camp. I came to an abrupt stop as I saw two forms on the snow-covered rocks ahead of me; their bodies were edged in ruby like hues.

Rune's human form was lying down in the snow, still, but unbroken. His head was in the Witch's lap, and she gently stroked his honey-colored hair. She was equally healed of the beatings Sondre and his men had inflicted. I rushed over and dropped into the snow next to them.

"Rune? Rune?" I gasped and took his hand.

His eyes drifted over to me, the warm light in them all but a flicker.

"You made it, Regh. Although, that means we are more doomed than ever." Rune smiled weakly.

I kissed his hand and held it to my cheek.

"Born doomed, remember?" I forced a laugh through the tears.

"I brought him here before they began, before they forced him to shift to skin his pelt." The Witch said quietly and nodded to a pair of amber stones in the dirt next to us, grounding crystals for a spell. "I dropped those here when they dragged me through the camp. I knew we could return when the spell started. He did not feel any of it once Sondre took the knife to him."

"That is what you were chanting into his blood?" I searched the Witch's face.

"Yes. No one deserves the horrors they put him through during the process…" She answered as she brushed his forehead. The Witch lifted her gaze to mine. "Neither of you did."

"How did you bring me here, like this?" I asked motioning to my form.

"Your blood." She said, her eyes tender. "It is soaking the floor of the tent now, puddles of it. It pooled enough for the spell to latch onto you, too. He did the rest."

Rune let out a soft chuckle.

"I pulled on the bond as hard as I could to rip you out of his grasp." Rune whispered. "Apparently, I just ripped you out of your own body. This spell stuff is not my strong suit, still your department."

There were tears in his eyes as he looked up at me, but they did not fall.

"I do not know how you did it, but you did just in time. I could not…I could not be there anymore." I shook my head as a shiver raked over my frame.

"I told you I would go to the Depths to find you. I only wish it had been sooner." Rune said with sadness in his voice.

"To the Depths." I choked back my own tears as I leaned over to kiss his temple.

"I—" Rune's breath hitched, and he glanced to the Witch.

"The spell is until the last drop of blood falls. We are almost out of time," She looked off in the direction of the tent.

"Brynn." He gasped out. "Brynn, I—"

"No. No, Rune. No, do not leave me." I sobbed as I held his hand to my chest and pressed my forehead to his. "We have lost too much, our littermates, Asta, now Halsten. Rune, stay with me. I cannot do this life without you, stay. Not you too, Rune. Not you."

"Brynn. I love you." He breathed as his gaze faltered.

He continued staring into my eyes, but I felt the bond dissolve.

"No, Rune. I love you. Please, no." I wept.

You are my life blood. My heart and soul. Find your way back to me.

The Witch let out a sigh and Rune's frame faded from view until he fully disappeared; a red tendril wove its way back to the tent. The weight I was pressing against him sent me unsteadily into her lap.

"No! You bring him back; you have to bring him back!" I pleaded as I gained my balance and gripped her arms.

"He is gone, Brynn. There is nothing for me to bring back anymore." The Witch said quietly.

"No!" I shook her shoulders, desperation blurring my vision. "Bring him back to me. He cannot be gone. He cannot leave me!"

Uncontrollable sobs overtook me.

The Witch pulled me close and let me weep.

"Death has already visited him." She somberly offered, "We cannot take anyone back from Her."

I pulled away, a plan forming in my swollen eyes.

"Is Valdis here? Can I see her like this? I can convince her to give him back." I started to get up, trembling as I scanned the camp. If I could shove Skai over Asta and still live, I could handle talking to Valdis for Rune.

What is the worst she can do, kill me? Then I will follow him to the Depths, as promised.

"No, Brynn. It does not work like that. She will not give him back." The Witch insisted and attempted to pull me back down to the snowy ground. "Stay out of the camp."

"Because I would see her, would I not? She is out here?" I glared down at the Witch, pulling my hand from her grip. "Is that why she was not at the temple?"

"No, because you will see her emissaries. The dead here do not only belong to your kingdom of Vik. The deities from Hoflin will come to claim their own too. We will not tempt the wraiths roaming between those tents." The Witch explained, glancing around carefully. "They all will be busy *in* the camp; we must stay out here to not gain their attention."

"Wraiths from Reykia will come for you, as well, will they not? That is why you came out here with Rune, to avoid them." I gazed into the camp to look for the emissaries.

I knew when wraiths had visited battlefields where I was a healer. All magic and life felt like it was sucked out of the air in their wake. I noticed how cold the air grew around us, a chill creeping far deeper than snow could reach on its own.

"They will," The Witch answered quietly and took my hand again.

This time I looked at her, surprised at the gentleness of her touch.

"I am on the table with you, now." The Witch whispered with a wince. "They have taken knives to our flesh, Little Witch. Before long, the wraiths will come for us, both. Then men will shift to their wolf forms soon enough and tear us apart."

"What can we do?" I stared back toward the tent where our bodies were kept.

"Brynn?" A voice behind us made us both turn with a start.

I squinted into the darkness as a figure approached. The Witch pulled me down to her level forcefully.

"No," The Witch rasped, her ethereal body paling. "Not *you.*"

Lerevna appeared from the shadows. She made no introduction; she only stared at my body.

"Depths, damn it all, what have they done to you?" Lerevna finally gritted out through clenched teeth.

I peered down but my current form showed no sign of the abuse happening to me. Lerevna must have been able to see my physical body through the spell.

"Doing. What are they *doing* to her, to us, is more like it." The Witch said staring up leerily at Lerevna.

"I am not here for you, Witch. Relax." Lerevna waved her off.

"You need to go and warn Aksel." The Witch cut in as she carefully got to her feet. "Sondre killed a Night Wolf, he aligned with a unit from the North *and killed him*."

Lerevna's brow furrowed but she remained silent.

"This was coordinated. He killed my Brede." The Witch's voice cracked and I remembered Sondre's taunts that it was the Night Wolf's love for the Witch that got him killed; the feelings seemed mutual. "Aksel will want to save her *and* to settle that debt. Even with my spell work, I do not know how long our bodies will last at this rate."

"He is already on his way. The whole pack is." Lerevna assured.

The Witch gasped and my form flickered.

"Bron has transitioned to his wolf form." The Witch rasped as she curled over.

I started to be able to feel the pain again, seeping into my frame from all sides.

"They will rip us to shreds." I whispered in horror. Pain seared into my back as I arched in agony.

"Alaris has taken you to the floor. I cannot hold on much longer. He is—" The Witch trembled and stumbled forward.

I stood to catch her from falling.

Lerevna let out a low curse.

We both looked at her and followed her gaze.

A black fog rolled in across the camp from the forest beyond.

"He is here." Lerevna gritted as she took a step away from us. The skin around her tattoos flushed red as her bonds activated.

The Witch looked at me, still leaning against me for support; a dark laugh tumbled out of her.

"I told you *he* would come for you." She wheezed. "It was just a matter of time."

"We have to get you two back to your bodies, now." Lerevna hissed.

"The wraiths are in there," The Witch spat. "They will force us to pass on in this state!"

"You are beyond the point of stopping that, regardless of where you hide in this camp. He will find her first." Lerevna shook her head and took my face in her hands. "Look at me, girl. Roderick is only steps away; I am sure of it. You do not have to trust me, hate me if you must, but trust *him*. Hold on until we get there."

She dropped her hands to draw a dagger from her belt that absorbed all light and pointed it at the Witch.

"Take Brynn back before I claim you for Tyr myself." Lerevna commanded without pulling away.

In a flash of red light, I could sense my body again; and all I felt was pain.

Chapter 20

Brynn

From the floor, I could see a glowing gentle face kneeling above me. I peered through the woman's ethereal visage to Alaris' wild expression covered in my blood.

"No. No, Little One." The woman in white cooed. "Your pain is almost over. Look at me, not him. I can take it all away."

I let my head lull to the side to see what was left of the Witch on the table above me and could hear myself gargling on my own blood. I saw a similar bright figure in a white flowing gown running a hand down the Witch's remaining arm as her life faded into nothing. The Witch went still, her yellow eyes staring vacantly at me. The magic within her went cold. Sondre and Bron, both in wolf form, plunged their bloodied erections into her mutilated body and remained unfazed. They tore at her flesh, already in ribbons, but this time, it elicited no response. They continued, oblivious of the wraith's presence.

The basin behind her collecting Rune's blood had long since stilled; his last drop of blood informing the tent of the finality of his death. I shut my eyes tight and turned back to the welcoming light.

I do not want to live in a world where he no longer exists.

"She is gone. Do not worry, she knows no more pain. Nor does he." The voice soothed and brushed my matted hair back. The wraith's skin was soft and gentle against my own, a stark contrast to the callouses and claws of Alaris. I slowly opened my eyes and focused on the tender wraith cradling my head from above.

Skai was right… He would not be the one to collect my soul after all.

I allowed my grip on this life to loosen.

A growl sounded somewhere outside the tent that caused the light in my vision to quake as the wraith trembled. That sound came from no wolf but could only be from a beast that fueled every living and dead creatures' nightmares. Sondre's wolf form yelped and sprinted out of the tent, his grey tail between his legs soaked in the Witch's and my blood. I felt Alaris startle within me as his half-shifted claws dug into my ribs. Darkness flooded the tent. Alaris yelled as pressure released from my center and the pain of sudden nothingness filled me. I could no longer feel him pressing my thighs open.

There was a ripping sound drowned out by Alaris' and Bron's screams of pain and horror. Their screams were cut short as blood sprayed on my skin and Rune's pelt beneath me; I heard the sickening thuds of body parts landing throughout the tent around me. A bloody hand emerged from the shadows to grip the wraith's throat as she peered above me. Feathered and leathered wings were inked up the arms of my savior.

"Not *her.*" A deep voice in the darkness demanded.

"*You…*" The wraith slowly removed her hands from my head, her eyes wide in reverence and terror. She gathered her white robes and fled the tent without further instruction.

A rustle of wings caused the shadows to dissipate as Roderick walked into the tent and assessed the space. He was dressed in fighting leathers of the North, but all died black. His face contorted in pain as he saw me in a pool of my own blood. He hurriedly took a step toward my frame, but paused as the being above me, blurred by my faltering vision, tilted his head toward the Blood Raven.

"Bring the wolf, and the blood." The voice in the dark ordered.

Roderick flexed and clenched his hands before walking to where Rune's body was to cut him down. The corners of my vision darkened as the shadows closest to me took shape. A pair of muscular arms covered in blood and ink lifted me from the floor and held me against a broad chest covered in leather. The mouth of a dragon tattooed on his throat came into focus. The scent of tonka bean and burning cedar brushed faintly against my senses.

"Call for Aksel. We are leaving." The voice rumbled against my temple.

"And what of Sondre?" Roderick asked the one holding me, his voice thick with grief.

"Let the Pack handle him. Come, she is fading." My rescuer urged dryly.

I saw Rune's form collapse across Roderick's shoulders and drape between the two large wings soaked in crimson. I closed my eyes and let the darkness take me.

Chapter 21

Roderick

Gunnar waited outside the tent and lowered himself for me to lay Rune across his broad black shoulders. The Night Wolf's fur stuck to Rune's exposed muscles, but Gunnar did not voice any contempt. He was already covered in blood from working his way through the camp. Screams echoed around us as his packmates wove their way through the tents, killing anyone in their path. Brede's death would be paid for with blood; a debt an entire legion's worth of bodies would not be able to repay.

I took a step toward my Master of War as Brynn's head lolled lifelessly against his shoulder. Lerevna landed in front of me in a gust of wind.

"Gunnar, go with Rhydar. We will follow shortly." She bit and walked into the tent. She grabbed my arm as she turned inside.

My bonds seared my flesh as I tried to approach Rhydar, but he was already briskly walking away toward the surrounding tree line. It felt like part of my soul fractured as I started to lose sight of Brynn again.

"What *the fuck* do you want?" I seethed at Lerevna as I leaned my head into the cursed tent. I found her kneeling on Rune's pelt.

"Brynn wears a black garnet amulet. It got ripped off during the struggle. I need it." Lerevna rushed as she threaded her fingers through the blood-soaked fur now covered in chunks of Alaris.

Everything in me stilled.

"Why?" I breathed.

Rune had made Brynn that amulet for her birthday. They had walked to the stream not far from here and he showed her his etchings on the grave marker for Yrsa. It was carved into a black garnet slab, much like the necklace Brynn had worn since childhood. The original pendant had been lost in one of the healing tents when Brynn had gone to the front, but Rune had made her an identical replacement from the stones he removed while carving. That was the first time I heard Brynn voice the end of the spell Rune had etched into the stone, one they quoted every time they visited since, *I release you now, rest in the Depths, oh, soul of Yrsa.* The quote was covered in various runes and staves for knowledge, magic, and the journey. I had never spoken of it to Lerevna, knowing this would be damning evidence in her case that Brynn was the witch she needed.

Lerevna stood, the small black stone slick in her now crimson hands.

"Fly with me." She demanded as she stepped out and took to the sky.

I followed as the mere thought of running after Rhydar set my oaths ablaze. Soon Lerevna banked to dip below the tree line in an all too familiar approach. We landed at the banks of the same stream just as Gunnar arrived with Rune on his back. Daegon followed them in his human form; the tub of blood sloshed in his grip. They both stopped at the carved gravestone.

The recent rain brought the water up to Rhydar's thighs as he waded into the stream with Brynn cradled against his chest. She barely resembled anything close to the human woman she had been when I kissed her in the castle. The fingers that stroked my chest were bent at differing angles; bones protruded out of some of them. Other fractures bulged against her marred skin, desperate to break free. Her wrists were raw from being tied down and fighting her restraints. The rest of her frame was punctured, slashed, whipped, cut, and defiled. Teeth marks tore into her from her thighs up to her throat. Her lips, usually revealing a smile as she helped and healed, were torn from being forced to open too wide. It felt like a part of me shattered with every injury as I took a tally. Bile rushed up my throat as Rhydar crouched and slowly plunged Brynn's body into the water.

"What is he doing?" My throat constricted as I took a step forward, but a strong hand grabbed my arm. I spun to see Aksel in human form.

Rage was alight in his eyes as he watched our Master of War, but he held firm.

Lerevna stepped just out of reach and wound the frayed leather necklace around her hand until only the stone dangled from it.

"Wake up, soul of Rune, Wake up. Awaken from the doors of the dead." Lerevna started to chant as she held the talisman out over the bank.

No!

I turned and shoved Aksel as hard as I could. The man fell back and shifted into his massive wolf form. His mouth foamed as he snapped his maw at me in reprimand. I drew my sword and pointed it at Lerevna.

"Stop this!" I bellowed.

The ink down my arm heated in an instant causing me to lose my grip. That was all that Aksel needed to barrel into me. We rolled on the ground, and I used our momentum to kick him as hard as I could to keep him tumbling away from me. I flared my wings and scrambled to my feet.

Ahead, Gunnar dipped his shoulder down to the slab of black garnet in the stream and Rune's mangled form splashed into the water. The gentle current held Rune's body against the stone.

My soul splintered at the sight of Brynn and him in the water, too similar to Brynn's relentless nightmares, "Do not do this, Lerevna!"

"The way ahead is long." Her voice cracked. "Guide, guide your dear Brynn. I cast the spell, release your memories, to lead her, though the way ahead is long."

Lerevna continued as she walled me off from our bond.

Aksel's teeth clamped down on my wing as I lunged at her. The oaths inked into my skin threatened to strangle me as I gasped against their restraint. I swung my blade and sliced the side of the big wolf's cheek. It was enough to force him to release me in surprise. I got to my feet just in time for another dark shape to plow into me, knocking me down on my back. Bragi, Brede's twin brother, snarled in my face, blood from the camp dripped off his teeth onto my forehead.

"Keep her along the road. Wake up, oh, soul of Rune. Wake up. Brynn calls to you. Imbue her with your knowledge of the road, for the way ahead is long." Lerevna chanted, her voice an eerie melody.

Daegon waded into the water upstream of Rune and tipped the tub of blood into the current.

A faint gasp sounded from Rhydar's arms, and I saw Brynn's eyes flick open.

"She is not strong enough!" I screamed at my mate, ignoring the beast of death in my face. "You will kill her!"

Lerevna did not look at me as Brynn took several shallow breaths before dipping back out of consciousness.

"Continue." Rhydar demanded as Brynn went limp in his grip again.

A black fog creeped in from the trees around us and settled on the banks. The stream turned red with Rune's blood, the last of his lifeblood. It washed over Brynn, sticking to her skin.

Lerevna breathed deeply.

"I cast the spell. Release your memories. She takes your blood. May you ever slumber in her." Lerevna's voice sounded strained as I noticed the skin around her tattoos flushed pink.

No, no, no!

"Roderick?" Brynn's gravelly voice pleaded, as her awareness fluttered.

"Enough!" I shouted as I threw every ounce of strength into the punch I laid into Bragi's jaw.

The wolf stumbled but recovered and bit down on my arm. I drew a dagger from my belt and plunged it under his eye.

Bragi howled and staggered back. I made my way to Lerevna. I reached out to grab her wing, my fingertips barely brushing her feathers when every muscle within my body locked up and sent me to my knees at her feet. Fingers threaded through my hair and wrenched my head back. Aksel's human form placed the dagger from Bragi's eye against my throat.

"Stop fighting, Roderick." He demanded.

I tried to shift from his grip, but my body was frozen in place, my inked oaths aflame. The pain forced an agonized groan from my mouth as I clenched my teeth. Aksel only shook his head before looking back at Rhydar and Brynn. A growl of undiluted rage ripped from my throat, but it was no use. Lerevna began the final verse of damnation, her voice sorrowful at the weight of her words.

"Wake up, oh, soul of Rune. Wake up. I bring Brynn to the doors, to the doors of the dead. She claims your memories. I release you now, rest in the Depths, oh, soul of Rune." Lerevna concluded and lowered the amulet in her hand.

A shadowy tendril floated up from the bank and plucked it from her grip. It crossed the stream and returned the amulet to rest on Brynn's chest.

Finally, Lerevna turned to me. Her skin was deep crimson under the ink as if she fought the chant the entire time. She knelt in the mud in front of me. Her eyes held an apology she would never voice.

"What have you done?" I breathed in horror.

"The spell was not from Yrsa's memories." Lerevna said sadly. "It was from Brynn's. She is the one we have needed *all along*."

She placed a hand caked in Brynn and Rune's blood on my cheek, but I pulled away as hatred filled my core.

A blanket of darkness crept from the shoreline and wrapped around Brynn's frame. It glowed a soft red under the shadows as it removed her from the water and warmed her body. Rhydar rested his hand on her ribs as black tendrils of magic wove around his palm and into her skin.

"No one touches her." Rhydar directed as he waded to the stream's edge.

The black fog dutifully carried Brynn's limp body beside him.

Without a thought, I barreled past Lerevna toward Rhydar. The Night Wolves did not motion to stop me this time, now that the damage had been done. I opened my mouth to berate the man who had just ruined whatever was left for the life of the woman I loved. As I approached, however, his hand covered in leathery and feathered wings raised and snapped his fingers. Every speck of ink in my body ignited and forced me into my raven form. Enraged, I croaked and took to the sky as I circled Brynn from above, forced to be all my kind was ever known for—an omen of a brutal, bloody death.

Acknowledgements:

Thank you, thank you, thank you.

Huge shout out to Tawnysha, my developmental editor, for seeing the vision and helping me fine tune what needed to be on the page. The story was able to stretch and spread its wings thanks to you. We're flying now!

My beloved artist Macarena, you made this come to life in a way I could never. You honor me. You took my jumble of inspiration pictures and descriptions and turned them into *EXACTLY* how I saw each character in my mind.

My beta readers, thank you for your time, dedication, and tears. Your encouragement, freak outs, and margin notes got me through this.

And to my sweet girls, thank you for all the late-night talks about this story. Your curiosity and creativity have been such a crucial part of making this a reality. Thank you for all your support and input.

I love you *all* to the Depths.